Cursed Dagger and Dragon
Clarima Syd Jones
Jan Toomer

Reality Undefined Publishing LLC

Contents

I dedicate this book to all those who have abilities and may feel out of place. The world is definitely a better place with you in it, so please embrace all of you.

Pre-Chapter One

Fifteen Years Earlier

She awoke with a start, her heart racing. Her parents often played their favorite oldies music after she went to bed. As she tiptoed to her bedroom door, she heard Herb Alpert and the Tijuana Brass jazzing down the hall. She knew her parents were talking, but the jazz music muffled what they were saying.

As she turned to go back to bed, her mother got louder. Her mother's voice shrilled like a cat whose tail was stepped on. "I'm telling you, she's not natural. And she does things that aren't natural, too. She's not right!" she screeched.

The now familiar dread came flooding back and shame blanketed her. With heart pounding, she blinked rapidly in hopes of quelling the tears that welled at her mother's words.

The atmosphere changed, as did her mother's voice. Both became toxic. "I'm going to contact a priest tomorrow and have her exorcized."

Her father's voice broke through the music barrier. "Leave her be, Miranda. She doesn't need an exorcism." Her father's voice faded back behind the music as he soothed her mother.

Her mother's words sat heavy on her soul. As though a rattlesnake was coiled and ready to strike in front of her, she took a couple of slow steps backward – away from the door – away from her mother's venom before she turned back to her bed. She crawled into her bed and cried herself back to sleep.

The heavens opened up as if they cried with her. At nine years old, she stood under the tent canopy that was provided to keep the mourners dry.

It was here she watched as her father's casket was being lowered into the ground. She'd cried so much since her father's death that she couldn't cry anymore. Thoughts of tomorrow, or of anything, didn't exist. Only numbness existed now – it was as if the world just stopped moving.

She stiffened when her mother stepped behind her. Her mother placed her hands on her shoulders and dug her nails in. Just like when their cat had attacked her, she knew she had to remain still; if she flinched or tried to pull away, the attack would be more vicious.

Her mother leaned forward and whispered so only her daughter could hear her. "Your father can't protect you anymore. No one can protect you now, you little freak."

She understood – she no longer had any protection.

Chapter One

> *But humankind continues to seek the answer to "What Am I?"*
> *And when one reaches an understanding of the answer "I Am", then all*
> *illusions shatter.*

She parked, forced open her door, stepped out of the air conditioned SUV and into the near gale force furnace-hot winds that threatened to slam her back into her vehicle.

Dressed in blue jeans, off-white linen blouse and dress flats, Clarima Syd Jones, or Clari, juggled her briefcase, coffee cup and keys. As a Level IV Energy Reader, she'd been hired part time by the police department to aid her assigned detective on his cases, and she was late. Again.

A sneeze erupted as she high-tailed it towards the building. The beautiful view of the mountains was missing, hidden behind an opaque russet wall of dust suspended in the air.

The two-story police station was stuccoed like many other structures in New Mexico. She figured they were made to not only blend into the desert landscape, but the desert-colored paints made the red dust coatings harder to see.

Compliant, she stood in line and watched those in front of her engaged by the uniformed officers as they directed people to remove metal items before going through the body scanner. She felt the now familiar, but still uncomfortable, energy residue that lingered in this part of the building. She wondered if the caustic emotional residue was the cause of the paint peeling in random spots on the walls. She Knew that the energy build-up of fear, anger and hate left behind from both victims and perpetrators permeated the walls and encouraged her, and others, to spend as little time as possible in the lobby.

The more private areas that housed the offices held less disruptive energy from years of exhaustion and frustration of the stretched too thin officers.

After she passed through the body scanners, she hustled upstairs for her meeting with Lieutenant Ted Avery and Detective Henry Morris.

Lieutenant Avery did not like her, or her abilities, while Detective Morris was still on the fence about her abilities. Of course, there were still teetotal unbelievers out in the world, as well as those people who saw using abilities as doing the "devil's work".

Then there were those who just outright feared abilities and those who had them...even if it was they who possessed the abilities.

Making a point of checking his watch when she entered the room, Lieutenant Avery, seated at the head of the conference table, tapped his pen on the table top and grumbled, "You're late. Again."

The conference room, like the other rooms designated for the detectives and officers, had the smell of dirty socks, sweat, old coffee, and pine. The pine wasn't working. The room's walls were barren and unwelcoming. The chairs in the conference room were the most comfortable in the station, except for maybe the ones in the Lieutenant's office.

Ignoring the tightness in his voice, she smiled as she put her coffee on the conference table and set her briefcase down. "Good morning to you too, Lieutenant."

She glanced over at Detective Morris. He sat with his chin propped up on his hand. His eyes twinkled as his eyebrows raised, silently asking, "Are you really poking the bear first thing this morning?"

Clari ducked her head as her smile grew bigger and she plopped down in the chair next to the one that held her briefcase.

The lieutenant wasn't known for pleasantries or niceties, especially when he wasn't too fond of the person, like Clari. They'd met three months earlier, and he'd made it crystal clear from the start that his division was only working with her since the Captain said that they had to because it would be "good for public relations". The Lieutenant let her know that he wasn't happy about this, nor was he happy that he was the one tasked to have her in his division. The Lieutenant's eyes, which were brown with gold speckles, flared when he had told Clari that he thought she was reckless. He also told her that he thought she had issues with authoritative figures, and that there was something about her that just rubbed him the wrong way.

Though the lieutenant appeared to be gruff, his energy let her know that he was a fair and just man, as well as protective of "his", though she knew that he still didn't see her as one of "his".

She glanced over at the detective. He contrasted the lieutenant in just about every way. The lieutenant was serious, big, and burly, and kept a tight buzz cut on his silver hair, where Detective Morris seemed the opposite. He was tall, about six foot two, with scruffy brown hair that had shimmers of red when the sun hit it just so. He had an average build and green eyes that sparkled with mischievousness.

The lieutenant interrupted her musings. "The Commander feels we aren't utilizing your 'consultant' abilities to the fullest and wants to expand you into other departments here. You would still report to me, but will be working with other internal departments."

The lieutenant was right; she had issues with authority figures. Her eyes became hard. "And who decided this without asking me first?"

She scowled when a soft chuckle emanated from the otherwise quiet Detective Morris.

Fuming, she turned back to the lieutenant. "I do not belong to the police department. They don't get to tell me what I'll do and where I'll go without my permission!"

The lieutenant didn't like anyone challenging him. His face clouded as he tried to keep his temper in check while holding Clari in a tense stare down.

The detective cleared his throat and in a smooth, soft voice, asked, "If I may?" When Clari and the lieutenant's attention turned to the detective, he continued. "Clari, the Commander feels that just about every department is showing strain trying to keep up with the multitude of paranormal abilities that have surfaced in some not-so-scrupulous people who have discovered new ways to commit crimes. In the hopes of alleviating some of the frustration and heavy caseloads, he thought that perhaps you would be willing to aid a bit here and there in other departments. You, of course, would be compensated for your services."

Clari's mouth fell open. "That is the most I've ever heard you talk in one week, much less in one sitting, Morris."

The detective's eyebrows rose up again, and a slight, almost imperceptible tug on his lips appeared.

The lieutenant had regained his composure while Morris had distracted Clari. The storm had passed and Lieutenant Avery released a heavy sigh as he rubbed his forehead. "So will you consider working with other departments here?"

She ticked her fingers off as she went through her questions. "Can I still keep my own clients? Do I have to take every case offered to me from the police department? Or can I say no to some?"

The lieutenant leaned back in his chair. "You are welcome to say no to any case presented that you're not comfortable with. You're also welcome to continue your own business away from the police department. So can I tell the Captain and Commander that you've agreed?"

After giving the lieutenant a curt nod, she answered, "Yes, I'll give it a try."

The lieutenant turned his attention to the detective. "Okay. Morris, you will be Clari's handler. I'll pass cases to you and you will brief Clari. If she accepts the case, you'll work with her on it."

"So I have a babysitter now?" Clari asked wanting to shoot fire from her narrowed hazel eyes.

Detective Morris turned his snicker into a discreet cough.

"Yes, deal with it." The lieutenant regarded his watch and rose to leave. "Any other questions?"

Morris answered for them both, "No, sir."

The lieutenant fled the conference room.

Meeting over, Clari stood and stomped her foot, then quickly switching gears, she figured she had just enough time to run to the grocery store, get home, unload and return in time for her afternoon client. She finger-waved bye to the detective and left.

After shopping, she began the drive home. For many people, the further they went into the desert, the more their eyes began to thirst for colors other than the dry sea of reddish brown that went on as far as one could see.

She thought that it would be cruel to bring any greenery to the desert out here only to make it struggle for survival in a harsh — and oftentimes, for plants, hostile — environment whose sole purpose appeared to be to find any moisture and suck it dry.

Anything planted in the desert also risked its existence by exposure to the animal life that forever searched for anything that might pass as something edible and have a bit of water in it. The javelina even dug up and ate cactus.

Yet contrary to first visual impressions, she saw the beauty of the desert.

One would think the starkness meant no place to hide, and that there shouldn't be any surprises in the desert. But she knew better. The desert dwellers blended in superbly, were adept in finding water as well as finding shade, and found ways to hide in plain sight.

Dust devils of varying sizes dotted the landscape. Having lived in what they called "Tornado Alley" in the Midwest, and then hurricane territory in the extreme south, these mini but mighty dirt tornadoes fascinated her. She loved watching them form, whirling the dust and small pebbles around and around, and then, for whatever mysterious reason, lose their momentum and fall apart.

Right now, Clari watched the ten dust devils of different sizes that were scattered across the plain. *Today must be a perfect recipe of wind and dust swirling together,* she thought.

She figured that there were two types of dust devils. The first one was a charging, thick-necked, unforgiving linebacker that insists on holding his form while taking down anything in his path.

The second, and her favorite, was the slender ballerina twirling on her toes while she performs her solo, and then gracefully dissipating only to begin anew at a different spot.

As she neared home, she viewed her ranch style house that, like so many others, had a stucco exterior finish painted a lighter color than the surrounding desert dirt. When she moved in, the painters recommended this color to have the house blend with the desert. She liked that idea; the house would be neutral and not stand out.

She recently had been unable to use the front patio. Each year the return of the barn swallows announced the end of winter. The barn swallows and other local birds had claimed the front porch for the shade during the scorching summers. She found the bird chatter calming while she was inside. Of course, like every family, there were squabbles. She had to go outside to break up one such squabble because it went on for three days. It began after the first round of babies were raised and to be on their own. All the new adults left, and then one came back, yelling for the parents to feed him. He even tried to bully his way back into the nest while the mom sat on the next clutch of eggs. Clari went out, shook her finger at the trouble maker. "You stop this right now. You're all grown up and need to go find your mate and live your life."

Otherwise it was peaceful out here. No city sounds and no one else's thoughts intruded her sanctuary. When she bought the ranch, the realtor voiced her concerns about Clari being so far out and isolated; Clari assured her it was perfect. What the realtor didn't know was that Clari sought a refuge where she wasn't inundated with the city sounds, which included being bombarded with even the unspoken thoughts of every individual around her.

As she pulled into her driveway she Scanned the property for any irregularities or disruptions. She learned to clear her, or her property's energy, by directing any negative energy be removed. Then she transformed the negative energy by visualizing it changing to pink or white energy. Next she brought down a bright white light and bubbled herself, or her property. The bubble of light was instructed to, "Only allow that which is highest and holiest may enter within." Her property energy shields seemed intact. All she noticed were the swallows doing acrobatics around her house.

She knew this meant she was able to use the front door now because the second round of nestlings had begun their flying lessons. The birds wouldn't be hanging out at the nests anymore since the evenings were starting to cool down a bit as fall begins showing itself. They were out building strength and preparing for their migration south. Winter would arrive not long after they headed south.

Finding nothing amiss, she unloaded her vehicle and brought the groceries inside the welcoming interior. The colors throughout the inside of her house were muted, offering her a subdued and calm energy to counter the stimulation generated by the different types of energy she was overwhelmed with every day. She preferred her belongings be tucked away instead of out on counters and shelves. Clari felt the surfaces in her house needed to be neat and tidy so energy could flow and not get stuck on bric-a-brac.

From the small foyer, one could go left down the hallway to her home office and further down to the master bedroom.

The hallway off to the right of the foyer had a guest bedroom, guest bathroom and the laundry room.

Across from the foyer was an open renovated kitchen and living room with high ceilings. She enjoyed watching renovation shows and picked her favorites from those shows and put them into her kitchen. The stainless steel appliances included a six burner gas stove, and the dark cabinets contrasted nicely with the off white with soft black streaks granite countertops. The black streaks, to her, spoke of movement and helped keep the energy in the kitchen from getting stagnant.

A clutter-free glass top kitchen table sat between the kitchen and living room and was in the front of sliding glass doors that led out back.

The living room was the heaviest looking room in the house. When Clari bought the house, the large fireplace demanded heavy furniture to compliment it, so she chose a large brown leather couch and two tan chairs that were a perfect fit.

Clari refined her property shielding over the years, until it ignored the few friends who visited the house or office. She did this too, because her shields set off her inner alarms each time anyone, friends included, would drop by. Now her shields would only warn her of an unknown presence.

After she put up the groceries, she felt the familiar tingle in the air as though it was electrically charged. This tingle announced the arrival of her lifelong companion, Aruta.

Aruta, an Arcturian, close friend, mentor and teacher is the prominent Being on her Team of guides. Each person has their own non-physical Team who guides, assists and stays with them throughout their Earth life journey.

Though Clari had many non-physical Other dimensional teachers on her Team, Aruta was visually present throughout Clari's life. Aruta was the one entity that she felt completely comfortable with being one hundred percent her true self.

Though a constant in Clari's life, she'd seen less of Aruta when Clari entered her teen years. Aruta's visits began tapering off until the only time Aruta came to visit was to warn Clari of something, to bring a message, or to provide a calming presence.

Clari had trouble with getting emotionally close to people. In Clari's past experiences, getting close to humans often brought emotional pain and betrayal...which she had found out the hard way, repeatedly. She also learned early in childhood that humans lie. However, animals, her Team, and energy never lied to her. It took her many years to trust humans, much less allow humans back into her life in the form of friends.

Clari, perched on the bar stool at her kitchen counter, bounced her knee as she eagerly awaited her friend, Aruta, to materialize in this dimension. When she did, Clari jumped off the stool and grabbed Aruta in a big hug. Clari had long ago become comfortable with Aruta's shimmering green hue and large unblinking eyes.

Communicating telepathically, Aruta would send emotions, feelings and mind pictures to Clari which she translated into words.

* Amusement - Greetings Clarima *

Clari beamed. "So what brings you here, Aruta?"

* Hesitancy - pressure building - stay safe - be aware *

"Any specifics, Aruta?"

* No - chaotic energies building - somehow touching you *

"Thank you, Aruta."

Aruta slightly bowed her head and disappeared.

"Ugh. More ambiguous warnings," Clari mumbled to herself. She enjoyed seeing Aruta, or communicating with her other spiritual guides, but the unclear messages frustrated her.

Checking the clock, Clari saw she still had plenty of time to run back into town for her appointment.

When she arrived at her office, she sat in her car for a moment, taking in the building. In contrast to the police department's building, Clari's office was in her small, unassuming adobe structure that was tucked in a corner lot. An ancient pine tree stood guard over her building. And, Clari recently discovered, the pine tree housed a large Horned Owl, who occasionally spat out its dinner remains near her front door. She was proud of her building and that she had saved to buy it. The older building was small and nothing fancy, but it was hers.

The simple sign painted on her one front window announced "C.S. Jones, Reader. By Appointment Only" followed by her phone number.

Clari got out, approached the door, unlocked it and stepped in. The gentle scent of sage and sweet grass greeted her. She stood in the lobby area where a deep green couch and complementary chairs provided a comfortable chatting space while the red Mexican-tiled floor brought a splash of color to the room.

The hallway was to the left of the lobby. The left side of that hallway had small windows, evenly spaced down the hallway, but placed high enough that she had to stand on tippy-toes to be able to see out of them.

The first door on the right contained the washroom and the door next to that was the supply closet.

The final door, located at the end of the hall, was her office. The office was as large as the lobby and spanned the width of the building. She opened her office door and entered. An executive ash wood desk was at the right and had the matching credenza behind it. Both had simple, clean lines. A simple, yet tasteful, hanging swag lamp hung over the desk.

Two guest chairs sat in front of the desk. A small brown sofa and coffee table were on the far left wall. There were two large area rugs — one placed under her desk and guest chairs and a smaller one under the sofa and coffee table. These gently colored rugs helped damper any echoing from the tiled floors. The office wasn't huge, but the furniture fit well.

While she waited for her next client, she straightened up her office, and then called her friend, Josie Parns, whom she adored and who was an Arch 3 energy Healer at The Whole Being Clinic. Josie's abilities included being able to trace energy imbalances back to the initiating event or incident. Clari hoped that Josie would be able to join her for dinner at Stefanie's, the local vegetarian restaurant and bar.

Josie answered her phone after the second ring. "Hi, girlfriend. I was just thinking about you. Are we going for dinner tonight? We are sorely in need of some face-to-face time." Clari could hear Josie's smile over the phone.

She and Josie met for dinner frequently, which gave them a chance to relax for a "normal" get together, but with someone who understood what their life was like.

"Yes. Want to meet at Stefanie's? I would like to share a dream with you and see what you think. I can call you when my last client leaves and we can decide on what time to meet."

"Ooh! I love your dreams; they are usually very...um...colorful. Call me when you're done."

"Will do," Clari said.

Clari focused on her next appointment which was a missing person's case. The mother of a missing teen had begged for Clari to take her case. Clari didn't take these types of cases very often; they were too hard for her – rather, the family's grief was too much for her. That and the fact that about ninety percent of the time, Clari had to tell them that their loved one was dead and all she could do was offer the families some details about where their loved one's remains were. This client coming in, the mother of the missing teen, was part of that ninety percent.

Clari took a deep breath as the client walked through the door.

Chapter Two

After speaking with the missing teen's mother, Clari handed the grieving mother the sheet of paper that contained all of the information Clari's abilities provided about the teenaged daughter and where her remains could be found. It never got easier. What Clari was able to do could never erase the family's pain, but might help bring closure to the wondering...and end the illusion of their daughter walking back through their door.

At the end of the work day, and after clearing the energy in her office building, Clari called Josie to let her know she was leaving for Stefanie's, a popular and upbeat restaurant, was in an historic building that had been a saloon and bordello. It still had the bar, but the bordello was long gone. Today, the main floor had the bar and restaurant, the basement was storage, and the offices are upstairs. The whole building was home to many ghosts.

When she arrived, she found her friend sitting at a corner table. Josie stood up and hugged Clari. Clari always felt a bit plain compared to Josie's exotic appearance. Josie had been blessed with a curvy body, long dark curly hair, and deep, dark brown eyes. It didn't help that every man around stopped and watched Josie, who appeared oblivious to their attention.

After ordering drinks, Clari asked, "How's work?"

Josie shifted in her seat, "Okay, I guess. I mean, I love what I do, and my clients rock! But the manager vacillates between letting everyone do their own thing to suddenly wanting to micromanage everyone and everything. I wish she'd find a happy medium. Oooh! 'Happy medium'. Did you get it?"

A smirk teased Clari's lips as she rolled her eyes. "Yeah, I caught that. Cute, Josie. Are you happy working at the Full Service Station?"

Josie cringed. "They don't like us calling it that, but yeah, I do. I wasn't sure if The Whole Being Clinic was going to make it, but it's doing fine. It was kind of bumpy for the first few months. The medical doctors and nurses seemed okay with all the other practitioners other than the energy Healers, Readers and Mediums on staff."

Clari frowned. "What are the other practitioners?'

"Well, there's a Holistic Food Dietitian, Massage Therapists, Chiropractor, and an Acupuncturist."

Impressed, Clari's eyebrows rose as she nodded.

Josie continued. "But things have started smoothing out now that everyone is actually trying to work together for the good of the client or patient. Well, everyone but the manager. I can't quite figure her out, so I stay out of her way the best that I can."

Clari twirled her straw. "Do you like being a full time Healer?"

"Yeah, I do," said Josie. "I think I get it now why you didn't jump on board to work at the clinic. You'd never be happy using the same ability over and over, would you? And there's the whole working for someone else. You seem happy being able to use whatever skills and abilities, whenever you want. For me? I love being an energy Healer and love the idea of having one central place that's not limited to just allopathic medicine. And they work to treat the whole person."

"That's great, Josie. And you're right, I like being my own boss and would go stir crazy using one or two abilities."

The waiter interrupted to bring their appetizer of complimentary chips and salsa and to take their food order. Clari ordered vegan fajitas with zucchini, peppers and onions with a side of Spanish rice and Josie opted for a green chile cheeseburger on a brioche bun with a side of fries.

After the waiter left, Clari excused herself and navigated the tables as she set out for the bathroom. She had to pass the bar, so she kept her eyes lowered, but her peripheral vision still Saw the ghostly patrons from yesteryears visiting the bar. If she made eye contact, they'd want to talk.

Clari entered the women's restroom and was almost to a stall when she Felt she was no longer alone, even though the door hadn't opened after she had entered. She looked back and Saw a cowboy ghost leaning against the wall by the entrance, his arms crossed over his chest. Their eyes met. Trying to not raise her voice, she went off on him, "This is the women's bathroom! What are you, a pervert?"

He started, and pushed off from the wall. "Whoa! I didn't think you could see me!"

"Yeah, well I can! You shouldn't be here," she hissed.

The cowboy ghost pouted. "I never go in. I just stand right here. I don't go no further."

"No! Go! And stay out. This is beyond rude!" It'd been some time since Clari had to use this degree of force to clear a space, but she didn't hesitate to Push energy at him to encourage him to leave the women's restroom.

He disappeared.

Geez, no privacy even in the bathroom. Clari thought back to when she was a kid. Excited to find someone who could Hear or See them, the ghosts often woke Clari so they could chit-chat. She was tired and cranky from being awakened night after night, so one night she tried energetically Pushing them away, and it worked. Sometimes it was exhausting seeing ghosts seemingly everywhere.

When Clari returned to the table, Josie asked her, "So what's new, girl-friend?" She tucked her hair behind her ear, took a sip of her drink, leaned back and waited for Clari to share.

"Okay, this is going to take a while to share it all. I've been having the same dream, on and off, for most of my life, and it always started the same way," she began.

I was walking through what bore a resemblance to an old European mountain village. The narrow streets were cobblestone and the buildings — from the late 1700's or early 1800's — would stand out in the modern world. It's always around the same time of the year – my guess is late September or early October. The air is a bit crisp, but not cold.

When the dreams first began, I often saw the older village people. Some villagers hung their wash while others swept their stoop and all gave me guarded, though not hostile, glances. The women usually wore white voluminous shirts and dark ankle-length skirts. Some of the women wore kerchiefs on their heads. The men were often in off-white or dingy grey shirts and dark pants, some with suspenders. My blue jeans, tennis shoes, and tee shirts did not belong. I was definitely an outsider there.

The path I took was downhill as I wove my way towards the outskirts of the old village. When I passed through the village, I walked a dirt trail back up a mountain. The trail opened up to a small hidden-from-the-view-be-low plateau, which contained a little old trailer sitting in the tiny dirt front yard and propped up on cinder blocks. Clothes hung out in the yard to dry during the warmer parts of the day.

The trailer was a 1950's thirty-foot Vagabond trailer. I could tell that it once had a coat of baby blue paint at one time, but now it was weath-er-worn, making the trailer look tired and sad. I remember thinking that a trailer out by the village seemed odd and out of place and time.

I climbed up the few rickety wood stairs to the door and knocked. The first time I had this particular dream, I realized — while I'd waited for someone to answer the door — that I had carried a large bag with me. It had made perfect sense in the dream.

It was also during the first dream that I had met the woman who lived in the little trailer. A tired and annoyed woman opened the door and scowled at me. Her faded floral housecoat mirrored her complexion. "We don't buy anything, we have our own church, and we want you to go away."

I spoke quickly as the woman began to close the door. "I have supplies for the kids." The door quit closing. I took this as an invitation to keep talking. "I'm sorry I came unannounced. I brought some stuff for the new baby and your daughter. And I came to help you a bit if you would like. I'm not selling anything, nor preaching. I traveled far and am tired and thirsty."

The woman opened the door some more. "You can come in and rest your feet a bit, but then you'll have to leave."

"Yes, ma'am. Thank you."

Moving like a woman many years her senior, she escorted me to a tiny, sparse living room which only had room enough for a small loveseat and an armchair, both of which were faded and worn. The mother pointed to a chair, and as I sat, the woman left the room. The woman and the furnishings, though definitely from our time, had, like the trailer, seen better days.

A young girl bounced into the room, eyes twinkling with excitement. "My name is Rebekkah, who are you?"

"My name is Clari, and it's nice to meet you, Rebekkah. How old are you?"

"Free," she proudly exclaimed.

"Three years old? My, what a big girl you are!"

Rebekkah tittered. When her mother entered the room, Rebekkah moved to sit on the loveseat across from me.

The mother had a glass of water in her hand and an infant cradled in her other arm. She handed me the water. She saw I was trying to catch a glimpse of the infant. "His name is Michael and he is three months old." The woman bent to show me her son.

I felt an immediate connection. I realized his eyes weren't a normal color — they were a beautiful gold with green flecks. Michael gifted me a beautiful, happy baby smile. It was that moment that I knew I'd play some part in his life, in a scene that had yet to unfold. I looked up at the mother and thanked her for showing Michael to me. "I'll leave the bag with you if that's okay."

"We don't accept charity."

"I understand. I'd rather not lug it all the way back home."

The woman turned her head away and nodded sharply.

I continued. "It won't be on a regular basis, but may I visit again? You have such a wonderful family."

Like the slow deliberate rotation of an owl's head, the woman turned back only enough for her eyes to meet mine. Her chin gave a sharp jab of agreement.

"Thank you for your hospitality, ma'am. Bye, Rebekkah." Rebekkah waved as I turned to leave.

And each time I had that dream, that's how it went. I'd go through the old village, carrying supplies, and ascend the dirt mountain road, meet with the wary mother, visit the two children and ask permission to visit again.

Each time I visited, which seemed to be about every two years or so, I noticed that the village had emptied a bit more. I saw more businesses boarded up and more homes abandoned. It appeared that the village was slowly dying out.

The last time I visited, which was last night's dream, was a special occasion. Michael had turned sixteen. Though it was almost two weeks past his actual birthday, I'd been eager to see him.

I knocked and a young woman of nineteen answered the door. "Hi, Rebekkah."

Rebekkah's panicked whisper interrupted anything else I was going to say. "You have to leave, now, before Mother knows you are here. Please hurry and go!"

Confused, I asked, "What? What's wrong, Rebekkah?"

Rebekkah was pushed aside and her mother's angry face was now in mine. Spit flew from her mouth as she started yelling at me. "You! You knew about this, didn't you? You knew he was an abomination. The spawn of Satan. And I let you into my home. Go back to hell, where you belong!"

Dread rose within me. "What's wrong? What happened? Where's Michael?"

The mother glared. "He's where he will never be able to harm anyone. He's where he belongs. I no longer have a son." The angry mother slammed the door in my face.

I wondered what the heck just happened. Dumbfounded, I turned to step down off the stairs when movement from a bedroom window caught my eye. I saw Rebekkah holding up a paper sign which read, "Meet at the bottom of the dirt road."

I hurried back down the dirt path and waited for Rebekkah.

Rebekkah, eyes wide in fear, finally showed up. She grabbed and hugged me. "I kept praying that you would show up. I knew you wouldn't let him suffer. I knew you'd come back and help him."

"Rebekkah, what's going on?"

"We have to hurry. I'll take you to him, but I have to be back before anyone misses me." She grabbed my hand and began climbing another trail that led up and away from the trailer.

We reached a ledge with a tiny path that led even higher up the mountain when Rebekkah stopped. "Follow that ledge. It'll lead you to the mouth of the cave. Here's the key. Please promise me you won't let him stay there. Take him with you." Rebekkah hugged me again. "Thank you for everything, and never come back here." Rebekkah fled, scurrying back to the trailer.

My heart pounded as I navigated the ledge that, as Rebekkah had told me, led me to the mouth of a cave. I found a large locked iron gate blocking entry. I took the key, opened the gate, and stepped into the darkness. The cave smelled damp and ancient.

Unable to see my way, I put my hand against the wall and used that to guide me as I moved further in and followed what felt like a worn path. The tunnel wall felt cold and a bit slimy, and I could feel it's slant as it led me deeper down into the cave.

Soon my eyes registered a light coming from somewhere in front of me. I continued on the path as it turned to the left. When I turned the corner, I stopped, shocked at the sight before me. A small scattering of battery operated lanterns hung in a rough circle in the enormous cavern, but their soft light was swallowed by darkness beyond their perimeter.

The dank, damp air was cold and I could feel it on the back of my throat. I hugged myself to try to keep warm.

I saw what looked like hundreds of swords hanging from the ceiling. They were stalactites, and their wet surfaces gleamed where the light was able to reach them.

But it was what I saw in the center of the cavern that made my jaw drop. I whispered, "Michael? Michael, is that you?"

The huge being slowly swung its head towards me. I gasped when I saw its large eyes — its gold with green flecks eyes. "Oh, Michael. What happened?"

I could Feel sorrow and fear radiate out from him. I Scanned the cavern. A sad Michael — I was pretty sure it was Michael — had some massive chains restraining him. He was a beautiful emerald green.

I thought, *Goes good with his eyes.*

I approached him. "Do you know how this happened?" I asked him.

I felt him touch my mind and could hear him speak to me inside my head. His voice sounded leathery. "On my sixteenth birthday, I started to change." A feeling of utter despair poured into me from Michael. "I became a monster on my birthday. My parents called me the spawn of Satan, and as punishment, God turned me into...into...this horrid beast." His emotions bombarded me.

"Michael, stop!" My voice reverberated off the cave walls. I took a slow deep breath and continued in a softer voice. "Your emotions are too strong and are overwhelming me. I need you to calm down, please." With guarded steps, I approached him, reached up and touched his face.

"You are not a beast, Michael. You are...well, you're a dragon. A dragon is not a spawn of Satan. You did nothing wrong. Your parents acted out of fear and just didn't understand. You did nothing wrong, Michael."

Anger came from Michael. "You knew this would happen, didn't you?"

"What? No, Michael, I didn't know that this was going to happen. I did know that I was in your life for a reason, I just didn't know what that reason was." I went on, "We need to get out of here. But first I need to get these chains off of you. Once we get you away, we will figure this out, okay Michael?"

The human gesture of nodding his head came across as unnatural and awkward on the large dragon.

After Michael informed me that the key also opened the massive locks holding the chains, I got busy unlocking them. One by one the chains dropped away from Michael.

We left the cave and traveled the mountains, away from the trailer and away from the village. By night time, we discovered another cave deeper in the mountains and moved into that to rest. Exhausted, I asked if we could get some sleep before we began discussing what to do next. Michael agreed. As the night deepened and the air cooled, we snuggled together to keep warm and eventually drifted off to sleep.

Refreshed in the morning, I told Michael a story. "I've had drag-on-themed dreams my whole life. Each one connected to dragons, and each time I dreamt of one of these three lifetimes, I was able to see a day in the life of each one.

"In one lifetime, I was a dragon rider. I bonded with a dragon and trained to ride him, to fight and protect with him. Dragons and humans lived and worked together.

"In another lifetime, I was a dragon slayer. At one time in human's history, humans became afraid of dragons and began hunting them down. They were slaughtered by the hundreds if not thousands.

"And in yet another lifetime, I was a dragon. I lived with other dragons. We had left Earth, and the humans, and moved to another dimension to live in peace and wait for the humans to once again be ready to live in harmony with the dragons.

"In this lifetime, my life as Clari, I've dreamt of talking with dragons. In these dreams I am called the Dragon Gatekeeper and told that I possess the ability to open the passage between Earth and their dimension. They said that I had these dreams to remember — remember that I had been a dragon once. And that I'd been a dragon rider once, as well as a dragon slayer. I needed to remember, so that I would know, without a doubt, when and why it's time to contact the dragons."

I stopped for a moment. I turned my attention back to Michael. "Michael, I think it's time. I'd like to contact them and ask them to help you. Is that okay?"

In my mind, Michael asked, "Does this mean I'm stuck this way forever?"

"Michael, I know it is hard to believe right now, but I think you wanted to be this way. Not a conscious decision as Michael, but rather before you became Michael. I think, together, you and I are the bridge between humans and dragons. Will you give it a try? We can talk to them and see what they have to say and what they know. Okay?"

Michael agreed.

"I've never done this before. Is it okay if I lean against you while I work to make a connection with them? I'm not sure how this works, so I'd like to be touching you when I make contact."

Michael moved to make himself comfortable. "Okay, I'm ready," he whispered into my mind.

I sat down with my back leaning against his side. I closed my eyes and sought out the thread I Knew existed for me to follow to the dragon dimension. I felt the energy shift and found myself standing before an impressive, and massive, iridescent silver dragon that had matching silver eyes. The dragon was more than twice the size of Michael. I felt my mouth drop open.

A new voice touched my mind. "Greetings, Gatekeeper."

Feeling overwhelmed and a bit clumsy, I actually bowed. "Greetings...uh, I'm sorry. I don't know your name."

He rumbled so deep, I felt it within me. "You do, you just don't remember. And in your human form you'll receive no dragon's name." Unlike Michael's mind-speak voice, which I heard in my head, this dragon's mind-speak voice was not limited to my mind. I could feel it throughout my body. It was, curiously, a familiar sensation, but I couldn't tell you from whom, or even when or where.

"Understood. My name is Clarima. What may I call you?"

"You may call me 'M'."

"Okay, M. I'm here on behalf of a human who recently turned into a dragon. I'd like to ask your counsel on this."

Another rumble. "You mean the youngling behind you?"

I swung around. Behind me, Michael had flattened himself on the ground as he supplicated to M. I hadn't realized we had come together. I turned back to M. "Oh, uh, yeah. M, may I present Michael."

While the two dragons checked each other out, I gently spun around to take in the scenery. The three of us were on a ledge high up in a mountain range, but this was no mountain range on Earth. These were mountains you were likely to see in some science fiction movie on television. The colors in the mountains were surreal. The pale pinks and purples looked like a Photoshopped scene. Underneath my feet was a very fine beige powder with some pebbles and rocks strewn about.

The ledge, in human standards, was large. Yet with two dragons and a human on it, there wasn't a whole lot of room to move around, and the drop was...well...so far down I couldn't see the bottom. Scary.

I tilted my head back and took in the sky, exhilarated yet nervous about what I saw. Fifty dragons or so, of different colors and sizes, flew above me, and I wanted to soar with them.

M teased, "You can soar with them if you can remember your dragon body, Gatekeeper." With that M charged me and pushed me off the ledge.

Terrified, I screamed as I fell, which was a good feat since I felt my stomach surging up towards my throat.

"Remember your dragon body, Gatekeeper," M commanded.

As I plummeted, I felt myself expand. I could feel wings grow as my feet became more talon-like. My soft, penetrable skin toughened and hardened...and I remembered. I flung out my wings and the wind caught them. I righted myself and gracefully moved back up towards the ledge M had just thrown me off of. After a clumsy landing on the ledge, I faced M and mind-shrieked, "What would've happened if I couldn't remember?"

"You would've died," he replied in a matter-of-fact way.

I turned to Michael, who was sitting like a rather large dog waiting for acknowledgement. *Was I Feeling a wave of amusement from Michael?*

Michael's mind-speak was tinged with humor, "Take a peek at yourself."

I looked down at my torso. "Pink!" My mind-speak seemed stuck in shriek mode. "I'm a pink dragon? Seriously? I don't even like pink."

While I was whining about my color, M charged Michael. He pushed Michael over the edge, and dove off the edge behind him.

I scrambled to the edge and yelled at M. "What are you doing? You're going to kill him!"

I watched as M moved himself into position under Michael, all the while instructing Michael on what he needed to do to fly. It didn't take long for Michael to get the hang of it.

I leapt off the ledge and followed behind the two dragons. The air felt as though water flowed around each individual scale. I wondered how I could feel and identify each scale as a separate part of my body when I never seemed to recognize my human outer covering unless something happened to part of it like a sunburn or mosquito bite.

My attention turned back to the M and Michael as they practiced, and it wasn't long before Michael begun whooping and hollering in my head.

"Clarima and Michael, fly back to the ledge."

After everyone landed, Michael bounced like an excited dog waiting for a ball to be tossed. He asked M, "I think I like it here. Can I stay?"

"Yes, but you will live the Dragon way and will follow without question. You'll not be able to visit Earth again until you've reached the dragon age of maturity, which is a long time in Earth years. And Clarima, you may visit whenever you would like."

Michael was home now.

I brought myself back to my dimension with M's parting words, "Farewell, Gatekeeper. We will meet again."

Clari ended with telling Josie, "I jolted awake and found tears falling on my pillow. I felt an emptiness I hadn't even known existed in me. I realized that I wasn't there just for Michael — I had been there because of my connection to M."

"Holy moly, Clari. That is a doozy of a dream, or rather dreams. After all that you did with, and for, Michael — how can you say the dreams were because of a connection with M?"

Clari threw up her hands. "Ugh! I don't know, Josie. I guess it was because of my response to M. His words touched my soul. I mean, I was there all those years for Michael, but I think he was the connector, or catalyst, to bring me and M together. I know it sounds lame, but I felt like some part of me was sad to be leaving M."

Josie tapped her fingernail against her tooth while she thought it over. "Maybe you shared lifetimes with M. You had past lifetimes with dragon connections. Are you feeling nostalgic for those times?"

Clari sighed. "You may be right. I don't know. I just don't have an answer. Yet." Clari paused, momentarily elsewhere with her thoughts, then snapped her attention back on Josie. "Oh, but I do have other news. I'm coming up on my ten year business anniversary and want to have a party at my office. Do you think that's a good idea?"

"Yeah. You know I'm the party girl! I'll be sure to be there. So what do you have in mind? Food, drink, music?"

"I was kind of hoping you could help me plan it. Do you think my office will be big enough? I was thinking of having it catered...you know, with finger foods. Oh, and it'll be casual or work dress." Clari revved up about beginning the planning.

Animated, Josie tucked her errant curls behind her ear. "Of course. I would love to help you plan." Josie rubbed her hands together, "Okay, what are you thinking for your party? I'm guessing you are definitely inviting Sebastian and Morris. Who else are you inviting?"

"I want to invite my most current clients and of course some of my first clients," Clari replied before taking another bite of her fajita.

"Remind me again, who was your very first client?" Josie asked.

"Oh, Mrs. Benton. She contacted me about her rescue, Miz Cozy. Mrs. Benton had explained that the little terrier mix refused to bond with her. She tearfully shared with me, 'I'm afraid my dog hates me.' So I sat with Miz Cozy and opened communication, of course speaking out loud for

Mrs. Benton's benefit. Miz Cozy lay on the floor with her head between her paws.

"The dog immediately shared overwhelming grief, and then showed me that she'd lost her human of many years. I asked Miz Cozy, 'Is the ghost standing by you your lost human?'

"Mrs. Benton gasped, but said nothing. The dog gave me feelings of terror and confusion followed by a profoundly deep grief.

"I told Mrs. Benton, 'It appears that Miz Cozy experienced a sudden tragedy and trauma before she came to you. She lost her human.'

Mrs. Benton nodded. I continued, 'She's confused and grieving, and she doesn't understand that if she can see her lost human, who stands beside her, why is she with you? She doesn't feel she can bond with you when her original human is right here with her. Miz Cozy feels she'd be betraying her first human.'

"Mrs. Benton started crying. She reached for a tissue, and then said, 'Yes, she did lose her human. There was a terrible accident and her human died. Miz Cozy saw her die. What can I do to make Miz Cozy comfortable?'

"I told her I needed to talk to Miz Cozy and the deceased woman. Miz Cozy lifted her head and looked at Clari. I said, 'I understand all that you both went through. Miz Cozy, I think your first human wanted to stay with you until she knew you were in a safe and loving home. She wants you to be happy and she thanks you for all the wonderful time that you two had together. But you, Miz Cozy, can love both women, and no longer feel like you're betraying your first human. She just wants you to be happy.'

"Miz Cozy looked at the ghost, and I swear they were having a private conversation. Miz Cozy suddenly looked back at me, slowly blinked her eyes, stood up, walked over to Mrs. Benton, and jumped up in Mrs. Benton's lap. Miz Cozy, as though she was feeling out Mrs. Benton's energy, circled a few times and then settled in. Mrs. Benton cried happy tears."

"And it wasn't long after that I met Mr. Hightower. He came to me because his show dog, a tiny Yorkshire terrier named Ridgewood Ernest Primrose Hightower, or Ridge for short, was depressed.

"When I spoke with Ridge, he said his whole life was all about the shows. He explained that he didn't mind the shows because, he shared, 'I am beautiful and others must see me', but he also wanted to have some fun as well with his human, who, he said, 'Was too stuffy all the time'.

"They worked out a balance of playtime with Mr. Hightower and Ridge and for work time. Last I heard, they were doing well."

Josie smiled, "Cool. So your first two cases were animal communication? Right up your alley."

They continued planning long after they finished their meal, and soon parted ways.

That night as Clari drifted off to sleep, she heard a loud bang, and then dismissed it. She knew that oftentimes, when she would start to drift, she would hear a loud bang or pop as she left her body.

But this time the night bangs and pops kept waking her throughout the night. She finally fell asleep shortly before dawn, and by morning she was cranky from lack of sleep.

Chapter Three

The WPO had developed standardized tests to help recognize and label the known Readers and Healers (those who have abilities); this also helps keep track of potential threats. ~ World Paranormal Organization (WPO) Information Pamphlet

Exhausted from a long day of doing readings, Clari crawled into bed. As she settled in, she heard movement on the deck outside of her room. When the sound didn't continue, she yawned and snuggled down for the night. As she drifted off to that in-between place right before sleep, she felt Sasha jump onto the bed and do the cat's version of tiptoeing up until she reached Clari's knee area. The feline circled a couple of times before she plopped down with a small thud.

Bang!

She bolted upright. *What the heck?* Sasha's head swiveled in the same direction as she let out a soft growl.

Clari heard a bang here, a pop there — all coming from the ceiling above her, and then it was quiet again. Sasha slunk off the bed and disappeared into the night.

Throughout the night, every time Clari began to doze off another round of bangs and pops began. Around five in the morning, her exhausted body gave in and went into a deep sleep.

Two short hours later the alarm clock jarred her awake and forced her focus away from the dream-world and back to the physical world. When she opened her eyes, she saw two blue eyes peering back at her from the foot of the bed. "So you fancied to grace me with your presence again, eh, Sasha?"

The Siamese cat responded with a "brrup" before she buried her nose and went back to sleep.

Smiling at the cat's response, Clari stretched as she gave her bedroom the once-over. Her room, like the rest of the house, stayed uncluttered. The walls throughout the house did have some artwork, but her favorites hung in her bedroom. Large paintings of her animal totems stood guard over her while she slept.

Otherwise the bedroom was pretty simple. The king-sized bed, which she usually slept right in the center of, was across and to the right of the door as Feng Shui recommended.

A simple stuffed and rather comfy retro chair with its faded blue fabric sat in the corner and a long dresser was against the wall to the left of the bed. There were no mirrors over her dresser or in her bedroom, and for a good reason. As a teen, when she'd still been naïve about her abilities, she'd been standing in front of her mirror and was brushing her hair like she had done every night for a few years. Lost in the rhythmic motions, she started when saw a stranger standing behind her in the mirror. She screamed and swung around to face...an empty bedroom. The terrifying introduction to being able to See images in reflective surfaces, which she learned many years later, was called "scrying", made her wary of mirrors.

It had affected her so much that she drew a sheet over the mirror and kept it covered until her mother finally relented and removed it from Clari's room. Ever since, she has only had mirrors in the bathrooms.

Still tired and foggy brained, she knew a shower would begin the process of perking her up, but first she grabbed her tape recorder, turned it on, placed it on her dresser, and made her way to the master bathroom.

As with most older homes, the master bath was barely large enough to contain a sink, toilet, and bathtub with a showerhead.

She scrutinized her reflection in the mirror as she brushed her teeth. Her hazel eyes, that changed their color depending on her mood as well as what she was wearing, happened to be blue today and were a bit tired. Her short auburn hair stuck out at weird angles. She remembered complaining to her mother that she'd stopped growing by the ninth grade, which left her an underwhelming five foot two and, when dripping wet, a hundred and fifteen pounds. Her mother had told her that, "Dynamite comes in little packages."

After her shower and while getting dressed, her Team spokesman popped into her head.

* Warning * the message began, and then continued on with:

* Movement - danger - large - your way. *

Clari rolled her eyes. "Great, guys. Can you be any more vague?"

* There is more happening than what you think * the spokesman added.

She thought, *Well, that was a clear message. Not.*

Showered and dressed, she closed her bedroom door behind her and made a beeline to the kitchen where the life-saving coffeemaker had the day's pot hot and ready for her. Once the coffee was in hand, she went to her home office.

An hour later, she retrieved the recorder from her bedroom, plugged it into her computer, and hit play. The bangs and pops were not alone. She also heard taps and knocks which continued up until the time she had begun to work on her computer, and the rest of the tape was quiet. That meant it mainly happened when she could hear it and it could bother her. That did not portend well.

Having decided she would mull over how to handle this while she was out and about, Clari gathered her purse and coffee and left for her office in town.

Her only scheduled in-office appointment was an Interview of Determination. When there had been an increase in hauntings and paranormal sightings reported, she had learned to do an Interview of Determination at her office to get a feel if the potential client was seeking attention or if it was a genuine case, and to allow the client a chance to share their story.

Her client, Jerry Armor, sat across from her in her office. "What can I do for you, Jerry?"

Dressed in cowboy boots, faded blue jeans and a tee shirt, Jerry shifted in his seat before answering. "I bought a house six months ago and I think it's haunted."

She didn't need her other-sight to know Jerry was nervous. He sat ramrod in the chair, and though he had his hands clasped and in his lap, the blaring white knuckles showed her just how uncomfortable he was talking about his experiences. She decided to ignore his nervousness for now. "What's happening to make you believe it's haunted?"

"When I first moved in, I felt a little uncomfortable, like someone was watching me, and I shrugged it off as feeling a bit jittery in a new place.

"As time went on, the house developed electrical problems. Every once and a while I feel like someone touched me — usually when I was alone. I would hear, and still hear, footsteps on a wood floor, and sometimes I hear what sounds like furniture moving across a wood floor.

"A few times I got up in the morning and when I got to the kitchen, I found the kitchen cabinets open."

"Did you have the electrical system, and the structure, checked?"

"Yes, ma'am. I had to bring it up to code, so I know the electric is all good. I did have the electrician come back, but everything checked out.

"I had the floors checked, too. The footsteps sound like boots on wood floors. I don't have wood floors. It's tiled all throughout the house.

"As for the cabinets, I've done everything I could think of to make them pop open, but nothing works. I even stayed up all night one night to see if maybe the vibrations from a truck driving down the road could cause the cabinets to rattle open. A truck did drive through, but the doors remained closed."

"I'm glad you did a thorough check. Anything else?" she asked.

"I have cold spots in the house. I never believed people's accounts of cold spots before. I figured they just had some drafts. Well, I'm a believer now. Those aren't drafts. They are cold spots and they aren't just in one place. Those spots move around, and they make my body feel completely drained of any warmth. I can feel the cold all the way down to my bones.

"And there's the voices. I can hear people talking, but can't quite make out the words. Or, at night, right as I'm drifting off to sleep, I'll hear someone say 'Hey!', but no one's there.

"Miss Jones, I'm at my wits end. Can you help me?"

After an hour and a half of asking detailed questions and letting him talk out his experiences, Clari decided it was time to go to his house.

"Jerry, I would like to go to your house and walk-through to see what we can find. Is this okay?"

His body sagged as though he no longer struggled to shoulder the weight of his experiences alone. A relieved sounding "Yes", was his reply

His home was a typical tan-colored adobe house that was over a hundred years old. Clari saw glimpses of the property's history as she approached. As she exited her car, she Felt several pairs of ghost eyes as they watched her. They were curious about her arrival. She Scanned the house as she moved to meet Jerry at the front door.

The house had thick adobe walls keeping the inside cool. The rooms were small compared to modern homes, but Jerry had them furnished in a comfortable Southwest theme that was tastefully done.

The kitchen and his bedroom were currently empty of any specters, but when they walked into the living room, Clari spotted a ghost standing in the corner. When he made eye contact, he asked, "Can you see me?"

Clari nodded. "Why are you here? Are you stuck?"

"Naw. I liked it here when I was alive, a long time ago, so I just stayed." The ghost nodded toward Jerry. "I like his energy. It's been a long time since a good hardworking man lived here. I mean a living man."

"Have you been harassing Jerry? Or do you know who has been?"

The ghost from yesteryears tilted his head forward. "Many ghosts come and go. They all seem to blend after a hundred years or so." He scratched his spectral beard. "Come to think of it, there was a youngster poking around. Foul mouth on that one."

"Is he still around?"

A slight head tilt again. "Hadn't seen him for a bit. Can't tell you how long ago, just not today."

"Thank you for your help. I'm going to be clearing the property today. You can hang around outside if you're ready to cross over. Otherwise, you might want to move elsewhere."

Clari continued through the house, then moved on to the shed and yard, and took notes, talked with the other non-physical entities who made their presence known, and listened to the stories of those who wanted to communicate.

Some wanted to talk about how they had died. Many entities just wanted to know that someone in the "real" world could hear them and to validate their existence. Some told her that they liked Jerry's energy, so hung out at his place.

After the walk-through, she explained, "Jerry, there are several Earth-bounds hanging out on your property. Earthbounds are those beings who used to have a physical body, died, and for whatever reason did not enter the Light to cross over."

Jerry's face paled. "What am I supposed to do? Do I have to move? Will they go away?"

"I think it will be fine. I believe that after we cleanse the property, we can get them to move along or cross over."

As she spoke, she noticed more Earthbounds had gathered on the outer edge of the property. The mass arrival of Earthbounds was, for her, a common occurrence. The Earthbound etheric pipeline had spread the word that Clari was preparing to aid those who were ready to cross over. This brought both those who wished help to cross over, as well as those who were curious or just wanted to watch.

Clari spoke out loud and with authority when she addressed the Earth-bounds in Jerry's house. "You all have to leave this property, either by crossing over or by moving somewhere else. Staying at Jerry's, or coming back after I leave is not an option."

Clari showed Jerry how to shield himself, and how to use sage to clear and cleanse the house, chasing the ghosts outside. When they finished, she also taught Jerry how to bless and seal the house.

They moved outside where she shielded herself, pulled down Light from above and called for angels to hold and protect the Light. She asked them to please assist those gathered. The Light came down, angels appeared and many Earthbounds started entering into the Light.

There were those in the group of Earthbounds, however, who were scared or still unsure. Clari took her time with each one. Even though all these Earthbounds showed up, not all would cross over. She would never force anyone into the Light; that violated the Law of Free Will, but spoke gently to them and did what she could. The ones who didn't cross over always had an angel with them until they were ready.

Afterwards, she talked to Jerry about regularly cleansing and shielding himself and his house to keep it free and clear of Earthbounds.

"Jerry, have you had any of these types of experiences before you moved here?"

Jerry shrugged and tried to not appear concerned about her question, but she noticed a Feeling of cautiousness coming from him. "Not really. Why?"

"The beings in your home were squatters, though they didn't have physical bodies. Squatters usually move into vacant places and hang out there. However, a person with medium abilities can also attract them like a flame attracts moths." She saw Jerry clench his jaw and Felt his energy shut her out. "I get it. You're not comfortable with the possibility of being a medium. I've shown you how to keep your property cleansed and shielded. If you want to learn more, feel free to contact me. Okay?"

"Yeah, okay. Thank you." Afraid she might pursue his past experiences, he politely encouraged Clari to get out of his house.

Worn out, she drove home. She wasn't done for the day though. She was anxious to get home and confront whomever, or whatever, was keeping her up at night.

When she got home, she shielded, closed her eyes and pulled in a golden light from the Source and filled herself up until she felt she couldn't hold it anymore. In one great push, Clari sent the golden light outwards, which pushed the light — and anything not of the same frequency as the golden light — out to the boundaries of her property.

She set the house and land property shield with an affirmation, "Only that which is highest and for my best may enter within."

She focused her Other-Sight on the outside of the shield to See what she had pushed away. "Oh, my god! Imps! What the heck are they doing here?" Imps resembled dark brown or black monkeys. They each had a nasty spike at the end of their tail and they loved to create havoc. But why were they at her house?

That night the ceiling remained quiet and she enjoyed blissful sleep. She awoke in the morning to a purring cat and a vision of a cartoonish blonde woman standing next to her bed. "Who are you and what do you want?" Clari asked her.

The intruder replied, "They know what you are planning and they don't like it. They want to stop you."

"I didn't think I was planning anything," Clari replied, but it was too late — the intruder had already disappeared. Sasha snorted, tucked her nose under her tail, and went back to sleep.

"Great," grumbled Clari. She knew there was no sense in trying to figure out what the blonde was talking about. Time didn't matter to the non-physical, or it seemed that time was an enigma to non-physicals. Sometimes they were a bit premature with their messages, often delivering them long before the incident. She was sure it, whatever "it" was, would unfold in due time.

Clari stepped outside. It was one of those rare mornings when the air was a little cooler and smelled so sweet. She locked the front door, and was halfway to her truck when inner alarms went off, the hair on the back of her neck rose, and she gagged in response to the smell in the air.

She closed her eyes and Scanned the area. She focused on the energy signatures around the house and found one behind the house that was connected to the awful smell.

Her eyes sprung open. What she Saw didn't make sense. It was eight feet tall, with long body hair and a terrible smell. Bigfoot? Here? She scratched her head…it didn't make sense. Why would one be in the Southwest's lower desert? She had heard of a scant number of sightings up north, but nothing down here.

After taking a deep breath through her mouth, she mentally touched the being she Sensed. He — most definitely a male — stood tall, self-assured, and had an intelligent, yet primitive feel to him. He acknowledged the mental contact with her and via emotions and mental pictures, let her know that he was passing through and stopped by because her energy intrigued him. He was just satisfying his curiosity. He Sent a message that he respected her "territory", and withdrew.

Wow! she thought, *I now have the energy signature of Bigfoot!* She found it amusing when she realized, based on the Bigfoot's smell, that the Floridian term 'Skunk Ape' was more accurate.

As she stood in her driveway contemplating the meaning of the arrival and departure of the Bigfoot, Sebastian Donahue's black Lexus pulled up. Sebastian was a longtime friend and a sometime client. Though he often called her "Belle" instead of her name. *And,* she thought, *he smells a whole lot nicer than Bigfoot.* She wondered which one he was today, friend or client.

In typical Sebastian-as-the-client fashion, and with effortless grace, he unfolded himself from the Lexus, approached her, handed her an item wrapped in a towel, and instructed her to "take care of it". Client it was.

Sebastian was tall, slender and had black hair. His eyes were a shocking blue that demanded your attention. He moved with the grace of a panther and had undertones of being a dangerous man. Her Other-Sight showed a vampiric genetic history. He was not someone you wanted to anger.

When Clari reached out to take the item, she Felt it was dormant. Nothing active stirred. She took a moment to put a protective bubble around it, for safety purposes since one never knew if an item might wake up and what it might do. She stashed it in the back of her car until she was able to work on it.

Sebastian relaxed a bit when they completed the business. "Did I interrupt anything, Belle? I'm guessing you weren't out here enjoying the landscape. Especially since the drought has made everything dry, brown, and dusty."

Clari harrumphed. "When do you *not* interrupt something, Sebastian? And no, I wasn't out here enjoying the drought-burnt landscape."

"Perhaps we need to petition either Zeus or Eudora for rain."

"I know Zeus, but who is Eudora?"

"Eudora is the Greek goddess of rain," Sebastian explained.

Clari frowned. "I don't believe in the old gods and goddesses. I often wondered if they were just stories to teach others lessons in life."

"Do you know Abi Habdul? Or maybe Sarah Freid?"

She wasn't sure where this new direction in their conversation was going. "Who? No."

"And neither of them, I'm sure, knows of you, yet you are real. Just because you don't believe in the gods and goddesses does not mean that they aren't real," he pointed out. "Your experiences are from what you allowed in your reality, and what you experienced was real to you. Your real life experiences are now just stories to others. Some may learn from your stories. For others, they are nothing more than fanciful fantasy stories."

"Huh, I never thought of it that way," Clari replied.

Sebastian puffed up. "My job here is done," he teased.

The conversation halted when the passenger door of the Lexus opened and released a tall, thin woman from its confines.

Sebastian smiled. "Belle, you remember my sister, Maria?"

"Wow. Hi, Maria! I've not seen you for what, four years?" Clari noticed the family resemblance in Maria's face. Her body was smaller than Sebastian's and her features were a bit softer. The resemblance stopped there. Her energy was closed off and, compared to Sebastian's energy, hers was a bit prickly.

Maria smoothed invisible wrinkles on her blouse before she answered. "Yes, it's been a while."

She didn't remember Maria being so serious, but, she thought, a lot can happen to a person in four years. "So what have you been into, Maria?"

Clari wasn't sure, but she thought she saw a flash in her eyes of disdain or embarrassment, like teens often show around older people. The flash was quick and gone before Maria answered.

Maria shrugged. "You know...graduated high school, and am now working in our dad's law office while I figure out what I want to do for my life career."

"Hey, remember the last time you and Sebastian were over here? We played Twister and Maria won." Clari snickered.

Sebastian smiled as he revisited the past. "We had pomegranate fizzies and music on in the background."

Maria gently shook her head, as if to say, "Ugh, children."

"It was on low, not like I normally crank it up," Clari defended. She looked over at Maria. "You were just coming into some changes then. I know it's rude to ask others about their abilities, but I have to know. Did you come into your abilities, Maria?"

A dispassionate half-shrug and eye roll, Maria answered, "Nothing to get excited about." She addressed Sebastian, "Are you ready? Father's waiting."

"Okay, off to work." Sebastian gave Clari a quick hug.

"Bye, Sebastian. And it was great to see you again, Maria!"

Maria smiled and she and Sebastian retreated back to his car.

Clari dismissed the deity conversation as he pulled away and focused on why Sebastian sought her out. She knew he had his reasons for giving the item to her. She also knew that she wasn't going to get any more information from him about the item, nor did he expect her to report back. He expected her to deal with it, period.

She settled in for the day and returned phone calls, saw clients, scheduled appointments and took care of emails. The demand for email mini-readings had increased, so instead of charging her hourly fee, she offered three questions for a small fee. This service was well utilized by the public.

When she finished for the day, she went out to her car and retrieved the item Sebastian had dropped off to her that morning.

Once she was back in the safety of her shielded and protected office, she unwrapped the towel to reveal what it hid. It was a beautiful ceremonial dagger. The whole length was just a little over a foot long with eight inches of it being the blade.

The pommel and guard, crafted of what she thought was sterling silver with an age-darkened patina, had intricate carvings of Celtic designs. At first the double-edged blade appeared to be glass, but closer inspection revealed it was a crystal blade.

She opened her other-sight to Look at the Celtic designs. They were pretty and she sensed no energy in the designs, pommel, guard or blade.

To begin the cleansing process, she dropped the protective bubble she had placed on the dagger when Sebastian had handed it over to her. She brought down gold light and started to sweep it over the dagger. The energy of the dagger awoke and energy tentacles snaked out and began to wrap themselves around Clari's arm. She started to feel lightheaded.

I don't bloody think so! Her mind screamed. Panicked, Clari immediately stopped the gold light, removed the tentacles, and slammed another protective bubble around it.

She had never encountered anything like it before. What the heck was going on? She considered contacting a local Wiccan for assistance, but decided against it. Sebastian could have brought it to a Wiccan and didn't. It was up to her.

She called on Mother God to protect and help her and asked the Archangels to stand guard around her office.

She once again dropped the protective bubble and immediately the energy of the dagger sprang to life. Working fast, she brought down the gold light and covered the dagger. The greedy tentacles began reaching for her and she could feel a strong hunger coming from them. She called Mother God and the tentacles froze in place.

The next thing Clari knew, she stood by a fallen log in a forest. A beautiful huntswoman approached. Her footfalls and body language showed that the huntswoman was not happy. "Who are you, and why have you stopped the energy sacrifice?" she demanded.

Clari wondered where she was and who the woman was. "I am not yours. I belong to Mother God."

"The blade has awoken and it must receive the giving of energy!"

Clari began to get a bit nervous. She still had no idea who she stood before. She repeated herself, "No, I owe you nothing. I am not yours. I belong to Mother God."

The beautiful woman turned into something hideous as she screeched her displeasure. Clawed hands reached out towards Clari...and she was back in her office.

She didn't waste any time dismantling the dagger's energy programming, stripping every energy thread and breaking any connections between her, the dagger, and the unknown "woman".

She re-programmed the dagger with a command to never reconnect with the "woman" or any other being and told the dagger to make itself get lost and to never be found by any beings. Clari visualized the dagger making it to the landfill to become lost in the rotting piles of garbage. She then commanded the dagger to never accept any other programming, ever. Clari felt a "pop" in the non-physical realm, signifying the energy commands had taken hold. It was done.

Exhausted, she placed the dagger back inside of the wrappings, sealed it, and then marched it out to the dumpster. She no longer considered it a threat, and Knew the dagger was neutralized and no longer carried any magikal programming.

Back inside, she sat and thanked Mother God and the Archangels for their guidance and protection.

She would definitely need to have a chat with Sebastian, but for now it was time to go home.

The gentle pitter patter of rain fell on her windshield as she left her office parking lot.

When she left the neighborhoods behind, she noticed heavier rains had already come and gone. The rain had cleansed everything of the reddish-brown dust and polished the landscape, allowing the desert's true colors to shine through.

When Clari drove by the car parked outside her house, she saw Detective Morris sitting inside of it. She giggled to herself, thinking that his car was as nondescript as the offices at the police station.

She parked in her driveway, and walked over to his car. "Detective, what brings you out this way? Is everything okay?"

The scowl on his face warned her of his mood. "Ever check your cell phone? I wasn't sure if something was wrong or not, so I stopped by after work. I didn't realize you lived way out in the boonies."

She winced. "Sorry, Morris, it's been a long couple of days. I guess I forgot to check for messages on my cell. Want to come in and talk?"

"No thanks, I've got to get going. Can you meet with me tomorrow at nine? Got some cases I want to run by you." He rubbed his arm and cleared his throat. "Oh, and I'm glad you're okay."

"Uh, okay. I'll see you at your office tomorrow. Night, Detective."

Morris started the engine and drove off.

She went into the house thinking the encounter with Morris was a bit odd. Her thoughts wandered to a bubble bath and relaxing music to soothe away the day's energies.

She dropped her purse and briefcase off in her home office and continued on to her bedroom, where she extracted her tired feet from the confines of her shoes.

The doorbell rang. She sighed and padded back to the front door. She opened it and found Sebastian on her front porch.

She noticed the amusement in his eyes when he saw her bare feet. "Did I interrupt something, Belle?" he asked in a silky voice.

"You know you did, and probably planned it that way if I know you." She turned towards the kitchen. "Come on then, you might as well come in."

"Hey, what happened to your front porch?"

"I don't know. What is wrong with it?"

"There are brown dots all over the place."

She grimaced. "Yeah. That happens each year. When the rains come, the race is on for the newly adult barn swallows to grab mud and make their nests. Little specks of brown mud are flung against the windows and walls. The birds, after placing their mud blob on the nest site, will shake their little heads to clean off the rest of the mud on their beaks. And, by the time the nest is complete, the patio mimics a brown mini-paintball war zone. I won't clean it off until the swallows move south for the winter.

"What's neat is when the young are ready for flying lessons, barn swallows from the whole area congregate here. They fly around, maneuvering through the obstacle course I call home. Everyone in the neighborhood helps train the new flyers."

She grabbed her pomegranate juice from the fridge. "Want some?"

"Uck. No, thank you."

She poured a glass, closed her eyes and took a sip. The cold, tart-with-a-hint of sweet juice filled her mouth and eased down her throat...ah...nectar. She opened her eyes and saw Sebastian watching her with open amusement. "What? I like my juice," she snapped.

Sebastian smirked as he turned away. That's when he noticed a pet food dish and small water bowl tucked in a corner. Both were empty. He pointed. "I didn't know you had a pet, Belle. What is it?"

She choked on her mouthful of juice. Sebastian patted her on the back. "You okay there?"

She bobbed her head and waved him back. "Just went down the wrong pipe."

Sebastian's raised eyebrows, waiting for Clari to answer his question about her pet. Clari feigned innocence. Confused by the whole incident, he shrugged it off, reached into his back pocket, pulled out a cream-colored envelope, and handed it to her.

She put her glass on the counter, took the envelope and peeked inside. "Holy cow, what is all this for?"

"Your payment for taking care of the last job."

Still inspecting the contents of the envelope, she asked, "How do you always know when I'm done?" She gasped. "Sebastian, there has to be a few thousand dollars here."

"Ten."

"Ten what?" asked Clari.

"Ten thousand."

Her mouth dropped open. "Dollars?"

Sebastian grinned as he moved towards the front door. "Uh hmm."

Confused, she started to follow him. "Wait Sebastian, why so mu..." she tapered off.

Sebastian looked back at her and saw the proverbial light bulb pop on.

"It is hazard pay! Crap! Why is it hazard pay?" she demanded.

Sebastian's eyes twinkled as he replied, "Only you, my dear, can royally anger a goddess you didn't even know existed."

He closed the door after himself.

Chapter Four

The WPO instituted a level standard to certify Readers and Healers, and is where WPO is mainly focused. This certification process legitimizes the process of hiring certified Readers and Healers. The WPO's certifications are recognized and are accepted as the standard worldwide. New abilities and talents have the possibility to spring up at any time, and anywhere, so our list is not inclusive. ~ World Paranormal Organization (WPO) Information Pamphlet

Clari knew she was dreaming, but it mimicked reality.

She was in her old hometown and had been hired to do a job there. Though in the dream, Clari didn't know what that job was. That told her that the dream wasn't about the job.

As she waited to see what the dream was about, she enjoyed the ambiance of the local laundromat as her clothes went through their routine in the washers and dryers.

Out the window she saw her childhood friend, Susan, coming out of the store across the parking lot. Susan had parked in front of the laundromat. Clari darted out and ran for her friend's car. Susan had already pressed the unlock button, so as she opened the door and settled herself behind the wheel, Clari slipped quickly in on the passenger side.

Startled, Susan jumped, and then relaxed when she saw Clari's smile. Their eyes connected but suddenly, Susan's eyes shuttered. Susan had shut down, but not before Clari saw the excitement and happiness followed by pain and the closing of the trust and connection.

It was this moment that Clari knew the truth. Her face fell as she told her friend, "I never meant to hurt you."

Clari got out of the car and began walking…walking away from her friend, away from her clean laundry, away from everyone.

As she moved away, animals began to follow her.

Awakening to an overcast morning, Clari discovered that a heavy grey pallor settled over everything, and it mirrored her mood exactly.

Other long repressed memories surfaced as a result of the dream she had just left behind. She sighed and decided she was ready for a shower. She stopped and cranked up her classic rock tunes in hopes that the music would beat back the melancholy blues that threatened to overtake her.

In the shower, Clari realized her brain wasn't done ruminating. She was back to thinking of her childhood friend. Her chuckle was bitter as she reviewed the dream. She hadn't been able to trust enough to get that close to people again, though she wasn't sure if it was the people she didn't trust, or herself. She always trusted animals — they never lied to her, used her, or treated her as an outcast or misfit.

Josie was the closest she'd gotten and that connection — compared to her childhood friendship with Susan — paled in the realm of friendship, but it suited Josie and Clari just fine.

Clari realized that the sadness and loneliness from that parting so many years ago still dogged her.

But she understood, as the dream reminded her, that you can never go back.

After her shower, and foregoing her coffee, she detoured from her regular morning routine and went to her meditation nook to begin a Reiki healing session to heal the past situations and all of the participants, including her.

Her mood improved on the way to the station when she saw the recent rains had dressed the regal mountains in a spectacular emerald green off-the-shoulder gown of new growth.

Even though she had stopped along the way to get some coffee, Clari was going to arrive on time for her meeting with Morris. She ignored the acerbic glares from some of the officers as she strode to his office.

His door stood open and she saw Morris slightly hunched over, his brows furrowed as he studied the file on his desk. The folder files sat neatly stacked on the corner of his desk.

She snickered to herself. She was pretty sure the detective's offices hadn't changed since the late twentieth century. As a matter of fact, Morris' pale green painted metal desk probably was from the earlier part of the twentieth century.

His office was tiny, almost claustrophobic. After having seen the other detectives' offices, she figured that they were made that way to discourage anyone from getting comfortable and wanting to chat.

Clari rapped her knuckles on his door and stepped into his office.

Morris rose, pointed to a chair, and went to his office door to close it from some curious, and some hostile, stares. He sighed heavily, sat down and asked, "How are you doing?"

She raised her travel coffee mug. "I'll be fine once I get some more of this in me. How are you, Morris?"

He grunted and grabbed the top folder from the stack on his desk. "Have some stuff to go over, see if you're interested."

"Yep. Let's get started."

Morris opened the folder. "Hmm, interesting. Coroner said it is suicide, but the detective's gut is telling him it is homicide. The detective has hit a dead end and needs a lead or two to follow if it is a homicide."

Clari asked, "Is the detective lazy, not good at his job or what?"

"No, it's like the lieutenant said. Everyone is spread so thin trying to keep up with all the new ways those with paranormal abilities are committing crimes. They just need some helping hands with their caseloads."

Clari asked to see one of the crime scene photos. She really didn't like working on current cases. The emotions of both the living and the dead were too fresh...too strong.

Morris handed her a shot of a deceased female, still hanging from the second story balcony and eyes bulging.

She slammed extra shields into place. Photo in hand, she closed her eyes and slipped into the grey void — the place in between dreams and nightmares.

She followed the energy signature back in time and began to Watch the scene unfold through the eyes of the woman.

She felt she was in a bedroom. The room was large with oversized and expensive furniture. The bed had fine linen and smelled faintly of lavender.

The woman awoke, panicked, when she felt a jab between her toes followed by a slight sting. She tried to sit up, but her arms and legs wouldn't respond. She heard movement in her room but she was unable to move to see who it was. The fear was immediate.

"Hello, my pet," a male voice cooed.

She knew that voice, and knew she was in deep trouble. Fear transformed into an all-consuming terror.

He resumed, his voice no longer cooing. It was the deep, oily voice of her former lover. "Sorry to wake you, but we don't have much time. It's a shame you wouldn't marry me...now I have to kill you and find me another rich target."

He continued to talk while he gently picked her up and carried her into the hallway. "In case you are wondering, *Hon*, the shot I gave paralyzes your limbs, but allows you to keep breathing and keeps you mentally alert. The drug disappears quickly, so we gotta move fast. It's been fun...well, not really." He sniggered, a sound that spoke of his dark and twisted mind.

He carried her to the railing on the landing, placed her on the floor and propped her up. She could see a noose lying on the floor and noticed it was the same tawny color as the carpet. Realization worked past the thoughts of the noose and struck...she was going to die tonight.

He'd set everything up before he'd jabbed her with the needle. He lifted the noose and gently placed it around her neck. He pulled the noose a little tighter, grabbed one of her hands and rubbed it on the noose. He dropped that hand and repeated the gesture with her other hand.

He lifted her up over the stair rail, and as the woman's mind screamed, "No!" he flung her. She heard a loud snap...and then nothing.

She found herself standing on the floor below, witnessing her own lifeless body swinging from the upper stairway railing.

Clari came back into her body, relayed what she had Seen and described the man's appearance. Despite the iron-clad alibi this man appeared to have, she told Morris that she'd Felt the man had done this before, so if the detective on the case looked deeper into this guy's past, he might find what he needed.

Clari excused herself and headed for the ladies room. Since current cases, especially homicides, took a lot out of her – which is why she rarely worked on them – she knew that Morris would probably go through the files to find something less traumatic to work on next.

Once inside the ladies room, Clari shakily splashed water on her face. She leaned against the bathroom wall with her eyes closed. She needed to take a few minutes to distance herself from what she'd just Seen and Experienced.

As she stood there, she suddenly Felt the presence of others. She opened her eyes but didn't see anyone. She opened her other-sight and Saw that there were ghosts standing all around her.

"What is it with you guys and public bathrooms?" she huffed, stormed out, leaving the ghosts behind as she returned to the office.

When she sat back down, she saw him studying her face.

He spoke softly. "You okay? You're looking a little pale there."

She smoothed her shirt. "Yeah, I'm okay. What else do you have?" He handed her a file. She opened it, read a bit, and asked, "Seriously?"

With the familiar twinkle in his eyes, he nodded. "No doubt someone's idea of a joke, but it is an active case."

She closed her eyes and began talking out loud, knowing Morris would take notes. "The so-called 'victim' gave his bike to an older boy, two blocks over. He did this in hopes of getting the new bike that he'd been begging his mom to get him. He figured if his old bike was 'stolen' she'd get him the new bike. The older boy who has the bike has the last name of Jensen or something that sounds like that."

She opened her eyes and handed the file back to him. They shared a knowing look...it was going to be a long morning.

They stopped at noon and were preparing to go out for lunch when Morris' phone rang. She only heard his side of the conversation, which consisted of a lot of "Yes, sir's," and not much else. His face showed surprise mixed with a touch of displeasure. He hung up and looked at her.

"Yes?" she asked.

"That was the lieutenant. He has requested our presence at a homicide site...now. Will you come?"

She'd never been asked to an active crime scene. She searched his face for a clue as to whether or not she should go, but found no answer there. She nodded.

"Have your department ID card?"

She dug it out of her purse and held it up.

He stood up. "Let's go."

As he drove, she asked, "Where are we going and what's the scenario?"

Morris shrugged. "Downtown and I guess we'll see when we get there. Put your ID on."

A few minutes later they arrived in the oldest part of the city where some of the buildings dated back to the late eighteen hundreds. Morris slowed as he watched for pedestrian gawkers and emergency vehicles while he searched for a place to park.

Clari people-watched out of the car window and caught Glimpses of a few people with attachments — some were Earthbounds and some were nasties. "Nasties' were those entities that had a negative, dark or ugly energy to them. This kind of energy usually indicated malice or hatred from that entity, and Clari not only did not trust that kind of energy, but preferred to not be around it.

While Morris found a spot and parked, Clari amped up her shields before she got out of the car. They aimed for one of the historic buildings as they moved through the crowd of onlookers.

The aged red brick was original to its construction, as was the large plate glass window that warbled the view inside. An old time sign, hung above the door, announced it was Abraham's Panoply of Past Procurements.

Stepping inside, they were greeted by a uniformed officer who checked their ID badges, wrote their names down, handed them blue disposable foot coverings for their shoes, and reminded them to touch nothing.

She put on the shoe covers, but wasn't ready to progress any further into the store. Eyes wide, she grabbed Morris' elbow and whispered, "What is this place?"

He frowned. "It's an old curio and book shop. Are you okay?"

"Yeah. Let's get started."

He led her towards the lead detective, stopped a bit away and raised a hand in greeting. The detective nodded and motioned that he'd be with them in a moment.

Clari Watched the other detective. His energy had a few dark spots which wasn't a good thing, but it could've been because of the Earthbound entity that was following him had negative energy. Her musing was interrupted when the lead detective approached Morris.

"I'm Detective Hargrove, and am the one who requested you and your consultant. I'd like you to walk through, do your thing, and let me know if you come up with anything."

"Understood. I'll take Clari around."

Normally Clari did not like people who talked about her as though she wasn't there, but she was being distracted by the store so didn't think much about it. She heard whisperings all around her. She wondered what kind of store this really was.

Morris nudged Clari. "Ready to do your thing?"

"What am I Looking for?"

"Guess we'll know when you find it. Let's roll."

They moved back to the front door. Clari closed her eyes, took a slow deep breath and opened her other-senses. She yelped, covered her ears and fell to her knees.

Morris instantly knelt down. "What is it? Are you okay?"

Though he was right in front of her, she didn't see him because her senses were in overdrive by all the items talking or yelling, and all of the energy in the space.

Once she shut down her other-senses, she noticed Morris was in her face with concern in his eyes. She gave him her hand to help her up. He brought her to a standing position as he rose.

"Care to tell me what the heck just happened?" Morris asked in a harsh whisper.

"It was too much at one time. This shop is loaded with active magickal or energy infused items and lots of beings. They are all talking at the same time and it caught me by surprise. It won't happen again."

Clari turned down the first aisle. She used her hands to filter and Read the items' energies. She did this by raising her hands with the palms facing the shelves; a hand for each side of the aisle. This technique would help keep her from being overwhelmed again and her filters would alert her to anything unusual. She Felt and Heard energies and magicks from old times to more recent — some negative, some more benign.

She made it to the end of the first aisle and was at the back of the shop when she Saw a shadow dart behind one of the other shelving units. She made a mental note to contact it before she left.

She noticed a shimmer develop as she turned to the next aisle, so she stopped to watch it materialize. It was a distraught little old man. "You can see me, can't you?"

"Yes, and my name is Clari. Who are you?"

"Abraham Snellerd. I own this place. I shouldn't be dead," he wrung his hands. "I knew I shouldn't have brought that cursed piece in here, but I did and I died because of it."

"What piece are you talking about?"

Hargrove joined Morris and asked, "Why aren't you walking with her?"

Morris shrugged. "She likes her space to do her thing. She can hear me just fine, and I can see her just fine."

Hargrove harrumphed. "She kind of looks like those crazy street people who hold a conversation with someone only they can see."

Morris countered, "Who knows? Maybe the street people aren't crazy. Maybe they see dead people, too."

He took a step away from Hargrove. Clari heard it all, and chuckled to herself.

Snellerd continued. "That cursed box! It was an iron box with the Sigil of Ameth carved on its top."

Her insides froze. "That is the Seal of God's Truth. Whatever was in that box was either good, or it was 'God have mercy on us' bad."

The ghost's head bobbed up and down. "When I was able to open it...well...it was bad. I didn't get to decipher much since I wasn't able to examine all of it, but I noticed the carving of the Sigil of Lucifer on the item inside the box. It appeared to be tanned human skin."

Eww. "Did you see who killed you?"

"No. Do you think you could find and take care of that box and its contents? It shouldn't be out there. Please." The desperation in his voice was heart wrenching.

Snellerd faded before Clari had a chance to answer him.

"Clari?"

She practically jumped out of her skin. She hadn't heard Morris come up beside her. She swung to face him.

"Are you okay?" He checked her face for signs of distress.

"Uh, yeah," she said, sounding distracted.

He gestured to the space she had been talking to. "Good, I was getting concerned by your facial expressions. Care to share with us mere mortals?"

Her brow wrinkled as she turned her attention to Morris. "Sure," she began as he jotted on his notepad. "That was Mr. Snellerd, who's extremely upset. Not only was he murdered, and no, he doesn't know by whom, but the killer left with a potentially dangerous item." She described the iron box and what she knew of its contents. "We *really* need to get that off the streets, Detective."

"I'll pass this information on to Detective Hargrove," Morris told her. "Can you provide more details like the information on the box carving and the known symbol on the suspected human skin?"

"Yes, I have a picture of the Sigil of Ameth at the office. I'll make a copy and fax it to you. The other, the symbol Snellerd was able to identify before being killed, I'll have to partially hand draw. It won't be complete, but enough to be used for identifying it if they run across it."

Morris continued to take notes so didn't look up when he asked, "And why a partial rendition?"

"Because it's the symbol to call Lucifer."

Morris' head popped up. His eyes searched her face. "You're serious?"

"Dead serious," she replied solemnly.

After faxing the information to Morris, who would turn it over to Detective Hargrove, she called Morris to schedule a late afternoon appointment for the next day to get back into Snellerd's shop. She told Morris that there was another being that she'd caught a glimpse of, but never got back to it. He agreed, and they decided to meet at his office at three-thirty and he would drive them back to the shop.

She leaned back in her office chair as she stared off into nothingness. Her thoughts tried to work on all the incidents that occurred over the last few days. It was like working on a large jigsaw puzzle without knowing what the big picture was.

Though nothing jumped out at her indicating a connection, Clari knew better. She just needed to find the common thread. She decided she needed to backtrack to what appeared to be the beginning, and find out who the goddess of the dagger was. She needed to prod gently. She didn't want to anger the goddess even more.

After a few hours on the internet all she had was a headache, a long list of goddesses' names, and no earthly idea which one she had tangled with.

She Sensed she wouldn't get the name from her Team, so she'd have to find it another way.

In the meantime, she would inquire about the missing iron box and Snellerd's death.

As she checked her list of contacts she stopped when she reached the Maestro. She didn't know his real name. She did know that to deal with Maestro could be costly, and not monetarily.

One could go to Maestro to get information, assistance, or be directed on whom to go to, but it would cost a favor at a later date. This favor would be equal to the effort, equipment, and quality of people and information you received.

The Maestro earned that name because he could orchestrate just about anything anyone would need, on short notice, *if* interested in your request and the possibility of what you could do to repay the debt.

She pondered the risk of asking for help to find the missing box. She decided it was worth it to get the box off the street. She called his number. After it rang a few times, it switched over to voicemail. Disappointed, she left a message as requested by the recording.

Clari checked her desk calendar. *Oh great*, she thought, *full moon in three days. That means the majority of the guys down at the police department are going to be cranky.* That thought triggered a trip down memory lane, back to when she began to see overlays.

When she was younger, some of her friends had developed some pretty awesome abilities and shortly thereafter, they disappeared. Not the abilities, the friends disappeared. She heard whispers about them being rated as Level X Readers. Level X meant someone thought they would be dangerous. Level X meant never to be seen again.

Truth be told, this was one reason she was afraid to let anyone know what she could do. She wasn't sure that her hidden talent, seeing what she called "overlays", actually did her any good. Overlays were when she could see the physical human and an energetic addition or trait of the human. She knew that the characteristics of the paranormal overlays gave her an idea about their possible behavior patterns...but what good was that?

It didn't seem to be that long ago when she had her first Sight of a paranormal overlay while driving home. It was still light outside as she drove through a subdivision and she passed a person on the sidewalk. She saw the human girl, and then she Saw a gnome overlay right on the back of the human, close enough to have been the girl's shadow. The gnome was not the garden statue kind of gnome, but rather the earth elemental. Still short in stature with a no-nonsense approach and dressed in earth tones.

Clari turned her attention back to the road, then back to the sidewalk again. Yep, it was still there.

She went a little numb as she continued her drive. Her mind did this when it was trying to make sense of what it was Feeling or Seeing.

She next passed a man on the sidewalk that had a blob overlay right behind him. An amorphous shape revealing nothing.

As she exited the subdivision, she hit the dirt road that announced her arrival in the undeveloped desert, and for the next twenty-five minutes, as she drove further and further away from civilization, she tried to digest what she had seen.

After that night, Clari began Seeing the paranormal beings overlayed on some humans. She wasn't sure what it meant and couldn't ask anyone. Over time, with a lot of observing, she realized that she was Seeing a human's overlay of paranormal DNA ancestry and that some of those abilities of their ancestors were being activated.

The Lieutenant, for example, had a wolf shifter overlay, as did a lot of officers at the police department — a lot, but not all. The wolf shifter attributes encouraged their pack mentality, and a lot of them started getting restless and agitated easily three to four days before a full moon. On the day of the full moon, Clari tried to be at home, behind locked doors. The wolf shifter overlays she saw were a bit unnerving on the full moon — it was, just like portrayed in the movies – when the wolf was closest to the surface.

The WPO knew that new abilities were surfacing, but no one ever said anything about anyone being able to *See* the paranormal or mythical aspects like she could.

Nope, she wasn't going to say a word.

She had, over time, learned what some of the overlays might represent or what might manifest in the human.

The vampiric overlays were sometimes Seen in people who were tall and pale. Early on when she sat and talked with a human with the vampiric overlay, Clari had felt totally drained. She learned that when she reinforced her shields when she Sensed or Saw one, they couldn't drain her energy. A human with this overlay didn't like to openly share information — Sebastian was proof of that trait — and one never knew where this overlay's loyalties lay.

The overlays of the nice Elves, also called the High Elves, were also tall, as well as lithe and beautiful. They had an etheric glow emanating from them.

The Dark Elf overlays were a lot like the High Elves in appearance, but their energy Felt slimy or dirty, and they worked to manipulate people and circumstances to their benefit or favor. She didn't trust any she Saw with this overlay.

Dealing with a human with either of the Elven overlays was an exercise in precision. You had to constantly be aware of how you worded things. If something could be interpreted any other way, some of the Elven would capitalize on the fact that it was open for interpretation, like a loophole. It was worse with the Dark Elf overlays. One had to be literal and specific in their wording to get the correct answer or information. Oh, and Clari really liked this part, they couldn't lie. They could evade, misdirect or avoid, but never lie. There were other mythical overlays she spotted. One Looked angelic. That overlay was a rather huge golden-winged being. The energy coming off that person was calming and loving.

Clari began to understand that it wasn't just paranormal traits surfacing...the mythological and mystical traits, as well as other planetary beings who currently wore the human bodysuit, were Showing up in the overlays.

She was still learning. Some overlays that she Saw, like the blob, were still a mystery to her — she had no idea what their attributes were.

Then there were the humans who displayed no overlays. Did this mean they didn't carry paranormal, mythological or mystical DNA? *Unlikely*, she thought. Or perhaps it meant it just hadn't been activated yet? *More likely*. She also didn't know what triggered the activation.

There were also the humans who kept her slightly off balance. She wasn't sure about them. They didn't show overlays, but Clari felt *something* coming from them. Detective Morris was one of these. He appeared one hundred percent human, but there was an energy about him that spoke to a whole lot more being there...she just couldn't get a handle on it.

Still so many questions.

Chapter Five

Reader Levels:

Reader Level I — Those who are able to Perceive positive and negative energy and can Sense lying/deception. ~ World Paranormal Organization (WPO) Information Pamphlet

There was nothing to do until her late afternoon meeting with Morris. Clari had already finished the day's paperwork and settled down with a book. Engrossed in the story, she jumped when her phone rang.

"Hello, Clarima. I am returning your call. What can I do for you?" Maestro's bass voice resonated deep within her body and produced a sense of familiarity, but she couldn't quite figure out why.

"Thanks for calling me back. I think I may need some assistance finding a stolen item." She filled Maestro in on the box and its contents. She waited nervously for his reply while she listened to air. Just when she thought he was no longer on the phone, he spoke in a formal manner, "You do understand the terms for acquiring my services? My terms are not conditional on the job's success. You are only hiring my assistance. Your payment will come at another time and will be equivalent to what services I rendered to you. Do you agree to my terms, Clarima?"

Some part deep within her knew that once she spoke the word, they were bound. She took in a shaky breath. "Yes."

"It is done. I'll contact you when I have information." He abruptly ended the call.

The mixed emotions and thoughts came on suddenly — she was nervous, relieved, and unsettled.

Later that afternoon, she met Morris and he accompanied him back to the last crime scene.

A little wary because of her last encounter at Abraham's Panoply of Past Procurements, Clari decided it would be prudent to open to energies in the store with a higher degree of guardedness. She took a slow deep breath and slowly opened to Feel, See and Hear the energies. She began her walk-through. Morris once again gave her enough room to do "her thing" but he stayed close enough to watch her.

Snellerd, dedicated to getting the box out of circulation, immediately approached Clari as soon as she opened to the energies. Clari quietly told him that they were still searching for the box. He mumbled under his non-existent breath as he drifted and faded away.

Clari hadn't realized how many beings were in the shop. She knew there were a lot of voices, but it had been mostly the items speaking to her. There were a lot of non-physicals as well. Not many were interested in talking with her though, which wasn't a bad thing.

Item after item Called to her, wanting to be Heard or Touched, but nothing that she Felt she needed to address right then.

Up one aisle, down another and up a third until she caught Sight of the shadow she'd Seen the first time she had come there.

She stopped and silently invited it to form in front of her and to talk to her. Her skin crawled as the energy in the air cranked up as if it was a massive buildup of static electricity. A light grey mist appeared. As the being manifested, the temperature dropped and goosebumps sprung up on her arms.

She Saw he was rather tall with skin the color of caramel. His short receding curly hair was graying and his eyes were an electric blue. His eyes darted back and forth, as though he was afraid he might get caught talking to her or get caught being there with her.

She craned her neck up to see his eyes. "My name is Clari. Who are you?"

His focus snapped to her as though he just fully realized she was there. His gaze was intense and drew her in...like nothing else existed.

She waited, lost in his eyes. He leaned forward, bending to be closer to her face. She felt he was searching for something in her eyes. Time came to a stop.

Clari jumped slightly when the being spoke to her. "Do you have the light?"

"Yes," she confidently replied. *Whoa! What?*

"Good. Good." He took one step away from her, and disappeared.

What the heck just happened? What was that about having a light? Why did I answer him like that? I don't even have a clue what he was talking about.

She stomped her foot on the floor.

Morris chuckled and muttered "This should be good. She never ceases to amaze me." Amused while watching her, "You okay over there?" he called to her.

"Peachy," she grumbled.

"Are you done here?"

"Yes." She stomped to the exit.

Morris continued as he ignored her foul mood. "How about we go grab a quick dinner and you can fill me in?"

Though she really didn't feel like talking, she knew she had to pass on to him what she had learned.

When he drove into the pancake house parking lot, she turned to him, frowned and hitched an eyebrow.

His eyes twinkled, "What? Pancakes are good for any meal. Besides, it's a more relaxed atmosphere here."

She shrugged. "Whatever."

Clari's insides froze when Morris placed his hand in the small of her back as they crossed the parking lot. Yet when he took his hand off to open the door for her, she became painfully aware of the void created by the absence of his touch.

Nestled across the booth from Morris, Clari shared her Experience while she indulged in her chocolate chip and whipped cream pancakes.

"So what did he mean, and what does that have to do with our case?" Morris was more traditional...walnuts with maple syrup.

"I don't think it does, or I'm not Seeing the connections yet."

He put his fork down. "I have a confession. I watched you doing...well, your thing, and am intrigued. Like today, I saw you weave your way through the shop, occasionally stopping and talking with someone – or something – I can't see. You'd get this faraway look in your eyes, or you'd freeze, or the color would drain from your face.

"I understand 'gut instinct'. Most cops have it and pay attention to it and it's saved many of our lives. Everything else was black and white; if we could experience it with at least one of our five senses, it was probably real. But you... you changed that. I can't deny the results that you get, so I have to admit something is going on. I'm just not sure what that something is."

Clari's fork was forgotten in mid-stride. "Wow, Morris. I'm not sure what to say. Uh, thanks?"

He smiled. "Okay, then," he looked down at his plate, "So what do you do for fun? Do you have any hobbies?"

Clari bristled. "Huh? Where did that come from?"

Morris put his hands up. "Whoa! It's after business hours. I just thought we could talk about something not work related."

She frowned and searched his face. *Dang,* she thought, *he's serious.* "I read paranormal mystery books, hang out in the desert with the wild critters, and every once and a while I leave for the lake or head out to the hot springs."

Morris let loose a full laugh. She liked that his eyes lit up from within when he whooped it up. When his laughter began to fade, he wiped his eyes and asked, "Paranormal mysteries, huh? Don't you get enough of that in real life?"

"Yeah, well, it's all wrapped up neatly in the books," she defended. "What about you? Same questions."

Morris leaned back and stretched his arms across the back of the booth seat. "I like pottery. I don't have my own kiln, but I have everything else I need to throw clay. When I finish a piece, I bring it in to have it fired."

She was pleasantly surprised by Morris' energy as he talked. She had noticed that when he was at work, his energy was tight and controlled. Yet, now as he spoke of his passion, his energy brightened and sparkled...it became alive.

"I'd love to see some of your work sometime," she told him, and meant it.

That night while Clari was doing her pre-bedtime energy check of the property and shields, she stopped by the sliding glass doors and noticed that the imps were gone, but standing outside the property shield were taller beings whose bodies were darker than the night and their eyes burned red. Sasha sat down next to Clari's feet. Clari glanced down and saw Sasha's tail snapping back and forth as her feline eyes fixated on the dark beings outside that were probably trying to find a way to encroach on Clari's space.

"I agree, Sasha. I'm not too happy about them being out there either. I'll reinforce the property shields tonight. Tomorrow I'm going to do some serious research. Hopefully that'll help me figure out who they are and why they're here."

Clari turned from the door and sat at the table. Sasha chirped, jumped on Clari's lap and settled in while Clari worked.

The next morning, she took a sip of her coffee, energetically checked the perimeter noting the absence of any would-be intruders. She headed to her office, set the cup on her desk, and crossed to the other side of the room where she had set up a little meditation area. This was her favorite spot in the house.

As she always did before any energy work, she cleansed and shielded herself and the space, and her mind focused on the dagger. She followed the dagger's energy back in time — back to the individual who'd programmed such dark intentions into the dagger.

When Clari Saw the dagger in her hands, she knew that she was Seeing and Feeling from the view of the woman who'd programmed the dagger — a dark practitioner.

Clari discovered that the dark practitioner's spell instructed the dagger to grab any active energy around it and to send that energy to Hecate. The first part of the practitioner's plan was to drain the life energy from the person who received the dagger. That energy would be sacrificed to Hecate. In return, Hecate would grant the dark practitioner the power and fortunes the practitioner felt she richly deserved.

Clari pulled away from the vision, re-cleaned and re-shielded herself after she disconnected any cords created by her viewing.

She moved over to her desktop computer and did a search for "Hecate". She read that Hecate's dark side did include commanding demons. *Well, that answers the question about the imps and night demons,* she thought.

But Hecate, the computer reported, gave her followers what they needed, not what they wanted. Clari knew that working with dark energies and intents often bit the practitioner in the behind.

She wondered...the practitioner had referred to the dagger/Hecate scheme as the "first part" of the plan...what exactly had this woman planned and against whom? Who was the practitioner? And, what was Clari going to do about being harassed by Hecate?

The questions still begged to be answered. She decided to do physical work which allowed her brain the alone time it needed to work problems out.

She cranked up the music, put in a load of laundry and danced as she dusted and vacuumed. She stood still to get a Feel of who or what the danger was and were it was coming from. She Felt a wrongness in the air, then a prickle on the back of her neck. Those were the only warnings she received, then everything went black.

She was dreaming, a weird dream. Why was she dreaming of Morris calling her?

As Clari pondered the dream, she slowly became aware of other noises. A lot of noises. Annoying noises. She opened her eyes, but everything was blurry, and her head hurt. *What the heck?*

"Hang on, Clari! They are going to move you now and get you to the hospital. You've been shot. You are going to be okay, just stay with us." She wanted to tell that voice that she had an awful headache and that whoever was talking needed to shut up...but darkness swallowed that thought, and everything else, up.

She was next aware of a consistent beeping noise. She wondered if it was the washer or the dryer. She struggled to open her eyes, but they fought her. She finally got them to respond, and she realized, as the light poured in, that it may have been a mistake...it hurt. She groaned and closed them again. An all-engulfing darkness followed.

She was awake, but couldn't tell if she was safe or not. The smells and sounds around her weren't those of home. She opened her eyes and took in her surroundings. She was in a hospital room, it was night, and Morris was asleep in a chair next to her. Aruta and other members of her Team stood around the room. Her head felt achy. She closed her eyes once again. As she drifted, she wondered what had happened. That was the last thought she had as a dream took her.

Clari found herself on a beach.

A horse ran up to her, stopped, and lowered for her to climb up. After she climbed up, he released his wings and Pegasus took off. He brought Clari to the top of a mountain, dropped her off, and told her to go inside the cave and get some help.

She entered the cave, and followed its twisting and curving path until it opened up to a dark chamber where a humongous dragon slumbered. Some unknown part of her rejoiced at the reunion. *Reunion?* It was a comfortable thought and feeling in the dream, but her non-dream self had no idea who this dragon was. The light was just too dim to see details. Was it M? She let go of her concern and let the dream take her.

She ran to the dragon's side and, as best as she could, grabbed his neck and hugged him. "I've missed you, my friend!" The giant awoke and swung his massive head towards her. A soft rumble sounded from within him.

"Tahini, I too have missed you." She felt him scanning her as he checked her energy. "You have been depleted, Tahini. Step away for a moment."

She hesitated again. *Tahini?* Again, it felt familiar, but she couldn't place it.

She stepped away from his large body. He kept his right eye close to her body. A large tear developed in his silver eye.

"Catch my tear and drink it down before it solidifies."

As soon as she swallowed the salty tear, her mind went kaleidoscope-y. Colorful unformed images swam before her, disorientating her, violently swirling within her. Her last thought, before her dream-body crumbled, was, *I don't think I can handle all of this...it's too strong and too much.*

The giant dragon caught Clari's energy dream-body as it collapsed and gently cradled her in his talons. He tucked her under his chin and went back to sleep, keeping her safe while her body struggled to adjust to his magical healing tear.

In her dream, Clari heard him telling her to sleep with the dragons at night until her body fully healed.

When she woke, she could tell by the sunlight filtering through her eyelids that it was daytime. She opened her eyes and saw a slightly blurry Morris staring at her. She blinked to clear her vision and saw Morris smiling at her.

"Hi." Compassion shown in his eyes.

"Hi," is what she tried to say, but it came out sounding like a croak.

Morris stood and pushed the nurses' button. "Don't try to talk yet. Let's have the nurse come in and see if we can get you some water."

The nurse came in.

"She's trying to talk, but needs some water. Can she have some?" Morris asked.

"Let's get the doctor in here first and then we'll see." She smiled at Clari. "Hang in there, sweetie. Let me get the doctor to check you over. I'll be back in a moment.

As far as she was concerned, the doctor, while pleasant to look at, didn't instill a high degree of confidence in his experience or knowledge. His brown eyes were warm and sharp and he had an athletic physique, but his smooth baby-face worried her. He looked all of nineteen years old. Unabashed, Clari croaked, "You sure you're a doctor? You look awfully young."

The nurse stood behind the doctor, but Clari still saw her roll her lips inward in an attempt to stifle either a smile or laugh, or both.

The edges of the doctor's eyes crinkled when he smiled. Unoffended, he answered, "Hi. My name is Doctor Firth. I promise. I'm not only a doctor, but graduated at the top of my class." He pulled out his stethoscope. "Let's take a look and see how you're doing."

Morris excused himself. "I'll be back in a minute."

Morris came back in after the doctor examined her.

The nurse was allowed to give her some water. Once she drank some, the doctor asked her some questions. Did she know her name? "Clarima Syd Jones." Did she know where she was? "The hospital." Did she know what day it was? "Well, no — it depends on how long I've been here." Did she remember what happened? Clari thought for a moment. "I was at home vacuuming. All of a sudden I felt like I felt a twinge of danger...then woke up here. No wait! I had a dream of Morris here jabbering at me and I wanted to tell him to shut up because my head hurt, and *then* I woke up here."

Morris' eyebrows rose and amusement sparkled in his eyes.

"Clarima, you were shot in the head," Dr. Firth told her.

"What do you mean I was shot in the head?" she demanded. Her gaze zeroed in on Morris. His face was solemn as he nodded slowly, confirming the doctor's announcement.

She ping-ponged back and forth, between Morris and the doctor, settling on Morris. "Why was I shot? Who shot me? Am I okay?"

Morris saw confusion and uncertainty in her eyes. "Clari, why don't you let the doctor explain what he knows. Okay?"

She returned her focus to the doctor.

Dr. Firth wrapped his stethoscope around the back of his neck. "You're a very lucky lady, Ms. Jones. Ninety percent of those who received gunshot wounds to the head don't survive. The bullet that hit you fortunately missed your thalamus and brainstem which is great news. The bullet entered at the back of the head and lodged in your frontal lobe. It was a pretty clean path and the bullet was small. However, it doesn't mean you're out of the woods. We'll need to figure out what the damage was or how it will affect you. Once the damage has been determined, we can provide you exercises, physical or mental as needed, to help your brain heal. The brain is resilient and works hard to repair itself and make new pathways.

"We do need to watch for any problems, like seizures. And you'll probably have a headache during the time the brain is healing.

"Your conversation with me so far has shown that your short term memory is a bit glitchy. That may improve as you heal. Your long term memory, so far, shows us that it appears to be intact, but you may discover some voids over time as you work to recall things from your past. You're also going to meet your neurologist who has the final say on the damage.

"When you leave here, you'll need to keep your bandage dry, so swimming is out, but you can use a shower cap for showering. Any questions?"

"Yeah. Who did this, and why? And is there going to be any permanent damage?"

"We won't know about permanent damage until your brain has had time to heal. So far, it's looking pretty good. As to who did this, I think we'll leave that to the local police to answer when they know."

Her head hurt. Tentative, she touched the bandage on her head. "When can I go home?"

"You can't go home yet. Let me watch you for a bit more and we'll see how you are doing. If I'm comfortable with your progress, then we can see about releasing you."

She sighed as the doctor jotted something down in her chart, then scurried from her room.

The nurse, Nurse Merriwether, gently patted her blanketed feet. "I'll bring some broth for you to try out. If it goes well, then we can try some other foods."

Clari thanked her before the nurse left to search for the promised broth.

Morris' presence made her feel safe, and she really appreciated that he didn't say anything while she tried to process all that she had just learned.

Morris stood and moved the table over to her to use when the promised broth arrived.

"Morris, how long have you been here? Better yet, how long have I been here? Who did this to me?" Clari began to panic again.

"Whoa, Clari. Don't get yourself all worked up. I can answer your questions *after* you have given your statement. Someone will be here shortly to talk to you."

"Why can't you do it?" Clari whined.

"First," he ticked his finger like Clari did. "Not my case. Second, conflict of interest."

"Conflict of interest?"

"Yes. You are my unofficial partner. Conflict. Of. Interest."

Chapter Six

While the detective assigned to her case, Detective Ambrose, scribbled notes in his notepad as she recalled what she knew, Clari mentally compared him to what she thought could be a younger version of Columbo.

Columbo had been a detective on a twentieth century television show who, like Ambrose, sported crumbled clothing and appeared to be scattered and distracted. But Clari wasn't fooled. She was sure, like Columbo, Ambrose didn't miss much.

He informed her that they currently didn't know who shot her or why.

After Ambrose left, the nurse brought her broth and saltines. The act of eating wore her out, and she soon slipped off to sleep.

When she woke a few hours later, there were flowers in her room.

Morris saw her admiring the flowers and explained, "You've had some visitors." He pointed to the cheery daisies. "Those are from a tall, creepy guy named Sebastian. And," pointing to a small bouquet, "those are from a pretty lady by the name of Josie." Clari made a face. "What's wrong?"

Her frown deepened as she answered. "Hmph. Pretty, huh?" Before he could answer, she asked, "How long have I been here, Morris?"

"You were shot two days ago. If you ask me, you're doing pretty well."

A tear slid down her face. It followed the curve of her neck and was sucked up by the hospital gown. Morris moved to the bed and sat on the side. "Are you okay, Clari?"

Both eyes welled up as she turned to him. He reached over and held her while she cried.

Clari woke up with a start. She hadn't realized she had cried herself to sleep. She looked around but saw no sign of Morris.

Nurse Merriwether shuffled in with a tray. "Oh good, you're awake! I've brought you some dry toast, jello, and apple juice. Hope you are hungry!"

Clari didn't hesitate. "Starved!" Then her voice dropped, hesitant as she asked, "Um, do you know what happened to Morris?"

Nurse Merriwether spoke as she set up Clari's table, "Honey, I sent him home." She saw Clari's face fall. "Oh, he didn't want to go, but he was still in the same clothes he was in when they brought you here. Honey, he *stunk*." Nurse Merriwether waved her hand under her nose. "I sent him home to clean up." She cackled. "Told him he'd better clean up before you realized how bad he smelled. I did tell him he needed to stay home and get some good sleep...but he scowled at me when I recommended that."

Clari's voice rose in disbelief. "He was here the whole time?"

"Yep. He came in with you. After your surgery, he planted himself beside you, even though only family members are allowed. He growled that you were his partner." Merriwether shook her head in amazement. "So they let him stay. He never left your side. He just sat there, waiting for you to wake up, reading those pamphlets." She pointed to the window sill, then followed her own finger to the sill, picked up the pamphlets, and handed them to Clari. They were WPO pamphlets.

Merriwether cackled again as she adjusted Clari's pillow. "I reckon you'll be seeing him soon. Now eat, and I'll check on you again later."

She actually enjoyed her meal. Afterwards, she leaned back and closed her eyes. She thought about having been shot. Something didn't make sense, but she just couldn't grab what it was. As she mulled it over, her nose caught a familiar and welcome scent. Her lips curved into a gentle smile and she opened her eyes.

Sebastian stood in the doorway, his hooded eyes watching her. Like a skater on smooth ice, he glided across the room, sat on the side of the bed and engulfed her in a hug. "I was so worried for you, Belle. I am so happy to see you awake." Sebastian waited for her to end the hug. When she did, he released her but stayed seated where he was.

"Hi, Sebastian. Thank you for the beautiful flowers."

"You are very welcome. I also brought a case of pomegranate juice, but they told me you weren't allowed to have it here, so you'll get it when you get back home."

Clari laughed, and then winced at the pain in her head. "Only you, Sebastian." She became serious. "Did anyone tell you what happened?" She wasn't sure if she had imagined it or not, but for just a moment, she thought Sebastian's blue eyes had turned a bottomless solid black.

Nonchalantly, Sebastian inspected his well-manicured fingernails. "Yes. You weren't awake yet, so that *interesting* man who glowers filled me in a bit. Not sure I like him. Who is he?"

"That's my unofficial partner, Detective Morris."

Sebastian's face puckered. "No accounting for some people's tastes in friends. I warned you about letting just anyone into your life, Belle. He kept sneering like he wanted to hit me and throw me out. He didn't, but man...intense."

Clari's face lit up as she chuckled.

It was Sebastian's turn to become serious. "What happened, Belle? I mean, I know what happened...but you are a Level IV Reader. How could someone get a drop on you?"

She took a long slow breath. "I don't know, Sebastian. I keep going over it. I keep feeling like I'm missing something important. I just don't know."

A head popped in the doorway. "Oh good, you're awake. Can I come in?"

Clari was pleasantly surprised. "Maria! Yes, please come in. How are you?"

Maria tilted her head. "Aren't I supposed to be asking you that? I'm not the one in the hospital."

"I guess you're right. Thank you for coming to see me."

Sebastian chimed in. "I dragged her with me. She needed a lift back to the office. I told her I was stopping here first."

Rolling her eyes at her big brother, Maria admonished, "You didn't drag me."

Clari smiled at their banter.

Sebastian turned back to Clari. "I guess you'll be canceling your anniversary celebration, at least until all of this is resolved." He watched Clari's face. His chuckle resonated in the room when the stubborn streak that she was well known to possess, surfaced.

"The anniversary celebration won't be canceled," she declared.

Someone by the door cleared their throat. Clari leaned forward to see past Sebastian. Propped against the door frame, arms crossed tightly, stood a frowning Morris. "Am I interrupting anything?"

Sebastian chirped, "No, Daddy. We were just talking."

An icy stare now accompanied Morris' frown.

Sebastian spoke in a loud stage whisper, "See, Belle? I told you he looked at me like he wanted to throw me out. He is one scary man."

Sebastian's drama often amused her. Clari knew that no one scared Sebastian.

Sebastian hugged her. "I'm going, Belle. Am so glad you are feeling better. I'll check in on you later. Come on, Maria." He kissed Clari on the cheek and moved towards the door. "All yours, Daddy. Bye." Clari imagined that, if Sebastian had been a cat, he would've flicked his tail as he regally passed by Morris.

Maria waved to Clari, and then both were gone.

Morris growled.

Clari's eyes beamed with amusement. "You should see your face, Morris. I take it you don't like Sebastian?"

"No."

"Why?"

"My cop instinct tells me he is really bad news."

Clari told Morris, "He's not to me. And thank you."

"For what?" Morris asked.

"For caring."

Morris held up a go bag. "I brought you a change of clothes, you know, for when you need them."

Clari felt her cheeks heat up. "Um, thank you. Did you pack it?"

Morris' ears flamed red and he shouted, "No!"

Clari jumped.

Morris cleared his throat and tried again without shouting, "I mean, no I didn't pack it. Josie met me at your house. She packed your bag and gave it to me to bring to you."

Amusement twinkled in Clari's eyes. "Thanks. Hopefully I'm going to need them soon." She scooched to get more comfortable in her hospital bed. "So you got to see the inside of my house. What did you think?"

Unabashed, Morris said, "Your house looks...well-ordered."

"Um, thanks? I'm not sure what that means."

Morris swept his arm as if he was showing her the open concept kitchen and living room. "Well, there's nothing on the counters or on the kitchen table or even the coffee and end tables."

Clari frowned and half shrugged, still cautious to share her life with others, even him...for now, "Yeah, I, uhm, don't like distractions or anything that might stop energy from flowing or make it sluggish. It, for me, helps keep my life less...complicated."

Morris sat down in "his" chair and changed the subject. "You're looking better, and I see you've eaten. What did you have?"

"Dry toast, jello, and apple juice, and they never tasted so good. Do you feel better after you were able to clean up?"

"Yeah. According to Merriwether I was starting to smell a little ripe." Morris waved his hand in front of his nose.

"You clean up nicely." Clari paused for a moment.. She held up a pamphlet and asked, "Something you would like to share with me, Morris?"

Morris' face flushed an interesting shade of red. "Well, I thought I'd try to understand a bit more about what you do."

"Hm...and did you?"

Confused, Morris asked, "Did I what?"

"Did you learn about what I do?"

"Sort of," he confessed. "I mean, I understand the words, but not *how* you do what you do...or *why*."

"Oh, okay. Uh, Morris, can we talk?"

"I thought we were already talking." Morris squirmed in his seat.

"Ha, ha. Seriously, Morris. Who found me?"Morris looked down at his hands in his lap. "Me."

"What were you doing way out there?"

Still studying his hands, he mumbled something. He began bouncing his knee. Unable to hear what he said, Clari craned her neck forward, wincing at the pain from the movement. "Uh, what?"

Morris chewed on his thumbnail and looked up. "I felt you were in danger and just showed up. When I got there, the door was open. I didn't think you were the type to leave your door open, so I quietly entered. I found you on the floor. The vacuum was still on and you had been shot." He took a deep breath. "I called for an ambulance and back up. The shooter was gone before I arrived. Fortunately, I arrived only a few minutes after you'd been shot."

"I'm sorry, Morris."

"Sorry for what?"

"I'm sorry for putting you through this."

His face twisted into an unpleasant sneer. "You're apologizing to me? You're the one who got shot. I should be apologizing to you. I didn't keep you safe!"

Eyebrows furrowed, she softly asked, "Morris, who said you had to keep me safe? Safe from what?"

Morris' eyes widened as though he'd been caught letting a secret escape from his lips.

Clari prompted, "Morris?"

He squirmed, became interested in his hands again, and then picked at a string on his shirt cuff.

"Morris?"

"What? Fine! I've wanted to protect you since I first laid eyes on you, okay?"

"What? Why?"

He threw his hands into the air. "I don't know," he grumped. "I just can't help myself! Apparently a separate section of my brain woke up when I met you, and you are all it can think about." This came out in an accusatory way, as though it was her fault.

Clari looked down to brush away non-existent crumbs from her lap to give herself the cover she needed so Morris couldn't see her reaction to his words. *Whoa,* Clari thought, *I can See and Feel, yet I did not see that coming.*

The neurologist finally cleared Clari, so after browbeating Dr. Firth, he agreed to release her once Morris promised she wouldn't be left alone until her follow-up appointment. That meant Morris was to be at her side for a week. She didn't mind if it meant she was free to leave the hospital. Hospitals weren't a fun place for someone who could See and Hear the deceased, and there are a lot of confused souls in hospitals. Every so often, Clari would go through the hospital and aid the wandering lost souls — but it was not something she would do when she was the patient and trying to recover.

Dr. Firth's voice broke through her musings as he instructed Morris and Clari, "You need to watch for any problems or anomalies. ANY. Eyesight, seizures, headaches getting worse, talking, thinking. If anything changes or gets worse, contact me immediately. Or go to the emergency room. Understood?" Morris and Clari nodded. "Okay, I will see you in a week."

A little unsteady on her feet, she needed the nurse's assistance to get dressed while Morris stood outside her room. Clari opened her go bag and pulled out soft grey yoga pants and a loose long sleeve shirt that Josie had packed for her. *Perfect clothes for going back home in*, she thought.

After the nurse had Morris and Clari sign the release paperwork, Morris left to get the car while the nurse saw to her wheelchair ride to the front entrance.

While Morris drove her home, she called Josie and asked her to stay a bit to Clari-sit while Morris ran home to pack a bag for his stay.

After she finished talking to Josie, Morris asked, "You understand why I need to be the one to stay with you, right?"

She was quiet. Morris glanced over her way, and then back to the road. He'd never seen that on her face before...fear. She spoke softly as she answered. "Yeah, I know why."

The rest of the drive was quiet with each person preoccupied with their own thoughts.

Josie, laden with grocery bags, was getting out of her car when Morris and Clari pulled up. Clari would catch Glimpses of silver wispy wings on Josie. Just wings, nothing else, so she had no idea of what Josie's overlay was.

When she got out of the car, Josie's voice sang out, "Ice cream and movies. We are so set." Clari giggled while Morris muttered something about females and chick flicks.

Sitting on the doorstep, as promised, was a case of pomegranate juice. Morris carried it into the kitchen, and over his shoulder on the way back out, he informed them, "I'll be back after I raid my house and the grocery store." He didn't wait for an answer, and locked the door behind him.

While Josie flitted around the kitchen, Clari could feel an emptiness in the house. She realized it was due to her own absence. She'd not been around to keep the energy moving in the house. Even though the shooting happened in her house, it was devoid of the trauma energy. *And come to think of it...* "Josie, who cleaned up the entryway?"

Josie stilled, and then looked over to Clari. "Morris did when the nurse sent him home to shower. He said he didn't want you to come home to that. I hope you don't mind that I let him in and helped him."

Emotions welled up. "Thank you, Josie. And I'll thank Morris. I appreciate all that you two have done, and are doing."

"You're welcome! I'm just so glad you're okay, girlfriend." Josie grabbed Clari in a big hug. "I was so worried seeing you lying still in the hospital bed. Never again, do you hear me?"

"Well, I hope never again."

Ice cream and movies in hand, Josie stormed the living room while Clari followed with soft cautious steps to avoid aggravating her still miserable head.

Before starting the movie, Josie wriggled her eyebrows. "You and Morris, here, together, for a whole week, eh?"

She smirked. "Nothing like that Josie."

Josie slid into serious-mode. "Let me ask you something. What happened? Or better yet, how could it have happened?"

Clari sighed. "I don't know, Josie. I keep going over it in my mind and it just doesn't make sense. But, I'm determined to figure it out."

"Are you okay? What I mean is, are you okay physically, emotionally, and ability-wise?"

Clari shifted uneasily on the couch. "I hope so, Josie. I guess we'll find out next week."

"Are you still having your party? The date is coming up pretty quick."

"I have all the invitations out and everything lined up. I *will* have that party."

"Good enough, girlfriend. What about your new roommate...is he invited too?"

Clari rolled her eyes. "Yes, Josie. I invited Morris and Lieutenant Avery."

A sudden thought occurred to Josie. "You aren't going through with your annual personal retreat, are you? I mean, you really shouldn't until the person who tried to kill you is caught, right?"

Clari's determination wavered. "I really don't want to cancel my retreat time, Josie. I've done this every year for the past five years, and it is important to me."

"You never talk about this 'retreat'. You leave every year. Where do you go and what do you do for that week you're gone?"

A relaxed smile appeared on her lips as she once again released a sigh, though this time it was a contented sigh. "It's my reconnection time, Josie. I disconnect from the everyday world and reconnect with myself and with nature. It's a week of solitude, regeneration, re-balancing and introspection. No phones, no electricity, and no people."

Josie snorted. "Seriously? How can you find that to be relaxing? Uck, nature and no electricity? Wait, no phone? I just couldn't do it. Not to mention you've been shot in the head! And you shouldn't do this, at least until your personal case is solved and you're no longer in danger."

Clari deflated a bit. "I know, Josie. I'll think about it." She mulled it over, and then crossed her arms.

Fueled by defiance, a spark ignited in her eyes, "But I'm not canceling the party."

Josie chose to ignore Clari's mini-outburst. "So you and Morris are getting closer? Are you and he getting more comfortable?" Josie wiggled her eyebrows again, but stopped when she noticed Clari's face. With a tight voice, Josie asked, "What's wrong, Clari? Did something happen? Did Morris hurt you?"

"What? No. I mean no, Morris didn't hurt me. Josie, something's wrong with me."

Josie leaned in, "What do you mean?" "Feelings are surfacing for some of the men in my life."

Josie bounced up and down on the couch, clapping her hands excitedly. "Yeah! Clari likes boys again," she teased in a sing-song voice. "So Morris broke through, eh?"

Clari turned beet red. "Josie, you know I don't want to get wrapped up in someone else's life."

Josie's voice dripped sarcasm. "Well that wasn't a self-centered statement in any way, shape, or form."

Clari rolled her eyes.

Josie tucked her hair, leaned forward and continued. "Maybe you getting shot, you know, your brush with death, has brought out the human desire to be with someone — a man to share your life with. This really isn't a bad thing."

"You know what I went through growing up. I was the family freak, ostracized in my own family unit. And outside the family? Ha! Anytime I allowed the real me to show…well, it was painful each time. I learned to not only keep most of my abilities to myself, but to keep to myself in general."

"Yeah, I remember you telling me you had an incident with a childhood friend's mother. What happened?"

"I had a friend, Susan, who had been my best friend.

"It had been bad enough that my mother couldn't decide if I was a freak of nature or demon-possessed, but she figured because of what I could do I had to be one of those, and in her mind, neither were to be tolerated. She also couldn't understand why anyone would want to be my friend.

"Anyway, Susan had been my first true friend. She never treated me as a freak, no matter what I did or said. We'd grown close and we each worked to protect the other from some of the cruel home realities we had to deal with. We defended each other and understood one another.

"When we became young adults, Susan's mother threatened to kill me if I ever contacted Susan again. Her mother told me, in a tone that dripped acid, that her daughter deserved a *normal* life and to be happy. She yelled, 'How can she have a normal life and be happy with someone like you in her life? You are by no means normal!'

"I Saw that her mother's energy was unstable and when I saw her pistol, I knew that she'd follow through on her threats.

"So, I walked away from my best friend. I'd often wondered if I'd left because I feared getting shot or because I felt that her mother's words might have had some validity." Filled with regret and unanswered questions, she sighed. "Maybe both reasons were why.

"I also learned back then that humans lie, but animals, my Team and energy in general never lied to me. I kept to myself. I felt safer. Lonely, but safer. Well, that was until I met you at a WPO meeting a few years ago and I didn't feel so alone again. But outside of you, the only time my 'abilities' are okay is when someone wants to hire me."

Josie was gentle. "I know it's hard for you to let people into your life. But you know what? You let me in. No betrayal here. And as for being alone? Not anymore, Clari."

Clari's eyes began to tear up. "And I'm scared all over again."

Josie hugged her until she relaxed. Josie sat back, clapped her hands and announced, "Okay, enough serious talk. It's time for some chick flicks." She punched "play" on the remote.

Sometime during the movie marathon, Morris returned and quietly slid into the guestroom so Clari and Josie could have their time together.

Many tears, glasses of pomegranate juice, and bowls of ice cream later, Josie left for home, and Clari sought her own bed.

Chapter Seven

Reader Level III — Includes Levels I & II plus: ability for at least Arch 1 level energy healing. ~ World Paranormal Organization (WPO) Information Pamphlet

Clari glanced into the mirror. The bandage was part way between the back of her ear and the center back of her head. She could feel the short prickly hairs where they had shaved her for surgery. Clari's fingers gingerly sought out the small bumps under her bandage that told her where the stitches were. Next she looked at her face. When she looked into her own eyes, she saw fear reflected in them. She hugged herself as the shaking began. Gut-wrenching tears followed.

She felt lighter when the crying stopped, but her head wound was pounding and her nose was stopped up.

After Clari put a shower cap on to protect her wound, she stepped underneath the warm soothing water, and allowed it to rinse away lingering residue from the emotional release. She still had an ongoing headache which was tiring in itself.

Shower done, Clari dried off and donned blue jeans paired with a blue long sleeved t-shirt that read *I don't have ducks in a row... I have squirrels and they're everywhere!* She took a deep breath and opened her bedroom door.

She usually wasn't thrilled to have anyone in her home, not only because she was most comfortable by herself, but having someone else in the house changed the balance of energy in her environment. She took a step into the hallway, once again stopping. Her stomach was doing something between being queasy and fluttering. It was then that she realized she was nervous and excited that Morris was in her house. She took another calming breath and headed to the kitchen.

From the open kitchen, Clari could see the table and the living room. She admired her eclectic assemblage of furnishings. She recalled Sebastian telling her that her home showed her flexibility in tastes and designs. He also said it reflected what kind of person she was.

She stood at the kitchen entrance and studied Morris. The newspaper Morris was reading hid his face. She knew Morris had earthly green eyes and she knew that when he was concentrating, his eyes took on an intense gaze. His energy was a soothing balm to her whole being, and she'd never met anyone before Morris that made her feel that way. A small smile played on her lips.

"Morning, Morris," Clari imparted in the direction of the upright newspaper at the kitchen table.

He lowered the paper, his green eyes taking her in. "The eggs and bacon are for you. I already ate since I wasn't sure how long you were going to sleep."

She mumbled her thanks, and grabbed a cup of coffee to go with her eggs and bacon. While she assembled her breakfast, she noticed another smell in the kitchen. She spotted canned cat food in Sasha's food bowl and fresh water in the water bowl.

Oops. "Thanks for taking care of my cat, Sasha, Morris, but she can't have that food. I only put out dry food."

"Sorry about that. I was hoping it was a cat. I noticed the bowls were about cat-sized and that both were empty, so I just picked up a few cans until I could talk to you. I take it 'Sasha' is a cat?"

She made a non-committal noise.

Morris continued. "I haven't seen her. Is she scared of new people in the house? Come to think of it, we didn't find a cat when you were shot. She must've been hiding. Was somebody taking care of her while you were in the hospital?"

"Um, a cat. Uh, yeah, she was fine," she muttered, hoping he didn't take notice of her being vague.

Morris hitched an eyebrow, letting her know that he didn't miss the fact she was vague and side-stepped the question. He shook his head and buried his nose back in the newspaper so Clari could eat in peace.

Clari's thoughts were still on her incident. In the past she always tried to use mundane tasks to either do a walking meditation or let her brain do some problem solving. Today was no different and while she ate, she worked on troubleshooting her attack. She knew she was missing something big, but couldn't quite grasp it yet.

She returned to the table after she finished washing breakfast dishes. Morris closed the newspaper and put it to the side.

"Uh, Morris? I want to thank you for everything you've done and everything you're doing for me. I really do appreciate you. Oh, and the whole saving my life thing too."

A smile teased his lips, "It's my pleasure, Clari."

She felt he wasn't looking at her, but looking within her...into her soul. Her heart raced and the butterflies reappeared in her stomach. She'd never felt as though anyone really Saw her – all of her – until this moment. Clari wasn't sure what to do, so in a panic, she blurted out, "So now what do we do, Morris?" *Smooth, Clari.* She mentally smacked her forehead.

"You mean aside from keeping you alive?"

She nodded at the solemn reminder as to why he was in her house. Some small part of her felt a twinge of disappointment. She wondered what that was all about.

He pointed to a box that sat next to the couch. "I thought we could work on some cases and, maybe, spend some time with you explaining more of how you do what you do and maybe how you perceive things."

She considered it. "We can do that, but I don't think it's going to take a week for any of that." She sat back down at the table. "Why don't you start with what you do know about what I do and we'll take it from there."

Morris sheepishly placed the WPO pamphlet he had been reading at the hospital on the table. "This is pretty much it."

She mentally rolled her eyes. "Okay, how do you think it applied to me?"

"Well, I know you are a Level IV Reader and I'm guessing you are an IV-B. And I say 'B' since I have seen for myself that you talk to ghosts, or dead people. So is that all you do, talk to the dead?"

"No, I don't just talk to dead people. I'm a Level IV, B & E. 'E' means that I can See and/or Sense magic spells, compulsion energy, wards or any other energy manipulations, though I don't always know what I'm Seeing if it is a new-to-me manipulation. I'm also able to do Levels I through III."

Morris read the Level descriptions again. "Okay, I understand Level I abilities. I don't understand 'psychometry' in Level II. What is that?"

"Psychometry, simplified, is the ability to access information by touching an object or person. It is a type of Reading and each Reader receives information in his or her own way. Some See it in their mind's eye, like watching a movie or flipping through photographs. Some Feel the information through emotions, such as sadness, fear, anger, joy and so on. Some Readers just Know information."

She picked up a pen. "When we touch an item, we usually receive the strongest, or the newest, imprint first. This energy imprint from, say your police force ring you are wearing, will Show me the most pronounced experience you've had recently. Like peeling the layers of an onion, we can move backward through time. No, we won't See everything going on, or all that transpired in your life. We just get Glimpses of the more intense energy moments that occurred during the time you wore the ring. Understand?"

His eyes opened wide. "Yeah, I think so. Kind of creepy though. Does this happen when you touch anything or anyone?"

"It can, especially for people whose primary focus, or ability, is psychometry. Those people are usually a bit withdrawn and may wear gloves to dampen the reception.

"For others, like me, if we are already overloaded energy-wise, we have to be careful of touching. If we aren't in a hyper-sensitive state, we have to tune into the frequency to get information. It's like a radio. I flip through the different channels or stations to find the one that I want to hear. When I do psychometry, I dial into that particular station and the reception is clearer.

"All of my channels, or stations, are active all the time, but I'm not listening all the time. Occasionally something will jump out at me, bypassing any station tuning. When that happens, it means I need to pay attention now."

He scratched his chin. "How can the stations be active all the time, but you aren't listening? How could you not listen if it was on?"

"Let's think about this in another way, Morris. How did you sleep last night?"

He sat back and shrugged. "Okay, I guess."

"Did you sleep as well here as you do at home?"

"No."

"Why?"

"Because it's not my bed. It's strange and new to me."

Her eyes lit up. "Exactly! The bed was different. The surroundings were different. The noises were different. So you were in a hyper-stimulated or hyper-sensitive mode. When you are at home, you know everything, sounds included. You only pay attention to sounds at home when they're outside the normal. The rest is pushed to the background; filtered. The noises are still there, still going on, but you no longer listen to them. Get it?"

He sat up straight. "I never thought about it that way, but you're right. So you can ignore the noise until you want to listen in?"

"Right, except when I am overloaded or hyper-stimulated."

Morris opened the pamphlet again. "Got it. Okay, next...what's 'energy manipulation'?"

"Energy healing is one form of energy manipulation. Energy healers bring in energy to their client and work to rebalance the energy flow. When someone is injured or ill, it is similar to a kink in a garden hose when the water flow becomes severely restricted or cut off. Energy healers work to unkink the hose and get the energy flowing back through again. Josie is an Arch 3, or advanced energy healer.

"Other forms of energy manipulation can be for positive or negative purposes. Spells, curses, blessings, and the like, are all forms of working to manipulate energy. There are also manipulators in what's considered the traditional sense. They are usually using it to get what they want, like talking someone into doing or buying something. Some people call that 'charisma' but they are actually manipulating the energy to make people feel good, or feel safe. Basically so they can get someone to do what they want."

Morris's brow furrowed. "Like what? Give me an example."

"Think of a salesman. His job is to get you excited and to buy, so he may manipulate your energy to make you more receptive to his suggestions to buy from him. This can be done with by using manipulating words, like many salesmen are trained to do, or by manipulating the other person's energy to make them more receptive to the salesman prompting them to buy from him or her."

He crossed his arms. "Hm. That sounds like cheating to me, but I do understand what you're saying. Can you tell me how you See? I mean, do you See ghosts like you see me? Or do they look transparent like some of the ghosts portrayed on the television?"

"That's a common question. Sometimes I See them as solidly as I see you. Other times they are full bodied and transparent. I can also See them as wisps of dark or light looking mist.

"I can See them in my mind's eye the same way you see memories. Or I can have a sudden Knowing of someone near me and what they may have looked like when they were alive. Any other questions, Morris?"

"Yes. I keep meaning to ask you, why do you stomp your foot? Is that the adult version of a temper tantrum?"

"Bwha! Ow!" Clari grabbed her head and fussed at Morris, "Don't make me laugh, it hurts!" She continued, "I do that when I'm frustrated or confused. Its purpose is the same as a ki-yap in martial arts, just quieter. It helps disperse the energy, and then I can shift back into a calmer energy." She shook her head and muttered, "Temper tantrum."

He shrugged. His eyes twinkled, "Well, it could've been a small temper tantrum."

She rolled her eyes. "Any other questions?"

"No, I think I need to digest what you've told me so far, though I'm sure I'll have more questions later. Is that okay?"

She nodded.

Morris continued, "Do you feel like trying a case or do you need to rest?"

"I'm not tired yet, Morris. I'm a bit nervous though. I don't know what this has done to my abilities...but I guess I'll never know until I try."

"Good! Oh, I meant to ask. What about your clients for this week?

She brushed his concern away with a dismissive hand wave. "Josie already handled that. We already had an emergency plan in place for both of us, so she'd already contacted my clients to let them know she could either assist them or they could wait until I returned."

Morris nodded. He stood, walked over to the couch, and grabbed the box of cases. He came back to the table and dropped it on the chair between the two of them, then flipped through the files to ferret out a case that wouldn't be emotionally charged for her to test her abilities on.

While he familiarized himself with the first case, Clari closed her eyes to center, balance and shield.

When she opened her eyes, he had a case ready. "A woman called in and said she keeps smelling cigarette smoke at night. She goes through the house but doesn't find anything burning. No one who lives in the house smokes.

"Police have been called several times. They proceeded through the house and around the outside of the house, but never found anything. The woman continued to call and the police continued to find nothing. The woman didn't appear to be on drugs or alcohol and seemed genuinely distraught."

While Morris talked, Clari wrote. He waited for her to finish writing. She glanced up at him. He motioned for her to share what she had gotten.

"What she has is a homeless person who comes around after the lights in the house have been off for a while. He's tall and thin, with short brown hair. His hair, though not close cropped, is disheveled. He rides a bicycle, wears tan canvas shoes, and smokes. He enters the screened-in patio and sleeps there. If he sees lights or hears anything, he flees before he can be seen or caught, and since the patio is on the opposite end of the house from the bedrooms, he receives plenty of notice to flee the area.

"There is some sort of rug or runner that he uses for a sleeping mat. His hair is oily and has left residue on it. He also left signs of his smoking — in a corner — where he put out his cigarettes.

"It will take more than one person to catch him. He is well versed in his routine and has his escape routes planned well."

She finished reading her notes. Morris had a huge grin on his face.

It confused her. "What?"

"It appears your abilities, as we know of them right now, weren't affected by the shooting."

"You're right! I didn't even realize it." Her eyes teared up. "Growing up I wanted my abilities to go away. Today, I was scared they were gone." A deep sigh escaped and Clari relaxed as they continued working on cases.

When they took a break mid-morning, Clari poured some pomegranate juice while Morris refreshed his coffee. As they sat back down, she pounced. "I have some questions for you before we continue on with work."

He raised his eyebrows.

She protested, "It's only fair. You're working on figuring out how I tick. Turnabout is fair play."

"Okay, but no guarantees I'll answer. Fire away."

"How did you end up with me?"

"What do you mean?"

"Me, Morris. It's obvious that many of the officers on your police force are hostile towards me, and to many of them I'm a freak of nature. Did you pull the short straw and get stuck with me?"

He shifted in his chair. She felt she'd hit a nerve, but she wanted an answer and wasn't going to let him off the hook. She sat quietly and waited.

Whatever turmoil he had going on inside settled. He studied her as he told his story. "Lieutenant Avery approached me and asked if I'd consider partnering, unofficially of course, with a contracted WPO Reader. Though, thinking back, I don't think I really had a choice." Morris squirmed a bit more before he continued. "I've had partners from the force before, but they usually requested a change of partners, or in some cases a transfer to another station.

"Though I'm known as a good cop, professionally and ethically, no one wants to partner with me. Some others said that there is something 'off' about me. They also claimed that they weren't comfortable with the 'weird' cases that seem to gravitate to me."

Morris took a sip of coffee and gathered his thoughts. "When the Captain approached Lieutenant Avery about bringing in a WPO certified Reader, which the Lieutenant had no choice about, he wasn't happy and didn't really want to deal with him or her. He called me to his office and asked if I'd be interested in pairing up with the WPO person. I asked if I could get some more information on this person before I answered.

"Lieutenant Avery's phone rang. He grunted acknowledgment a few times and said, 'We'll be down shortly.' He hung up and told me that we needed to go downstairs. The phone call had announced the arrival of the WPO Reader. 'Now's your chance, Morris. Let's go meet this person.'

"When we got downstairs, I could *feel* you. My eyes searched the room until I found you. I knew right then and there I'd accept the Lieutenant's offer to work with you."

Her heart raced. She wasn't sure she wanted to hear more.

He glanced down at his hands, took a deep breath and released it. A red blush crept up his face and his ears flamed. When he spoke again, he kept his eyes on his hands while he picked on the ragged cuticle on his thumb. "And I knew I had to protect you. It was a call that came from...I don't know...my soul?" The cuticle ripped a bit.

While he was focused on his thumb, she crossed her arms over her chest in an unconscious act of trying to protect her heart.

"Before we even reached you, I grabbed the Lieutenant's arm. He swung back at me. I nodded and mouthed 'I accept.' His eyebrows rose, but instead of asking, he just gave me a nod back and we moved to meet you."

Morris lifted his head and made and made soulful eye contact. "So no, I didn't draw the short stick, Clari. I was the lucky one."

Bewildered and pleasantly surprised, she managed to say, "Thank you, Morris." But she wasn't sure if the thanks was because he shared something so personal with her, because he'd felt like the lucky one to be able to work with her, or because of something more...something bigger.

Making a decision, Clari stood and proclaimed, "Enough work for to-day. My head is sore, so I'm declaring it game time. Let's get the cards." They spent the rest of the day playing card games and chatting about nothing in particular.

When it was bedtime, she moved towards her bedroom. She stopped and called back. "Hey, Morris? Thank you."

Startled, he beamed. "You're welcome. For what?"

"Everything. Just thank you for everything." She entered her bedroom and shut the door.

In bed she closed her eyes only to pop them back open. "What the heck?" she whispered. She closed her eyes again. With them closed, she could see a black and white x-ray-like image of her room. But, she also saw a glow emanating from each object in her room. She felt like it was the life force of each item. She turned her focus to talking with her guides.

What am I Seeing? She asked her guides.

* Life forces *

But how can inanimate objects have a life force?

* Everything's energy – it takes energy to create all you see – all is imbued with life force – just a much denser energy *

Whoa, that's cool. Is this a new ability?

* No – you just never paid attention before – really no new abilities – just different forms of energy use or energy perceptions *

"Neat," she whispered as she snuggled in to go to sleep.

Chapter Eight

Clari found Morris preparing fried bologna sandwiches with a side of cheese crackers and chocolate milk. Delighted, she asked, "And who did you talk to, because I know you didn't think of this yourself?"

Morris' face lit up. "Josie called me to see how you were doing. She sang like a canary when I asked for lunch ideas."

Morris paused and read Clari's T-shirt. "Underestimate me. That'll be fun." Morris snickered. "Cute, Clari."

Her eyes twinkled. "I thought so."

Morris asked, "How did you sleep last night?"

"I had to shift now and again from the pain in my head. But once I found the perfect position, I was out. How about you?"

"I did fine. Let's eat." Morris motioned to the table.

As they sat eating, Clari realized she'd become comfortable with Morris in her house. *Maybe it wouldn't be so bad living with someone, if it's the right someone.*

Morris interrupted her inner musings. "Have you ever tried using your abilities to help with your own unresolved cases or incidents? You know, like the shooting?"

She thought about it before she answered. "I hadn't thought about it for the shooting. I have, in the past, been able to Read for myself if it wasn't something I was too emotionally involved in. The more emotion an incident stirs up in me, the less information I can get."

Clari could feel his wheels turning.

He asked, "Is there a way to, I don't know, detach yourself and treat it like someone else's case?"

She hesitated. "I don't know."

"Want to try?"

"I can try, but can't guarantee it'll work. How do you think we should do this?"

Morris leaned back. "What if we did it similar to some other cases? You prepare yourself, and when you are in your zone I'll ask questions and help guide you. Want to try?"

She could feel hope and excitement building in him. "No guarantees, Morris. We don't know if this will work or not."

He gulped down the rest of his lunch, and cleared the table.

Clari settled on the couch, closed her eyes, and went through her cleansing and shielding process. She opened her eyes.

He sat across from her in a chair. He shook his head. "Uh-uh. You need to close your eyes again. Just listen to my voice."

She closed her eyes.

Morris began, "We have a female. She was at home vacuuming. She was shot. Do you have her?"

Clari answered in a quiet, unsure voice. "Yes."

Morris continued, "Okay, so she was vacuuming. Tell me what you see."

"She's wearing dark colored baggy sweats and a light colored tee shirt. The music is cranked up and she's vacuuming when she suddenly feels the hair stand on the back of her neck. She freezes. Something is wrong. She begins to slowly turn around..."

He prompted, "She began to turn around and what? What did she see?"

Clari opened her eyes. "Nothing. Darkness came. Next thing was you telling me to hang on." The darkness, or void, and of not knowing what had happened, scared her. Clari began to feel the same panic that she'd felt at the hospital start to well up again. She took a deep breath in an attempt to calm herself.

He lightly chewed on this thumbnail. "You mentioned the music was cranked up. What were you listening to?"

"Ugh! You should know, Morris. You were the one who found me."

Absorbed in thought, his teeth sawed at his thumbnail. He stopped, met her eyes, "I'll be right back." He grabbed his phone and punched in a number as he walked away from her.

She heard him talking, but couldn't make out the words.

When he came back into the room, he told her, "Detective Ambrose is on his way over to talk with you."

"Why? What is going on, Morris?" She felt like she'd missed something.

"I'll let Ambrose handle it. He'll be here shortly." Morris refused any further attempts to get information from him.

When the doorbell rang, she was once again reminded of why Morris was there when he drew his weapon and motioned for her to stay on the couch. He cautiously moved to the front door. After seeing it was Ambrose, he holstered his weapon, let Ambrose in and led him to Clari.

She moved to stand but Ambrose waved her to stay seated. He took the chair recently vacated by Morris. "Hello, Ms. Jones. It's good to see you again. Morris informed me that you two have been revisiting the day you were shot. Can you share with me what you told him?"

Clari shot a questioning glance at Morris who nodded to let her know that it was okay. "I was just telling him about what I was doing. I described wearing dark sweats and a light tee shirt, had the music cranked up, and was jamming to classic rock while I was vacuuming."

"I see. Do you remember what song was playing?"

"I know one of them was 'Smoke on the Water' because I was singing to it, though I can't remember if that was the one I was singing to when I got shot."

"Do you often 'jam' to classic rock?" Ambrose inquired.

She jutted her chin forward. "Yes I do, and I'm not ashamed of it. It's one of the many reasons I live way out here. I can crank my music so loud you can see the windows vibrate. And out here, there is no one to complain about how loud I put it. I never clean without my music on — it gives me the boost needed to keep working."

Ambrose looked over at Morris and motioned to him. Morris left the room.

"Detective, what's going on?" As she asked this, Morris returned with another person.

Ambrose explained, "This officer is from the lab. He is going to dust your sound system for fingerprints. Ms. Jones, when Detective Morris arrived, there was no music playing. The only thing on and making noise was your vacuum. Do you know of anyone who would turn your stereo off?"

"Uh...I...no. I can't think of anyone who would. Why would they?"

"That's what we would like to know, Ms. Jones." Ambrose stood and handed her his card. "If you remember anything else, please let me know."

After she took his card, Morris escorted him and the lab officer out, and then re-joined her in the living room.

Clari stood. "Morris, I need to tell you something. Well, actually a couple of things."

His forehead puckered. "What?"

"First, I'm glad you shared with me about how you got 'stuck' with me. And, in the spirit of, shall we say, mostly 'full disclosure', I want to share with you one of my...uh...quirks."

She noticed that wrinkles appeared at the corner of his eyes when he was in a mischievous mood. "You only have one quirk, eh?"

"Oh, I'm sure I have more than one. It's just that some aren't so easy for me to share."

The wrinkles disappeared. "Okay, I'm listening."

"Sasha, my cat, died about three years ago."

Morris squinted his eyes at her. She knew that look...it was the one someone gives you when they think you aren't firing on all cylinders. Without realizing it, Morris took a step back. "What do you mean?"

Resigned, she shared, "Sasha, my blue-eyed Siamese cat died three years ago of old age, only she doesn't realize she's dead. Well, I don't think she realizes she is dead. She comes and goes and sometimes begs for food, but since she's dead, she can't really eat. I just keep recycling the same old dry food." She waited. Was he going to think she was a total loon? And it wasn't quite "full disclosure" yet. She also hadn't mentioned that Sasha wasn't the only unseen-to-others cat with her.

Apparently reaching a decision, Morris sighed. He shrugged his shoulders. "Okay."

She wasn't sure she had heard him correctly. "What? Okay? That's it?"

His spontaneous laughter made her feel light and safe. "You talk to dead people. So what's so bad about talking to a dead cat?"

She was a little shocked that he took the news so easily, but she also felt relieved, like she'd just passed some sort of test. She realized that she felt Morris had just accepted another aspect of her.

With a lighter heart, she told him to go through the cases to see which one they should start with while she made them sandwiches.

Morris lifted a box and opened the lid. "Clari?"

"Mmmm?" Clari mumbled as she smeared mayo on his sandwich.

"How's your head feeling after you did...well, what you do...after we worked on your case? Did you get a bigger headache or did anything else, like a side effect from pushing your ability show up?"

Clari took a moment to tune into her body, and more importantly her head to see how everything Felt. "My head is still throbbing, but it hasn't gotten worse and I don't think anything else has happened. I think I'm good to go on."

Morris turned his attention back to the box of files. "Okay, great! But let me know the second you feel there's a problem."

Clari came to the table carrying the two lunch plates. "I'll let you know."

He read to her as they sat and ate. "Jewelry started disappearing. The mother thought it was when her son had friends over, but she wasn't sure exactly when they disappeared since she doesn't wear jewelry every day.

"She keeps the most expensive stuff locked away. The jewelry she left out was the silver with the less expensive semi-precious stones."

Clari closed her eyes to focus inward. "It's her son. He has a substance addiction and is pawning her jewelry to get his fix. He makes sure to snag something when there are others in the house so that it will create confusion and take suspicion away from him."

She opened her eyes and asked enthusiastically, "Don't you guys have that invisible ink stuff that turns purple when someone touches it? We could so catch him that way!"

"Or we could just put in a hidden camera and catch him that way."

"Oh, yeah. But that's not as exciting," she whined. She stood and began to gather her dishes to help clear off the table. As she worked she continued on in a more serious tone. "That was too easy. What gives?"

He shook his head. "I don't know. I guess they are more short-handed than I thought."

"Well, for this case, that's just going to be the first part. Next they have to deal with the stealing as well as his addiction. It is sad really — this kid stealing from his mother. That really sucks."

"Yeah, it's worse when it's someone you know."

Clari could feel the blood as it drained from her face. She was vaguely aware of Morris cleaning up his spot at the table. Clari fell back into the chair with a thud.

"Clari?"

She whispered, "What did you say?'

He frowned. "What? I said it is worse when it's someone you know."

She felt a weird numbing effect crawling up her body.

Oh. My. God.

She could feel all of the little snippets of information – the puzzle pieces – begin to click in place. Her mind whirled in a chaotic way, but she knew better than to get excited. She also knew to just sit still while her brain worked to reorganize the information. She stilled, except for that one thought that had escaped the whirlwind. That one that kept repeating in her mind.

Oh. My. God.

Morris stood still. He recognized the look on her face. He called it the "magic moment". It was the moment when everything began to come together...to solidify. It was also known as the "eureka moment". It was the truth gathering and preparing to reveal itself. The pieces needed to finish coming together before anyone spoke or moved. It was like trying to remember a dream...if you got distracted by the physical world, the dream was lost.

"I don't understand why," whispered a dazed Clari.

Her phone rang. She absentmindedly picked it up and answered before she realized she had her phone in her hand. "We traced the iron box to your neck of the woods, Clarima," the familiar voice of Maestro informed her.

"Um, okay," she stammered.

"It never left your town. Someone local has it, though we've not been able to narrow it down to an individual yet."

"It is okay, Maestro. I'll take it from here. I think I know who has it. And thank you."

"You are welcome, Clarima. I heard about the shooting. How are you feeling since your incident?"

"The physical is healing quite well, thank you, but I'll have to get back to you on the emotional part. Thanks again, Maestro."

"Again, you are welcome. I will seek payment another day." He disconnected the call.

She looked over at Morris. "We need to talk. And I need your help."

They moved into the living room.

Clari sat cross-legged on the couch, hugged a pillow, took a deep breath and released it. "I think I need to fill you in on what else has been going on because I'm beginning to see that they are all interconnected, or at least some of it is. And need to give you some more background so you'll know where I'm coming from with all of this."

His silence encouraged her to continue.

"You know how we talked about the different levels in the WPO pamphlet?" Morris nodded. "Well, there are more levels, levels that are normally not public knowledge, and I need to talk about those for a bit."

She struggled with sharing. The fear and indecision showed on her face. Morris nodded, but didn't say anything, which made the space feel safe to Clari.

"To help differentiate these from the public levels they are labeled with the Roman numerals." She began pointing to her fingers as she made her way through the list. "There's Level C. The Readers in this level are 'wild'. Wild is what the WPO calls the untested, uncertified, unregistered, and probably untrained Readers.

"There is a Level D. These are certified Readers, but the details are deemed 'classified' by WPO. All we have are speculations, and even those who are regularly certified don't know what this level means.

"There is a Level M. This means that their certification, or renewal, is pending. This is usually due to an investigation being done on that individual. Once they're cleared, they're reclassified and put back into service. If they aren't cleared, their certification is revoked.

"And finally, as far as I know, there's the last level…Level X. These abilities, and therefore the individuals with these abilities, are designated — I think — as dangerous, deadly, or uncontrollable. These people usually disappear, never to be seen or heard from again. Ever. You with me so far?"

He crossed his legs. "Yep."

She took a deep breath. "Next, I want to share a theory with you. Well, a theory as far as the rest of the human population is concerned. Through my observations of physical patterns and energetic patterns, coupled with information my Team has provided…well, this is what I've come up with and ask you to keep an open mind. Please?"

Morris leaned forward. "You helped me develop an open mind, which I promise to keep, at least until I've heard all you have to say."

"Thank you." Clari went on to explain her theory. "I believe that paranormals were prevalent in the days of old, but the hunting and killing of the predatory paranormals — like the different kinds of shapeshifters and vampires — had severely reduced their numbers. Human fear of the predatory paranormals leaked over to other paranormal species, and eventually dangerously reduced their numbers as well."

Her hands helped to weave the story. "The paranormal survivors had quietly co-mingled and bred with humans, significantly weakening the paranormal species bloodlines and abilities until the paranormals were nothing more than ancient scary or mystical stories."

Her fingers found her earring and began fidgeting with it. She had that far-away look and it sounded to Morris that she was thinking out loud. "I don't think that it's just the paranormal traits that are surfacing. The traits of mythical beings are showing up as well, but, so far as I can tell, they're only in the overlays."

She looked up and focused on Morris. "Throughout history, an occasional throwback was born, but never with the full paranormal abilities of their ancestors, only some with enough abilities to perform an extraordinary feat or two.

"Today, so far, there aren't any 'real' vampires, shape shifters, and fae or other mythological and mystical beings in our dimension, but some of their attributes, or abilities, are showing up in the physical world.

"My theory is that the energy shifts that began in force in the year twenty-twelve had begun to activate the previously dormant paranormal and mythical attributes in DNA and began bringing them back.

"Our ancestor's blood awakens within us," she finished.

Morris paled. "So does that mean we are going to have shape shifters shredding people and vampires draining people of their blood?"

"Oh, gods no, Morris. The paranormal and mythical *attributes* are showing up, and those who have paranormal DNA are probably unaware of it. They aren't going to be the actual creatures or beings. It just means that some aspects, like increased speed, heightened senses, and an increase in abilities, are going to surface. We're not going to need silver bullets or wooden stakes. Not in our lifetime, anyway.

"Those who have wolf shifter DNA may have the stockier appearance of their shifter animal and show traits of extreme spouse or mate protectiveness or jealousy as well as protecting those under their care or considered to be part of their pack. They may also exhibit an increased sense of smell, enhanced hearing, or extra-human strength. Lieutenant Avery, for example, is one, and he is very protective of 'his'. You know, those who work for him?"

"Like you and me?"

She flinched. "You, yes. Me, not so much."

Morris interrupted her thought flow. "Isn't a wolf shifter the same thing as a werewolf? And what about vampires?"

"A wolf shifter is not a werewolf. The werewolves of horror shows only have a single thought of hunting to kill. Wolves, and other shifters, are more like the wild version of their animals, and the wild animals try to avoid contact with humans."

She continued, reabsorbed in sharing her thoughts. "Vampiric attributes could show in the ability to drain another's energy. Some have become energy vampires as opposed to physical bloodsucking vampires. Like the wolf shifter traits, the vampire traits may show up in increased speed, a heightened sense of hearing and smell and increased strength.

"And the humans whose overlays are angelic-like beings may start exhibiting a noticeable calming effect on those around them, or perhaps have healing abilities show up.

"For those whose attributes are earth-connected, you may find some that have a green thumb on steroids, or someone who has animals following them around."

She took another deep breath and blew it out. "Those with fae attributes will have a variety of abilities. I'm also able to See a lot of those attributes in some people's energy overlays."

Morris held up his hand. "I feel like I'm in school. What is an overlay?"

"Okay, let's say you are showing a home movie on a blank screen or wall. You see the images on the surface it is being projected on. What happens if someone stands up in between the projector and the wall? The images are now projected, at least in part, on the person's body. You can see both the person's body — the physical world — and a see-through scene being shown on this person — the overlay.

"I can see both the person and the see-through scene, or picture, at the same time. The overlay is the see-through projection associated with that particular person or place. Understand?"

He nodded. "Yeah, I think so. So, do I have an overlay? What does it look like?"

"I don't know. I've not been able to See one with, or on you." Her fingers fidgeted with her earring again. "Morris, no one, except you, knows that I can do this and I'm scared of being labeled Level X if anyone ever found out."

"I'm honored you shared that with me, Clari. Your secret is safe with me."

Clari released a breath she hadn't realized she held. She next shared with him about the dagger experience and the vague warnings she had received from her Other-World friends. "So with all of that, along with me getting shot, and what you said about it being hard with it being someone you know...it kind of made things click into place for me. For example, my shields only alert me if someone I don't know crosses them. The shields are programmed to ignore the people I consider friends and to ignore those energy signatures. That means..."

Morris interrupted her, "That whoever shot you was someone you consider a friend. Since Sebastian gave you that dagger, I think he's the one who is trying to kill you."

Tickled by his assumption, she teased, "You *really* don't like Sebastian, do you?"

His eyes flashed. "No, I don't."

"As much delight as it would provide you, I assure you it's not Sebastian. But, I think I know who, and need your help to prove it."

He jumped at the request. "I'm in."

Chapter Nine

Reader Level V — Most of all the Levels plus: able to trace the weaker energy manipulation signatures. Usually Vs work at WPO as investigators, researchers, or instructors or they police WPO certified members.
~ World Paranormal Organization (WPO) Information Pamphlet

Clari and Josie watched as the caterers bustled in. The office lobby had been transformed — it now had long buffet tables along the walls. The caterers set up tapas for Clari's guests. The tapas ranged from cucumber finger sandwiches and classic bruschetta, to charcuterie platters, as well as an offering of sliced fruits and potato salads. Another table had been set up for non-alcoholic drinks. A banner proudly displayed the reason for the party, "Congratulations on your 10th Anniversary!"

"Josie, you look awesome!"

Josie, dressed in an off-the-shoulder with an overlapping soft beige neckline and color blocked with a black skirt, swirled, "I know," she giggled. "And look at you in your fancy black three piece pant suit with a black and white geometric shapes duster. Pretty!"

Clari looked away, embarrassed by the praise, and then looked back at Josie. "Thanks for all the work you've done on this, Josie. I couldn't have pulled it off. Thank you for handling it."

Josie grabbed and hugged Clari. "You're welcome. I'm just glad you're feeling better. But, are you sure this is safe for you? We still don't know who tried to kill you."

Clari stood up a bit taller. "I'm not letting that stop me from living my life. So, shall we enjoy our celebration tonight?"

Josie did a little dance. "Bring on the party!"

The guests began arriving as the caterers finished up. One of the first to arrive was Mrs. Benton with Miz Cozy. Clari felt it was appropriate that her first client was one of the first to arrive. Mrs. Benton, Clari's first ever client, grabbed Clari in a warm hug. "Thank you so much, Clari," she whispered in her ear as they hugged. Mrs. Benton and Miz Cozy, whose tail was wagging, took off to walk the room to meet others at the party. The room soon filled with the guests.

Client Jerry, in his blue jeans and cowboy hat, stood holding his soda and looking like he felt out of place. Clari went over to him. "Jerry, thank you so much for coming tonight. I really appreciate it."

A smile lit up his face. "Yes, ma'am. Least I could do for all your help."

"So everything's still good at home? No problems?"

Standing taller and looking more self-assured, he replied, "No problems at all, and that's the way I like it."

Clari was happy to hear that. "Good! Please help yourself to the food, Jerry. And thank you again for coming."

Jerry nodded and walked off towards the food tables.

As Clari turned, she saw that Mr. Hightower had joined the party. He was wearing a tweed jacket and had his nose in the air. He strutted with his Grand Champion Yorkshire, Ernest, on leash. Clari chuckled as she watched them work the room as though they were on the AKC show floor.

Her breath caught as she saw Morris enter. He was dressed in dark dress pants and a long sleeve oxford shirt. These clothes were a lot nicer than his work clothes. She watched his confident approach, which was occasionally halted by someone stopping him to chat. She noticed that he kept an eye on her no matter where he was in the room.

Her eyes softened as he finally made it to her. He placed his hand on her lower back, leaned into her and asked, "You look amazing. How are you doing? Nervous?"

Absorbed into his green eyes, she felt the whole room disappear...only his eyes existed. She tilted her head slightly while she tried to figure out what was different about his eyes. *Fierce, with a hard glint*, her mind whispered. It dawned on her that he was in protector-mode.

He cleared his throat. "Um...Clari?"

"Yes?" Her blink was slow. She started and shook her head. "Oh! I mean I'm fine, Morris. And yes, I'm nervous." She could feel the embarrassment slowly creeping up her face. "You?"

"You got this, Clari. And you're not alone." He didn't have a chance to say anymore as others approached and congratulated Clari. Morris left her side to go mingle, but made sure Clari stayed in his sights.

She wove around the room making sure she thanked each guest for coming. Clari was pleased that people mingled comfortably, and that her lobby was the perfect size for the gathering.

Clari saw Lieutenant Avery and Morris standing together and approached them, "Thank you both for coming, Lieutenant and Morris." Still poking the bear, she hitched one eyebrow and told the lieutenant, "You clean up nice. I like the dress blues."

Avery rolled his eyes. "I'm attending as a representative of our police department."

Morris chuckled as he nodded to Avery and Clari, and then headed off to talk with others.

Clari smiled. "Well, you look really nice. And I do appreciate you coming. Now, if you'll excuse me, there are more people I'd like to thank. I hope you enjoy yourself, Lieutenant Avery."

An hour into the party, Josie asked for everyone's attention. The room stilled. "Thank you all for coming. Clari would like to say a few words now." Josie swept her arm towards Clari. "The floor is yours."

Clari placed her drink down on a nearby table and turned to face her guests. "Thank you, Josie. I wanted to thank you all, but not only for coming tonight. It was your support, and your business, that made this celebration possible. I want to give a great big thank you to Josie for putting this all together." Clari's eyes sought out Lieutenant Avery. Avery came in his dress police blues. "And I'd like to thank Lieutenant Avery and the police department for everything they've done. Now, please enjoy the food and conversation." Some people clapped and conversations throughout started up again.

She turned to pick up her glass, but stopped when she saw it in Sebastian's hand. Dressed in typical Sebastian style, he wore a soft charcoal grey Armani slim fit jacket with matching pants. He held her glass out to her, and as she reached for it, his voice caressed her energy with one word, "Belle. You look stunning tonight."

She suddenly felt shy. She took her glass. "Thank you, Sebastian. I'm glad you made it tonight."

Josie walked up to Sebastian and Clari. "Hey, Sebastian." Sebastian nodded to Josie. Josie turned to Clari and asked, "So, who is your bodyguard tonight?"

Clari faced Josie. "No one. I no longer have a bodyguard."

Josie angrily shoved the errant locks behind her ears as she spoke. "Holy moly! What? You are kidding, right?"

"No, I am not kidding."

Josie's energy prickled. "But the person who tried to kill you is still out there."

"I think it was just an isolated, random incident. Nothing has happened since, so I refused any more protection."

Josie's mouth hung open. Clari refused to look at Sebastian. She could Feel waves of anger roll off him. Before anyone else could say something to her, Clari murmured, "Excuse me. I need to circulate the room," and walked away.

She stopped and chatted every so often as she worked her way through the room. She kept Josie in her peripheral and saw her stomp off and go straight for Morris.

Clari snuck a peek back to Sebastian and saw that his normally blue eyes were now black, and locked on her. She'd never seen him angry before. She Knew he was angry with her for being so reckless with her life. With a deepening scowl, Sebastian turned and stormed out into the night.

Clari looked back at Josie and Morris. Josie had her hands on her hips. Morris shook his head no, and then shrugged.

A party guest asked Clari a question. After she answered, she looked back and saw Josie throw her hands up and march back to the buffet table.

As the party began to wind down, Josie helped Clari make take-home plates for the guests. "I'm staying with you until you're ready to go home", Josie said in a clipped tone of voice. Josie was, Clari guessed, as mad as Sebastian had been for Clari dismissing her bodyguard. Josie continued, "Let's clean up before we go."

Clari rebuffed offers to help clean up. "Josie, the room is fine. We don't need to clean up. I have the cleaning crew coming in the morning. Thank you again for everything, but please, just go home and I'll talk to you later."

Tears built in Josie's eyes as she turned, slamming the door behind her when she left.

Clari plopped down at the almost empty buffet table. The party was over. The squeak of the door opening hit Clari's ears. Her heart beat sped up as unease slithered like a snake up her spine.

Maria stepped in, gun drawn and pointed at Clari. Maria crossed the room, and stopped a few feet from Clari.

Regret and resignation had stripped the life from Clari's words, making them sound hollow. "Hello, Maria."

This Maria was barely recognizable from the one Clari knew from Maria's youth, and even from the last two times she saw her. Madness danced in Maria's eyes, her lips pressed tight and soured emotions filled the room as Maria ground out, "You aren't surprised to see me? What gave it away?"

Maybe I'm not supposed to survive this time. Can Maria smell my fear? Clari wondered before she answered. "The music. I had the stereo on loud when you shot me. But when the police found me, there was no music on. I remembered that when I saw you four years ago, your hearing had become sensitive. When you and Sebastian visited me back then, I had to turn the stereo off even though it had been playing softly."

Maria's jaw clenched and eyes narrowed as she spit her response to Clari, "You just won't die. You somehow managed to escape every attempt, even shooting you point-blank in the head. This time I'm going to make sure you die and stay dead!" Her eyes became cold and flat as she took aim.

Clari was driven to understand, "Wait, Maria! Why? Why have you been trying to kill me? What did I do to you?"

"I've worked hard my whole life so I could work beside my brother. So that I could be his partner. But even when I became an adult, Sebastian still went to you." Maria pounded her chest with her pointer finger. "I'm family. I can do the work. He doesn't need you. Yet he still comes to you. He still gives you the hard magick or energy cases. No one takes me seriously." Maria's anger spilled over making her hands shake as she kept the gun pointed at Clari.

Clari's body sagged. The sadness bled through as she spoke. "You're the one who cursed the dagger and made sure it found its way to Sebastian so he would bring it to me. You're the one who made a deal with Hecate to have me killed. When that failed, you stole the seal to summon Lucifer." Clari's anger began rising from the depths of that place within where she had stuffed it. The bitterness bit her words, "What happened, Maria, the seal wouldn't work?"

Maria's face contorted in fury as she waved the gun with contempt. "Yeah, that stupid thing wouldn't work, so I had no choice but to shoot you. And yet, you're still here. Tonight you die." She refocused the gun on Clari, but before she could pull the trigger, Sebastian appeared out of thin air behind Maria.

Like a striking snake, Sebastian's right arm lashed out, wrapped around to the front of her, not only pinning Maria against his chest, but also securing the forearm of the hand that held the gun. At the same time, his left hand came around the other side. It held a knife which he used to slice Maria's lower arm enough to force her to drop the gun. Sebastian transferred the knife to Maria's neck, growled a warning to Maria to not move. They both suddenly disappeared, leaving behind blood drops on the floor where Maria once stood.

Clari sat, stunned by what transpired as Lieutenant Avery and Morris stormed through the door, their bodies taunt and ready for battle. When the other officers entered after them, Avery motioned for them to fan out and search the premises. Morris rushed over to Clari. He knelt down and gently cradled Clari's face. "Are you okay? Are you hurt?"

Clari shook her head, "She didn't touch me."

His shoulders dropped and a heavy sigh escaped his lips, "Thank goodness."

He pulled up a chair next to Clari. She leaned into him as they waited together for the officers to secure the property.

After they cleared the building, Lieutenant Avery approached Clari, "Can you talk me through what happened tonight? We need an official statement."

Following an extensive debriefing with Lieutenant Avery, Avery asked Morris to bring Clari home. When they were alone in the car, Clari asked Morris, "Because you guys bugged my office building before the party, I know you have Maria's confession on tape, but what happens now that she's literally disappeared?"

"I don't know. We are in uncharted waters as far as policy and laws go. It's not up to me anyway."

She stared out into the night. "I hated to deceive Sebastian and Josie, but I knew neither one of them would like me being bait. Thank you for helping me."

Feeling no words were necessary, he just rested his hand on her thigh as he drove.

When they arrived at Clari's house, Morris went through the house first and checked everything before he allowed her to enter.

"I know I took all my belongings home, but I can stay tonight if you'd like, Clari, especially since we don't know where Maria is."

Weariness had hit. "No, I think I'm safe, but thank you."

He put his hand on her cheek. "I'm so glad she didn't kill you." He leaned over, gently kissed her. "Goodnight, Clari."

Wait. What? Her mouth dropped open as he turned to walk back to his car. She battled within, fighting the desire to call him back to her. Bewildered by both her and Morris' actions just then, she continued watching until his car was swallowed by the dark of the night.

Clari curled up on the couch. Hugging a pillow, she cried until she fell asleep.

The next morning, following a lot of verbal groveling and a lot of explaining about Maria's attempts and disappearance, Josie forgave Clari.

The house felt surprisingly empty without Morris. She did laundry and solemnly, without her loud music, cleaned the house.

Morris called to let her know that they'd finished searching Maria's apartment. While they hadn't found her, they did find a room dedicated to her black arts. "We also found the iron box that had been stolen from Abrahams Panoply of Past Procurements shop." He assured her, "The box has been turned over to the WPO's artifact caretakers. It's safe."

"Perfect. Can we go back to the shop after lunch so I can let Mr. Snellerd know that the box has been recovered and is safe?"

Morris agreed and assured her that he'd pick her up at three. The flutters in Clari's belly gave away her excitement at being with Morris again.

Clari's thought moved to the upcoming visit to Abrahams Panoply of Past Procurements and hoped her news would convince Mr. Snellerd to be at peace and cross over.

Morris waited just inside the door as Clari went further in. She felt safe under his watchful eyes.

The store felt like it was holding its breath. She softly called to Mr. Snellerd as she trekked down the first aisle.

Mr. Snellerd materialized just as she rounded the corner. "Did you find it? Did you get the box?" His eyes, both hopeful and fearful, bore into hers.

She nodded. "Yes, Mr. Snellerd. The box, and its contents, has been recovered."

"Good. Good. Did anyone have a chance to use it for summoning?"

"The person said she couldn't get it to work, so I'm guessing we're okay."

Concern crossed his ghostly face. "That's no guarantee. We don't know if it actually works. We also don't know if it does work, or how long after a summoning ceremony would it take to see the results. Where is the box now?"

"It's under lock and key at WPO," Clari assured him. "The artifact caretakers will watch over it."

His ghost shoulders dropped as he released his concerns. "Excellent. That's all I can ask for."

She saw the light come down a few feet behind Mr. Snellerd. "Are you ready to cross over now, Mr. Snellerd? Someone came to greet you." She pointed behind him.

He turned towards the light. "Ah, my sweet Sally." He turned back to Clari. His face beamed. "Thank you."

He stepped forward where the light quickly embraced him. The store felt a little lighter.

The best part of my job. She sighed and smiled as she headed back to Morris. They were done here.

Pomegranate juice in hand, she was in route to her home office when she saw Sebastian standing in the entryway. She was unsure of Sebastian's intent.

As if he could hear her thoughts, he softly confessed, "I'll never harm you, Belle...ever."

Her heart pounded in her ears, and even with her uncertainty and fears, deep down she trusted him. She whispered, "Sebastian?" She took a deep gulp of air and tried for more words. "Where's Maria, Sebastian? What happened to her? The police want to talk to her."

With a slack face and dull voice, he told Clari, "I'm so very sorry, Belle. She'll not be able to harm anyone else, ever again." Weariness in his words spoke of his exhaustion from carrying a heavy burden. "My family's honor has been damaged. We're in your debt until such time that our honor has been restored."

In a half whisper Clari asked, "What are you, Sebastian? I know you have a vampiric overlay, but your vampire traits seem more pronounced. You appeared out of nowhere, and then disappeared as quickly."

Literally in a blink of her eye, he stood before her, gazing into her now brown eyes, searching for something there. Or was it her soul that he searched?

He whispered, "I hear your heartbeat. I hear your blood coursing through your veins, and I can smell your fear." He leaned over to the side of her neck. He deeply inhaled her scent as he moved up her neck towards her ear. When he reached her ear, he whispered, "I know you can See the ancients' blood awakening...you aren't the only one aware of this. Some beings don't want their new secrets revealed, and some want to use you for their own unpleasant reasons. Be careful, Belle."

Clari could feel the truth in his warning; it settled like a lead weight dropped down into her stomach as a wave of grief for Sebastian rolled over her.

He pulled back, his gaze bore deep into her eyes. "I promise I'll do my best to keep you safe. As for your question, I think you know what I am. The real question, Belle, is...what are you?"

Clari sat on a rocking chair on the porch of her rented cabin. The smell of pine trees, the cooler air, and the isolation up in the mountains was just what she needed.

The wind gently caressed the pine trees, coaxing them into whispering their secrets, a soft pleasant sound that calmed the restlessness seated deep within her.

This was her annual retreat time — her time to unwind and regenerate. Only this time, she had more to think about.

She had feelings for both Morris and Sebastian. She also had questions about both of them. She trusted both, and felt an attraction to them in different ways. She didn't trust herself with her new feelings towards them. She let out a grunt of frustration, and then chided herself, "This is not relaxing."

She stood up, moved off the porch, and strolled down to a patch of sunlight filtering through the trees. She plopped down, took a couple of deep breaths, and entered her meditative state.

She wasn't sure when she was Aware of the presence behind her, but she didn't feel threatened, so took her time coming out of meditation. Without standing or turning, she opened her eyes and addressed the one behind her. "Hello, Maestro."

"Greetings, Clarima."

She stood and turned around for her first glimpse of the infamous Maestro. Her breath caught. He exuded ancient and forbidden power and all wrapped up in the package of the beautiful male body before her. He wore black jeans and a deep purple oxford shirt with a black lightweight jacket, unzipped. His blonde, almost white hair and his olive skin were alluring...but what really got her attention were his eyes.

His silver eyes.

A dangerous recognition ignited deep within, the attraction going to a cellular level as warning alarm bells went off in her soul. Too many men were showing up in her life and it was beginning to get complicated.

He smiled. "I could say, 'Greetings, Tahini', or perhaps you would prefer, 'We meet again, my pink dragon'?"

Stunned silent, her mouth dropped open.

Maestro hitched an eyebrow and gently clamped his lips together in effort to not laugh. He cleared his throat and asked, "Might we have some tea?"

She still hadn't uttered a word as she put water on the stove, and then pulled out the tea and teacups. As she prepared the tea, Maestro took a short, self-guided tour around the small cabin.

The living room and kitchen shared the same space, with an old wood dining table set close to the designated kitchen area. The living room had a wood-burning fireplace. Off to the back of the dining room was the door to the bedroom and bathroom.

Small, but it served her well.

She had regained her mental balance and found her voice again by the time she announced that the tea was ready. They both moved towards the rustic table.

"What brings you out here, Maestro? Is it time to collect your fee?"

"I just came to visit with you, Tahini. I worry about you with all that transpired. I'm glad you are feeling well after the shooting. I also thought you'd like to meet."

"My name is Clari. I'm confused, Maestro. You're not known to let others see who you are. You work in trading of services only and yet you sit across from me to drink tea and chit chat? Oh, and let's not forget, you are also a dragon as well as sporting a gorgeous human body. Did I cover everything?"

She recognized what the deep rumble meant — Maestro was chuckling. "Did you say I have a gorgeous body?" His gaze became predatory.

"No, Maestro. Don't go there. Not interested and not playing that game."

Disappointed, he sighed. "Fair enough, Tahini."

"It's Clari. Now, why are you here?"

Maestro peered into his teacup. "I knew you'd figure out who I was because of our dragon connection. I just thought I'd speed the process up."

Everything inside of her Knew there was more — a lot more — to his sudden appearance than what he divulged.

She felt conflicted. As a dragon, his energy showed an honorable being, but she wasn't too fond of the energy from him in his human form. In his human body, his energy read darker, more self-serving. If she'd met him on the street, he'd be someone she would know not to trust. Sebastian's warning echoed in her thoughts.

She redirected her thoughts. "How's Michael doing?"

"He's adjusted quite well and has been fully accepted. I'm glad you brought him to us." Maestro mulled something over. "Tahini, I've been approached by a client and am afraid I have found myself in a position I've never been in before." Maestro stared deeply into his tea as though he expected it to reveal the answers that he sought.

She waited.

Maestro stilled, then raised his head and met Clari's eyes. When he spoke again, she could See his hesitation and conflict in his energy. "My client asked me to find a person for her. That person she is seeking is you."

She raised her eyebrows, the silent question hanging between them.

Maestro stood and strode over to the window. "I've not told her where you are or that I know you. She's not told me why she seeks you, and at this point, I can't ask her, though I intend to do a little digging on her to see if I could figure out why she wants you."

Maestro rejoined her at the table and leaned forward. "I have to ask you, Tahini...what are you?"

Her mind whispered, *there is no such thing as a coincidence.* She frowned. "It's Clari. What do you mean 'What am I'?" Her voice dropped into a whisper, afraid of his answer. "Did you accept the job from her, Maestro?"

"No, Tahini. I told her my plate was currently full, but if I had an opening that I'd contact her. Again, I ask you...what are you?"

A shrug accompanied her answer. "I don't know. I'm just Clari."

Maestro snorted in frustration at Clari's answer. Clari almost expected to see smoke coming out of his nostrils.

Maestro, with a promise to see her again, left, leaving them both with more questions than answers.

In the morning she grabbed healthy snacks and water and put them in her backpack. She enjoyed doing some light hiking when she came up to the mountains and now was the ideal time to begin.

Cool, crisp air welcomed her as she hiked uphill, weaving through the tall pine trees. She'd traveled for about half an hour when she came upon the little body of water that the locals called "the lake", which was really more of a seasonal pond. This was one of her favorite spots — it was secluded, peaceful and of course had "the lake".

She climbed onto a large boulder. This was her preferred perch. It overlooked the lake and had a bit of a view of the mountain.

After settling in, she closed her eyes and listened to the sounds around her. She took in the sounds of the occasional bird chirp, water movement, and little critters shuffling in the ground debris.

She focused on her breathing. Slow deep breath in, hold, and slow release. The scent from the pine trees soothed her. A few more deep cleansing breaths and she reached out to connect with her Team. Their welcome/greeting was immediate. She thanked them for their help and support, especially lately with all that had transpired. "Guys, I'm a little confused. Sebastian and Maestro both asked me what I am...is there something I need to know?"

* You are Clari — you are who you are *

"Not very helpful, guys."

* Labels, boxes, boundaries are not part of who you are *

"So, what you are saying is that I shouldn't try to answer their question because it limits my potential and possibilities? Makes sense...if I accept a label, then I'm liable to not step out beyond that."

* Agreement *

She sat quietly while she thought through this conversation. She then refocused her attention towards her Team and opened her energy to receive any information that they wanted to share with her.

She first Felt wobbly. A tightening sensation in her stomach let her know that this was not a good thing.

She Saw a mind picture of the Earth and Saw red spots light up here and there. She focused in on one of the red dots close to where she lived.

She pictured zooming in like when she used the map programs online. She Saw a disturbance in Dulce, New Mexico.

She pulled back out and zoomed in on other red dots and found a few in central Illinois, another few in Georgia, several in Texas and some in Utah. Confused, she asked her Team what she was Looking at, but before she could get an answer, her nose picked up a newly familiar scent at the same time she heard someone tromp, noisily, towards her.

She stretched her mind towards the intruder.

* Peace, little one *

Bigfoot? The same one from her house? What the heck was he doing out here? She opened her eyes, swiveled her head towards the noise. He stopped about fifteen feet from her. He remained within the shade of the trees and moved into a squat, making himself less of a threat to her.

She waved her hand and spoke as she Sent mental pictures and emotions to him. "Hi. Um...care to tell me why you followed me here?"

His response was to Send her the same sensations she'd just had, the wobbly feeling as well as the unease in her stomach. She had the Sense that a question was coming from him next, but they were interrupted. Clari turned away from Bigfoot to find the source of the new sound as intruders crashed through the woods. Two people talked loudly as they approached the other side of the lake.

When Clari swung back to Bigfoot, she found that Bigfoot had disappeared. She slid down off the boulder and quietly retreated. When she made it back to the cabin, she set up the energy equivalence of a "Do Not Disturb" sign. She programmed the energy around the cabin and surrounding land to gently dissuade intrusion. She next asked her Team to help keep her isolated for the remainder of her stay.

Chapter Ten

WPO Meetings – *Regularly scheduled local meetings for registered WPO members. These are not only to meet and greet other WPO Readers and Healers in your area, but also where Readers and Healers can share organizational news and updates. Open and free to all registered WPO members.* ~ World Paranormal Organization (WPO) Information Pamphlet

Back in her office, Clari listened to the voicemail messages.

"Hello, Ms. Jones. This is Elizabeth Rayden. Melinda's mother. I'm calling to let you know that Melinda is doing well. She's still in counseling; her grades have improved; and I only see Melinda when I look into her eyes. I guess what I'm calling to say is thank you for giving us our daughter back. We remain hopeful that she'll continue on this path. Hopeful, but watchful."

She had helped Mrs. Rayden when her daughter ran into trouble with an entity attaching itself to the daughter. Clari had removed the attachment and recommended the daughter receive counseling. Apparently all was going well. Clari leaned back in her chair. *This is why I love my job.*

The deep silkiness of Maestro's voice was next. "Please call me at your earliest convenience. I'd like to arrange an appointment."

She dialed Maestro's number and her heart skipped a beat when he picked up on the third ring.

"Thank you for calling me back, Tahini. How was your vacation?"

"It's Clari, and my trip was fine. What do you need, Maestro? It's time for me to pay my debt?"

Amused, he rumbled, "No, Tahini. I promise that when it's time I'll say that up front so you needn't worry all the time. Actually, I'd like to discuss a case with you. When would be a convenient time for us to get together?"

"How about tomorrow morning, say ten thirty? Where would you like to meet?"

"Ten thirty's fine, thank you. How about we meet at my office?" He gave her the address and directions. "I anticipate seeing you again, Tahini."

"It's Clari," she proclaimed, apparently to herself. Maestro had already hung up.

She called Morris next. They chatted briefly and agreed to spend Wednesday going over cases.

She dialed Josie's number.

"Girlfriend, you're back! How was isolation? Oh, I mean your vacation. Meet any hunky dudes?"

Clari snorted. "Who says 'hunky dudes'? I'm back and was wondering if you have time to come by the house tonight? I'll provide pizza and your favorite soda."

As though narrating a wildlife program, Josie replied, "She spoke softly and slowly so as to not frighten the elusive Clari-cat back into hiding." She snorted, amused at her own cleverness. "I'll be there. How's five thirty?"

Clari giggled. "That works. See you then."

Eyes twinkling, Josie asked, "So *did* you meet any hunky dudes?"

Feeling mischievous, and still not ready to discuss the reason she asked Josie to come, she leaned forward slightly. "Does six foot plus, pushing seven easily, with a lot of hair sound right?"

Josie's eyes lit up. "Oh...do tell!"

"Well, we met up by the lake. I was sitting on a boulder, relaxing..."

"Yes?" Josie prompted.

"...when I smelled him."

"Wait. You *smelled* him?"

"Yes, it was a cross between...oh, I don't know...a cross between wet deer and skunk spray."

"Ew. What are you talking about?"

Laughing, Clari told her, "You should have seen your face. Bigfoot showed up to 'talk' but we were interrupted by two noisy hikers. It was the same Bigfoot that showed up here before the shooting."

Josie was not pleased. "Uh, Bigfoot? Here? Hello. Why am I just now hearing about this? What did he want, and why did he show up at your retreat?"

Clari caught her up on the Bigfoot experiences.

"So what do you think is going on with him?" Josie asked.

"I don't know. I'll Google the places I Saw when I get a chance later this week. But there is something else I wanted to talk about, but I want your promise to not make fun of what I'm going to share. I'm asking for help from you."

Josie nodded.

She blurted, "He, uh, kissed my cheek the other night, and I'm not sure what to think about it."

"Bigfoot kissed you?"

"What? Ew. No. Morris kissed me."

Josie grinned.

Clari glared.

Out waiting Clari, Josie blinked with wide, innocent eyes and pushed some errant strands of her hair back behind her ears.

Clari continued. "And I'm not even sure what to call this thing between Sebastian and me. There's no romantic feeling, but there is an intense attraction."

Josie clapped her hands. "I'm so excited for you! But I don't understand why this upsets you."

"I told you before that this was difficult for me. I spend half my time keeping people at arm's length. The other half is spent with me in an almost pleasant state of disbelief knowing that someone, especially the opposite sex, sees me and cares about me. And that's terrifying. And sometimes I feel as though the guys currently in my life either want to rename me or are stalking me."

"Whoa, wait just a minute. Who's stalking you?"

"Oops. I guess I forgot to finish filling you in. Well, one stalker, though definitely not dating material, is Bob."

Josie, a bit exasperated, threw her hands into the air. "Who is Bob?"

"Oh, I just decided to name the Bigfoot that I just told you about. Bob is a whole lot easier to say than 'the Bigfoot who is stalking me, showing up at my house and at the cabin', don't you agree? So, we shall call him Bob." Her eyes sparkled.

Josie rolled her eyes.

Clari asked, "Do you, uh, know anything about someone called Maestro?"

Josie froze. "Please tell me you haven't gotten yourself mixed up with him?"

"Uh, maybe a little bit?"

Josie jumped up and began to pace the floor. "That's like saying you are a little bit pregnant. Either you are or you aren't. Have you gotten mixed up with The Maestro? Oh, this is so not good. Why in heaven's name did you do that? How can we get you out?"

"Josie, stop. What's wrong with Maestro?"

Josie sat back down. "He's kind of like the Godfather of the underworld. You know, like the mob? Once you're in, you don't ever get out."

"Where did you hear that?"

"Everyone knows it. Where have you been? Man, wait until Morris and Sebastian hear about this."

"Sebastian is the one who electronically introduced me to Maestro."

Josie sprang up, her face reddening. "I'll kill that blankety-blank. Holy moly! What was he thinking? We need to call Morris now and see if he can help."

Clari began to laugh, and once she started, she couldn't stop. The confusion on Josie's face only fueled her laughter.

When she wound down, she apologized. "I'm sorry, Josie. I couldn't help it. I didn't see any of the nefarious godfather energy around Maestro. He's pleasant to look at, but I think I can hold my own."

Clari watched the color completely drain out of her friend's face as Josie dropped onto the couch. She lowered her voice and spoke in a breathy whisper, "You met The Maestro? No one's ever seen The Maestro. You saw him and you're still alive?"

"I don't know what the big deal is. He's just a guy. We sat, had tea, and chatted at the cabin."

"Maybe it was better when you didn't have men in your life. I never realized how naïve you are."

"Hey, that's not nice. Maestro is not a romantic interest, and I was asking you for help, not insults or fears." Miffed, Clari stomped off to the kitchen.

Josie followed. "I'm sorry. I didn't mean to hurt you. But honey, you were recently shot and I kept praying I wasn't going to lose you. You survived, but now are consorting with The Maestro? I do not want to see you hurt again...or killed."

Clari sighed. "I understand, but I really don't feel I'm in any danger with him, and I'm cautious."

Josie hugged her. "Can you at least not hang out with him? Maybe he'll forget about you."

"Yeah, I could see him forgetting about me. Not. But I do promise to be careful."

Clari followed the directions Maestro provided. She found herself facing a door which bore a placard stating, "J.R.'s Consulting Services". As she debated whether she was in the right place, the door opened and Maestro greeted her. His silver eyes were complimented by his expensive charcoal grey slacks with a matching suit coat with a white shirt. He invited her in and led her through a luxurious lobby. Clari nodded in greeting as they passed by the curvaceous secretary seated at her desk, and they entered Maestro's office. Just like a high-priced lawyer's office, Maestro's had dark paneling, rich carpet and oversized leather chairs next to an oversized desk. There was also plenty of room for a table for four and a three-seater leather couch.

"It's wonderful to see you again, Tahini. Please be seated." She sat while Maestro closed the office door and moved towards his desk. He removed his jacket and hung it on a nearby butler coat rack.

"It's Clari."

"What? Of course, my dear." He sat at his desk.

"So who is J.R.?"

"I am."

"But you're Maestro. Oh, and you're M. So now you're J.R.? Is that for 'Junior' or do the initials mean anything?"

He broke eye contact and tugged on his shirt cuffs. He muttered, "Jury Rigging."

"What? Seriously?"

He looked back up. "Yes. J.R. stands for Jury Rigging."

She rubbed her temple. "I don't get it. And, how many names do you have?"

His words were precise, but carried a weight. "'Maestro' is for my online and unseen presence. It means I can orchestrate operations. I needed a physical presence as well and that is where J.R. comes in. J.R. denotes the ability to work with the tools on hand or what is available. However, the public thinks that J.R. is either my initials or my name. I don't tell them otherwise."

"So you want me to call you J.R. in public?"

"Correct."

"Okay, I'll try to remember that. Now, why am I here, J.R.?"

"Well, Tahini..."

To avoid yelling out of frustration, she gritted her teeth and hissed, "It's Clari."

"...I figured by now you'd have some questions about me, personally, and when we've satisfied that topic, where I'll answer any questions to the best of my ability, I may have a job referral for you if you are interested. So, let's start with your questions. Mind you, Tahini, what's said here stays here and is for you and me only. Understood and agreed?"

She knew an agreement between, or with, dragons was binding. "Agreed." She could feel the agreement binding settle in her, and knew that he'd felt the same.

She began by confessing that she told Josie about meeting Maestro and how worried Josie had been. Suddenly concerned, she asked him, "You're not going to kill her, or me, are you? I mean, the agreement wasn't until today."

J.R. rumbled as he leaned back in his chair. The rumble was a cross between someone expressing amusement and a purr. The energy from the rumble welcomed Clari at a cellular level. Clari was awed and comforted by the sound. *Must be a dragon thing*, Clari thought.

J.R. regained Clari's attention as he spoke. "I'm not going to kill either of you. But let's just allow 'Maestro' to quietly disappear from your life so your friends will no longer worry."

That sounded good to her. "So I can ask you any questions I want?"

"Yes. It doesn't mean you'll get an answer, but feel free to ask."

She snuggled into the chair while she formulated her questions. "I know you as M the dragon, Maestro, and now J.R. The dragon energy I respect and feel safe around and I felt him to be an honorable being." She noticed J.R. sit a bit taller. "But," she continued, "your energy as a human is dark and definitely something I don't wholly trust. Shouldn't they be the same energy?"

She saw a subtle shift, and if she had blinked she would've missed it. He tugged his cuffs again and she saw his energy leak regret as he internally revisited something from his past. She didn't want to miss a word of this.

J.R. focused back on her and began to explain. "You're a guardian of the dragon portal and you've memories of many lives that involved dragon interaction. You're also a dimensional-walker, which is why you can visit the realm of dragons and live as a human. This is how you could bring Michael over to the dragon realm."

She sat up straighter and her eyes bright with excitement. "That means you're a dimensional-walker too, since you're a dragon there and a human here," she blurted.

"No, Tahini. I'm not. I'm a human, and I'm a dragon. Unlike you, my essence, my soul, had been fractured and divided between the two. I live both simultaneously."

She frowned. "How? And why would you want to?"

"It's not a matter of wanting to. It's my punishment. I had been a dimensional-walker, but in my human form I was ruthless, self-serving, and greedy. I didn't care who I trampled to get what I wanted. I used humans to gain more wealth and power.

"The Dragon Council wasn't happy when they learned that their fair and just leader of the Avonish Clan in the Dragon Realm was the same being who, as a human, was such a monster." He spread his hands out. "As punishment, I'm bound to wear, like a cloak, the negative energy I created so long ago, to live in this human body while I try to work to rebalance what I did; to repay the debt I created.

"The crux is that I must carry this human body with that darker, un-trustworthy energy while working to rebalance the scales and give back to the human race. Most humans sense the dark energy and stay away from me.

"That meant, and continues to mean, that I've had to work even harder to make any headway. Over the years, I realized that I needed to mainly work unseen, such as with the Maestro persona, to be able to get my work done to help others. My working for trade instead of monetary gain is how I'm doing it."

Clari frowned, "But doesn't that mean you gain as well?"

"No, the services others provide as repayment are never for me; instead they help someone else in need. I'm just the conduit the energy passes through to make those two connections. I work hard for no personal gain."

Captivated by this revelation, she leaned forward and asked, "How long have you been doing this?"

"Seven hundred and fifty years."

Clari leaned back. She recognized that his words were weighted with regret and repentance. The silence stretched out between them as she tried to visualize what his life had been like. She couldn't. She focused back on J.R.

He continued. "The invention of the web and email made it so I could work unseen. These modern conveniences also made it a lot easier to work on repaying my debts from a distance. This way, the energy I carry doesn't scare others away as much. But, as your friend demonstrated, some people still sense it and are scared of it...and of me."

"Is that dark energy what you truly are or are you something else?" Clari asked.

He fiddled with his shirt cuffs. "Tahini, I'm cursed. The curse is that I have to wear, like a cloak, the corrupted energy I had created. Most people sense that cloak and want nothing to do with me. That has been my challenge; to work to help others with that curse in place. And it'll stay in place until the council feels I've paid my penance and worked off my debt.

When my debt is paid off, my two halves will be rejoined. I'll be a complete dragon and a dimensional-walker again."

She knew the enormity of what J.R. just shared. Even with the agreement binding, he took a big chance sharing that. "Thank you for telling me, J.R."

"I told you so that you'd understand why I work the way I do, Tahini. Now, this brings us to the job I wanted to talk to you about. I'm just the intermediary, the one to hook you two up. If you accept the job, they'll pay you directly."

She shifted in the chair. "Let's hear it. Oh, and J.R.?"

"Yes?"

"It's Clari."

He gave her an indulgent smile. "I've arranged for this potential client to be here in about an hour."

Annoyed, Clari interrupted. "You're that certain I'll take the case?"

J.R. raised his hand. "I'm having him come here to get an answer, whether you take his case or not. Also, if you need, it gives you time to sit and discuss the case with him before you answer. It is a convenience, not a pressure tactic. I'll honor whatever you decide."

Mollified, she relaxed a bit. "My apologies. Actually, that's smart planning. Okay, why don't you fill me in on what this case is about?"

J.R. pulled a slim folder out of his desk drawer and placed it on his mostly empty desktop. "The gentleman is a representative of an unusual group. It's a group of scientists who are investigating a rather substantial chunk of land. This land is...shall we say...unique."

Inner alarms began to stir, encouraging her to proceed with caution. "What is it they are investigating, and what does it have to do with me?"

"There are anomalies they are investigating. They're discreetly trying to locate a Reader who can See what they're talking about, would like some input, and hopefully help them."

"J.R., I have the feeling that you're making this sound a lot more innocuous than it really is. Perhaps I should speak with the representative myself."

J.R. nodded. "I think that'd be wise."

"So how did you get involved with this group of scientists, J.R.?" Clari queried.

"I have worked in the past with the gentleman who owns the property. He's also the one who brought in the scientists."

Clari's curiosity wasn't sated. "How did you meet the owner?"

J.R. smoothed his cuff. "Tahini, I help connect people who have – shall we say – "special needs", including discretion with those who can help them. Like I mentioned, I've worked with him before, and discretion is usually utmost important to my clients. And while we're talking about this, I'll need you to sign both my, and his, confidentiality agreements before you meet with him." He slid two forms to her, along with a pen. She took time to read the contract and noticed it only had business names on each one, no personal names. She signed both.

J.R. stood. "We have time to grab a bite to eat before our guest arrives. I had Rachel get us some Thai food which now awaits us in my small, but adequate kitchen." He held his hand out to Clari, offering assistance. She readily accepted. She'd been worried about how she was going to gracefully extract herself from the massive leather chair that had attempted to swallow her whole.

As they finished their meal, Rachel came in to announce that their guest had arrived.

Clari and J.R. moved back to his office where J.R. motioned for her to sit at the table. She was secretly pleased. These chairs wouldn't try to swallow her.

At his desk, he buzzed Rachel and asked her to escort their guest to his office. J.R. joined Clari at the table.

The door opened and Rachel motioned for the guest to enter, softly closing the door behind him. The guest was a short, balding, middle-aged man with a somewhat pudgy belly and who sported thick black rimmed glasses. To Clari's thinking, he mirrored the stereotypical geek from the early twentieth century. He hugged a well-worn leather briefcase to his chest and his eyes were opened a little too wide.

She switched to her other-sight and Saw he was clearly scared. His over-lay Showed something along the lines of what she could only describe as a mole-man.

J.R. stood and shook hands with the mole-man. "Clarima, I'd like you to meet Dr. Samuel Hidl. Dr. Hidl, this is Clarima Jones." She gave him a tight smile. She wasn't about to shake hands with someone broadcasting so much fear.

While J.R. spoke, he motioned to Dr. Hidl to sit. "Dr. Hidl, Clarima would like to know more specifics before she makes a decision. She's already signed your confidentiality agreement." He handed the signed document to Hidl.

Hidl slid the paper into his briefcase and then pushed his slipping glasses back up the bridge of his nose. His voice came out a bit nasal sounding. "Thank you, J.R., and please, both of you call me Samuel, or just Sam."

J.R. swept his hand towards Clari, turning the floor over to her. "Samuel, I'd like to know more about what you're investigating and what exactly it is you expect from me." She saw Samuel's energy spike. She once again wondered what was frightening him.

Samuel nervously cleared his throat. "I work for a group of privately funded scientists who are investigating anomalies and bizarre occurrences at a specific location.

"For the past six years we've been living, on site, at a ranch located in an otherwise desolate area. This ranch and the surrounding area have hundreds of years of sightings and stories behind them. Are you aware of the place I'm speaking of?"

"Yes."

Samuel hadn't continued on, so she figured he wanted to know what she knew, so she continued. "I know that the indigenous tribes, of many years past, had stories of shape-shifters and that the tribal leaders banned their members from talking about, wandering near or entering those areas. I also know that these anomalies you're referring to are dimensional portals which have been active for...well...like forever."

In the back of her mind, she began Seeing some pieces of information she had Seen on her retreat start weaving themselves into Samuel's information. She Watched as Bob's interaction wove itself in as well. This was her brain's way of showing her that these were somehow connected.

Samuel's silence encouraged her to continue. "These portals, or wormholes, have been used by other-world beings to come and hunt here. There are additional portals that other beings who aren't here to hunt, use. But, the area you are talking about is mainly hunting grounds.

"The reason those portals were so successful for the other-world hunters was the desolation and isolation of the area where they entered and left our dimension. Then some early white man decided to ignore all the locals' warnings passed down from generation to generation and he built a home there.

"This just made the hunters appreciate having lunch a lot closer to their entry points, so they tolerated the ranch and people as long as food was available.

"When food became scarce, the hunters became less tolerant of humans in their hunting grounds. How am I doing so far?"

Samuel snapped his mouth shut, glanced quickly over to J.R. and back to Clari. "Uh, pretty good."

She closed her eyes and mentally rolled them. This guy wanted her to perform to prove herself. She opened her eyes and pierced into Samuel's while she continued, "With all the 'investigating' you've been doing, you've ticked off the regular hunters.

"The poking and prodding you've done has agitated the energy involved with these portals. I'm guessing attacks have increased on you and your fellow scientists?" She energetically slid into her self-protective mode. Her personal shields and her resolve hardened...all signs to her that this was not good energy. No wonder Samuel was so scared.

Samuel's mouth hung open again. His head nodding was as hesitant as his words. "The portal has enlarged immensely and continues to grow in size and now more portals are opening. The beings, rather beasts or creatures, emerging are larger, more vicious, and less afraid of humans."

Enough on proving what I can do, she thought. "Samuel, what is it you want, or even think I could do for you?"

Samuel's Adam's apple bobbed. "We need someone to fix it. We've tried everything we could think of to close those cursed portals. Instead, we've fed them somehow."

She stood. "I have to think this over. Are you okay with me giving you an answer on Friday?" she asked them both.

Samuel, relieved that she hadn't walked away completely, replied, "Yes, Clarima, that'd be fine. I'll stay in town until I receive your answer on

Friday. I'll leave my contact information with J.R. And thank you for considering it."

As she left, she thought, *Great, first a cursed dagger and a dragon and now cursed portals. Definitely never a dull moment.*

Chapter Eleven

Clari poured herself a cold glass of pomegranate juice and savored its slightly tart flavor as she proceeded to her home office.

At her computer, she typed in "anomalies, ranches". The entries confirmed what she'd Seen when she was Shown the picture of Earth with what looked like randomly placed holiday lights.

She next searched anomalies in Central Illinois followed by those in Georgia, and Texas, and she finished up with Dulce, New Mexico.

She finished her juice and strode out the back door. It was time to chat with Bigfoot Bob, if she could get him to come over.

She grabbed a garden chair, moved away from the house, and dropped into it. She closed her eyes and did a few cleansing breaths. As she centered, she turned her thoughts to Bob. She talked out loud as she used her mind-pictures to See him and Ask him to come Talk to her.

She sat for quite a while. When she thought of going back inside, she Felt Bob's mind-touch and smelled his pungent odor.

She opened her eyes and saw him out by the scrub line and watched as he crouched down. As Bob opened up communication, she began to receive mind-pictures of the red dot locations.

Clari in turn Shared the memories of the information she'd found on those locations, the information about the heavy UFO activity and strange animal sighting reports.

Bigfoot Bob batted the UFO information away as though he was swatting at a fly. He Shared his information on what he had Seen and found in his travels.

Once again, she felt a question beginning to form from Bob. As the new information came in, she realized it wasn't a question...it was more like a summons.

Bob faded into the shadows.

She continued to sit outside to enjoy the evening. She thought about those who visited her way out here. Pigeons, who were city dwellers, sought her out when one was ill. If it was able, it would make its way out to Clari's for healing. She noted that the ill pigeon was often accompanied, or perhaps escorted, by another pigeon. If it appeared to be a mate, it would stay with the ill bird until the bird was healthy enough to return to the city. If it was not a mate, the accompanying pigeon only stayed long enough to ensure that Clari had seen the ill bird and had begun energy healing treatments.

She giggled. City dwellers of any kind didn't usually come out to her house unless they felt they had no other options, and she was okay with that.

While she relaxed, she saw a mockingbird land nearby. She found them entertaining, especially since they love to sing other birds' songs that they heard along their travels, and this one was no exception. She closed her eyes and listened to this birds' concert. Mid-concert, Clari's eyes popped open as she bolted upright and let out a gut busting laugh. The mockingbird had mimicked the police sirens from town...definitely a visiting city bird.

At the police station, Clari climbed the tired grey steps to get a bit of exercise on her way to see Morris.

Morris' door was open and Clari saw he was bent over looking at a file. She decided that all of the detectives shopped at the same clothing store, and that the generic short sleeve shirts, tan or black pants and an easy-to-forget jacket were the mandatory uniform. *Perhaps that's why they dress that way...so they don't stand out and are easily forgotten.* As though he sensed her presence, he looked up. His face smoothed when he saw Clari standing in the doorway. A welcoming smile graced his lips. "Good morning, Clari."

Clari moved into the office and plunked down across from him. "Good morning, Morris." Her heart was beating a little faster, and she knew it had nothing to do with the stair climb. "Did you miss me?" she asked him.

He chuckled, and then asked, "Have you had your coffee? Ready to get started?"

"Let's do it!"

Morris shifted in his chair. "You remember me telling you that weird cases find me?"

"Uh, yeah. Why?"

"Well, while you were gone, a doozy came in, but it's a messy one. Interested?"

Clari's eyebrows rose. "How can I say no after an introduction like that?"

Morris normally just read the highlights to her, but this time he handed her the whole file. Her stomach dropped as she rifled through some rather gruesome photographs of what she thought must be of cattle mutilations. The attached report also included sightings of animals that didn't fit any known earth animal descriptions. The officer who took the report annotated that the rancher who had called this in appeared to be "lucid, agitated, and spoke in a matter-of-fact manner." The officer wrote that he did not smell alcohol on the rancher, nor had he seen any evidence or signs of substance abuse. He went on to state he couldn't find any trace of animal tracks, vehicle tracks or any noticeable disturbances near or around the mutilated cattle.

The officer's report continued, stating the rancher claimed he'd seen something "large, hairy with a slightly hunched back with a hump and it walked both two-legged and four-legged with an odd gait", that it was larger than a full grown man, and, "truth be told, it would be what I might imagine a werewolf from the old scary movies might've looked like. But there's no such thing as werewolves."

She looked up and Morris shrugged, "Haven't a clue. I've heard of these occurring in places like Dulce, but never here."

Her stomach acid cranked up. "Are you supposed to be working on the cattle mutilations?"

Morris shook his head. "No. Though we're receiving reports of suspicious deaths of ranch animals and pets, this is different from the mutilations. We're supposed to be investigating the unexplained, unusual animal sightings connected to missing animals."

Clari frowned. "Then why do we have a cattle mutilations file if we're not doing those?"

Morris shrugged. "Because some ranches have both – mutilated and missing livestock. The mutilations have been reported way back before our time. Local police only record the suspicious mutilations and disappearances for insurance claims only. No one has ever figured out what is happening. Our division has the same policy for ranchers if they have had a history of mutilations and disappearances."

She gently rubbed her temple. "So you are working on the unknown animal sightings? But doesn't that make this a cryptozoology investigation?"

He shared, "Yes, but they wouldn't call it that, and the department wants us to check it out. The commotion started after you left for your retreat. We've had a lot of freaked out people make reports about weird or unusual creature sightings. However, all the reports mirror one another, even if the witnesses don't know each other or live near one another.

"At first I thought maybe people were seeing one of those Bigfoot beings, but with each of these recent creature reports, most of the witnesses stated they felt that it was a predator. Some were just terrified.

"None of the witness reports of Bigfoot sightings in history — that I'm aware of — match our witness accounts. I may be wrong, but I don't think our mystery creature is Bigfoot."

Her mind whispered once again, *there's no such thing as coincidences.*

Morris asked, "Are you okay? You look a little off. I know this case is unusual even for us. Are you up to working on it?" The edge to his voice exposed his concern.

"Uh, yeah. Morris, have you ever had a case that made you doubt yourself along with your abilities, skills, and knowledge?"

"You mean besides you coming into my life and turning it, and my belief systems, completely upside down?"

A cynical snort escaped Clari. "Yeah, besides all of that."

His voice softened. "It happens to all of us at one time or another."

"So what do you do? I feel like I'm frozen in one place and I need to get unstuck."

His eyebrows rose. "That sounds like fear. Fear can mask itself as doubt and freeze you in place. It makes you afraid to take the next step forward. You freeze so you don't have to see or know. But you and I both know that you have to step forward to set yourself free from that fear." He stood up and moved to the front of the desk, sat on the corner, and leaned closer. "You and I are both survivors. We adapt and keep moving forward. I'm, unofficially, your partner and being partners means that we are here to support one another. We cover each other's backs. We push each other forward when one of us gets stuck."

Her voice softly quivered. "But what if you doubt whether or not you can protect your partner from what created the fear in you?"

"Then we go down fighting...together."

"But Morris, you've had to adjust to quite a lot when I began to introduce you into my world, and what I did introduce you to is barely the tip of a huge iceberg. I don't want to scare you off...or make you go nuts trying to forget what you've seen or experienced with me."

"Have you run away, or gone nuts, from anything I introduced to you from my world?" he challenged.

"No."

"Haven't I always said you can choose whether to work on a case or not?"

"Yes, you told me I could reject any case I wasn't comfortable with."

He crossed his arms over his chest. "So why are you trying to decide what I can or can't handle? Don't you think that I should be the one who gets to decide that?"

Ouch.

Morris continued, "Okay, partner, what's got you all worked up? What's the case you're talking about that we'll be working on together?"

"I signed a confidentiality agreement so I can't talk about it yet. If you're serious, I'll contact the potential client and tell him I want you to sign one too, so that I can see if you'll work with me on this."

Morris' energy prickled and she cringed at the hard edge in his voice, "Clari, what's going on? If this is about my case, you are obligated, by law, to tell me."

Crap. "I'm not sure if it's connected to your case." She grabbed her phone. "I'll be back shortly, okay?"

"Like I have a choice?" he grumbled.

Unable to locate a private place to make a call, she maneuvered through the hallways until she decided on the women's restroom.

She got through to J.R. – formerly known as Maestro – quickly, but had to wait for him to call back with Samuel's answer.

"Samuel has agreed. Are you sure bringing Morris in on this is a good idea, Tahini?"

"J.R., I'm not sure of anything at the moment."

"I'll have Rachel send a blank agreement to you. You can print it out now and after he signs it, just fax it back to me. You can bring me the original on Friday."

"Thank you, J.R. Oh, and my name is Clari."

Upon her return, she noticed he'd moved back to his chair and his energy was agitated. "Sorry, Morris, but before I say anything, I have the confidentiality agreement for you to sign. I've sent it to your email. Can you print it out? After you read it and sign it, I can openly discuss...well what I currently know... what I'll be working on.

"You're a police officer, Morris, so not only may there be some gray areas to discuss, I'll more than likely be traveling for this. So I guess if you're interested, we need to talk this over with Lieutenant Avery."

Morris scrubbed his jawline while he mulled it over. "I'm a detective, not a police officer. I can't sign anything without talking with the Lieutenant first. If my case and yours are somehow connected, then – if the Lieutenant okays it – I'll head out with you. Besides, I've quite a lot of vacation time that I've never touched. I'm sure something could be worked out."

Morris picked up his phone. Within fifteen minutes both seated across from an unhappy Lieutenant Avery. "What's this about, Morris?" he demanded.

"I think perhaps Clari should fill you in, sir."

Avery's penetrating gaze moved to Clari. "Well?"

"I find myself in a situation, sir, and have probably, by association, dragged Morris into it. I signed a contract, a confidentiality agreement with a potential client. In order for me to talk to Morris, he needs to sign the agreement. However, there is a question of a conflict of interest with a new case Morris has."

A vein throbbed in Avery's forehead, and then Clari Felt and Saw Avery's energy prickle followed by a fire engine red color building in his aura. As he opened his mouth, Clari raised her hand to hold Avery from commenting. "Please, sir, let me finish."

Avery rubbed the tension in his forehead.

Clari learned early on that Avery's energy had a tendency to run hot when he felt his authority was being challenged. The fire engine red energy is where the terms "hot headed" and "seeing red" came from. She also learned that Avery tended to mostly maintain control. With considerable restraint, Avery's energy began to cool. He took a deep breath and conceded to Clari.

Feeling safe to continue, Clari told him, "I can't guarantee one case is connected with the other. I do feel both have at least a toe in the realms I deal with, and that if I, or we, solve the puzzle the potential client has brought forward, it *may* help with the case here. And, since you don't like grey areas or surprises, I figured we needed to present it to you and see what you thought should be done, officially or unofficially."

Avery nodded and took a moment to think it through. "So, if Morris signs the confidentiality agreement, you can share with him something that might have relevance to his case. But by Morris signing the agreement, he can't divulge what he learned to solve his case, correct?"

She nodded. "I know there's a fine line here, but what if Morris signs the agreement and comes with me, say as a consultant or partner through my firm? What he learns there, though he can't share or divulge the information, may give him enough knowledge or insights to aid him with the investigation here."

Clari was getting concerned when Avery's energy morphed from being cooled down to fire engine red, then to chocolate cosmos red. *Oh, chocolate sounds nice right now. Ugh, focus, Clari*, she admonished herself.

Agitated, their boss stood and paced. When Avery reached some sort of decision, Clari Saw the reds begin to fade. Avery sat back down and glared at Clari. "You seem to like walking that fine line, Ms. Jones." He turned to address Morris. "What do you think?"

"Well sir, I could take vacation time and head out with her, that way I won't be there in an official capacity. And, if I unofficially learn something there, I could use it to investigate the case here." Morris nodded, more to himself than anyone else. "Yes, sir, it just might work."

Lieutenant Avery's eyes bored into hers. "You know I could charge you with obstruction, Jones."

Clari capitulated. She averted her eyes as she answered, "Yes, sir." She knew when to pick her battles.

Avery stroked his chin. "Okay. I can't order you what to do with your vacation, Morris. Let me, unofficially, know where you're going, though, so I won't get any unpleasant surprise phone calls about you two." He turned to her as he continued, "Because I'm pretty sure I'll hear something...trouble does follow you, Ms. Jones."

Avery busied himself with papers on his desk. Without looking up he barked, "Dismissed. Oh, and have your leave papers on my desk before you sign the agreement, Morris. I'll sign as soon as you get them to me. Now, out."

Morris had the approved vacation form in hand within the hour, and within two, the agreement had been signed, faxed to J.R., and they left for Clari's office.

Clari locked the front door to avoid interruptions. Seated in her office, Clari began filling Morris in, "J.R., of J.R.'s Consulting Services, was formerly known as Maestro. Long story there, for another time. Anyway, J.R. coordinated a sit down with Samuel to discuss hiring me," she waved her hand back and forth between her and Morris, "now us, to see if we can help with some problems Samuel and his team of scientists are having on the ranch where they're working. Some of those problems include sightings of some strange looking cryptids – or unknown or unsubstantiated animals. This is why I think your case and possibly Samuel's are connected.

"But," she continued, "before J.R. contacted me, I had my own cryptid encounter." She told Morris about her Bigfoot, aka Bob, encounters and his summons.

Morris interrupted the briefing when he burst out laughing.

"What? Why are you laughing?"

"Bob? You not only met, and named Bigfoot, but you called him Bob? Unbelievable!"

Clari crossed her arms over her chest. "Well, he needed a name. I can't keep calling him 'Bigfoot'. What if I run across another one? How am I supposed to keep them straight? How are you supposed to know which Bigfoot I'm talking about?"

Morris howled louder. She huffed out of the room.

She came back in after she thought he was under control. "Are you finished? Can I continue now?"

He smirked, nodded, but stayed quiet as she described her conversation with Samuel.

When she finished, he asked, "If you think these two cases may be related, then you must think they both involve portals and these hunting creatures?"

"Yes, but what I don't understand is that Dulce, this ranch, central Illinois, and some of Texas has had these reports, intermittently, for well over fifty years. Why are there reports spreading and moving northward in Texas? Why are they increasing and why are we experiencing them here?

"I think that if we take the ranch case, and we figure out what to do there, then we might be able to do it here."

Morris scratched the back of his head. "All right. You are the lead on this, so what's our next step?"

"Call J.R. and set up an appointment with Samuel. You can ask him your questions. We can tell him whether or not we'll take the case and, if so, set up our arrangements for going out there. Oh, and we need to discuss your consulting fees for this case. Thoughts or questions?"

Morris rubbed the back of his neck. "The detective side of me doesn't like this whole Maestro/J.R. thing – it reeks of deception and I'm not sure if I can trust him. What are your Feelings about him?"

"He shared with me his story – but that's for him to tell, not me. My Feeling is that he is okay and trying to do the right thing. As for Samuel, I guess we'll know more when we sit down and talk with him," Clari told him

"Fair enough," Morris conceded. "Now, what do you suggest for my consulting fees?"

Clari recommended an amount for the job.

Morris' eyebrows rose, chasing after his hairline. "Whoa! Are you serious, Clari?"

Clari laughed. "You look like one of those people on those old antique appraisal shows after they were told how much their treasure was worth. Some of those people looked like they were going to pass out from the shock." She continued after a couple of deep breaths, "Though you and I are working on different aspects of this case, neither aspect can be considered 'safe' with all that I know about what's going on there. I suggest we ask for a hazard pay amount for each of us. Of course, we can negotiate if it's too high for Samuel – but I don't think it will be."

Morris' voice went up an octave, "Do you always make that much per case?"

"Sometimes, Morris. But not with the police department. Why?"

His Adam's apple bobbed. "I, uh, I'm just...that's a lot of money, Clari."

"Morris, I'm not ripping anyone off – truly. It really is a fair amount."

"I guess I'm in the wrong business." He gave a nervous laugh.

After they finished hashing out Morris' pay, Clari made the call to J.R., who shortly returned a call to confirm their meeting with Samuel. They were to get-together at J.R.'s office after lunch.

After a round of introductions, Clari turned over the original of Morris' signed agreement to Samuel. "Are you ready for some questions, Samuel?"

"Yes. I'll answer what I can."

Morris asked, "Have there been any police actions or investigations on your experiences?"

"No. As part of our research on the past history of the area, we requested information from the local authorities. Some people reported incidents, but only when insurance claims were involved. The other people quit trying to report anything since the local authorities weren't able to do anything." Samuel paused for a moment. "The authorities were at a loss. How can they protect against something they can't see or find? For incidents that are visible, they still don't know what it is or what to do about it."

"What do you mean about the stuff that is visible?" Morris queried.

In what was a well-oiled move, Samuel pushed his glasses back into place. "When the previous ranch owners moved in, they were approached by a rather large wolf that was nice to the people, but then tried to take one of their calves. It's said that the owner shot the wolf several times with different firearms. The wolf never fell and didn't appear to be affected by the bullets. It ran off and the owner took off after it. The tracks eventually stopped, but they stopped as though the beast just disappeared into thin air."

Clari spoke up when Samuel paused. "I noticed there was an influx of UFO sightings in the area as well. Did you want us to investigate that aspect too?"

"No, we are only interested in the windows, or portals, on the property. Also, our investigators will be monitoring the area as you investigate. I just wanted to let you know up front that you'll be observed and we'll be monitoring to see if anything changes throughout. Do either of you have a problem with that?"

They spoke in tandem, "No."

When she and Morris asked all of their questions, they excused themselves to reach a decision as to whether or not they'd work with Samuel. It didn't take long. They accepted the job.

After they agreed on Clari and Morris' rates, Samuel sighed and his shoulder relaxed. "Okay. The company plane will be leaving for Utah on Friday at 9 a.m. sharp." He wrote down directions and handed them to Morris. "I suggest you be there no later than eight thirty."

Back at her office, she and Morris went inside, but before they had a chance to talk, they heard a commotion out on the street. Outside, they found two stray dogs fighting. Clari stood still a moment to take in the scene.

Morris stood beside her. "Don't get too close to them. When dogs fight over territory or possessions, they only see others as either a pack member or someone that is not part of their pack. They may only recognize you as not one of their pack and attack you. I'll call in to dispatch to have them send someone to tranquilize them and bring them into town." Morris grabbed his cell phone.

She strode forward towards the dogs. She stopped about two feet away and took a slow deep breath and projected one word. "Enough."

Morris stopped talking to dispatch, mid-sentence, and swung around to face Clari. His mouth hung open.

Both dogs had quit fighting and sat facing her, their heads hung low. Morris could tell she was talking to the dogs, but he couldn't hear her words. He knew she was scolding them by the way she was shaking a finger at one, and then the other.

Morris refocused on the cell phone. "I don't think tranquilizers will be needed after all, Louise. Just have someone come pick them up please."

He called back to Clari. "Someone will be here soon to pick them up."

All four of them started towards the office entrance. Clari stopped right outside the door and told the dogs to sit down, stay put and that she'd be back shortly.

Morris watched as the dogs did as she requested.

A few minutes later she came out with two bowls of water and placed one in front of each dog. As they began lapping at the water, Clari leaned up against the building, folded her arms across her chest, and waited for the officer from animal control to show up.

"What did you do back there?" Morris pointed to where the dogs had been fighting.

"I told them that their fighting annoyed me."

"No, I know that part, but before that, when you spoke the word, 'Enough'. You didn't yell it, but I felt it reverberate *within* me. It felt like even my blood cells heard you."

"That was the Voice of God."

"The what?"

She turned her head to look into Morris' eyes. "The Voice of God."

Morris motioned for her to elaborate.

She pushed off of the wall and turned so that her whole body faced him. "The Voice of God — or whatever your belief system calls the Creator. We have been granted the authority of God's power behind our word or words.

"I've only used this to break up a fight between two beings; human or animal. Since it comes with the power of God," Clari ticked them off her fingers as she listed them, "then I use it sparingly, and, It will be obeyed."

"Seriously?"

She nodded.

"I don't...I'd never ...I didn't know such..." Morris shook his head to try to clear it. "I don't even know what to say. That's amazing."

"No, it's really not, Morris. Most everyone has the right to use it, but they don't believe it's within their ability. They don't believe it's possible, so they nullify the ability within themselves."

Morris sounded annoyed. "You say it like it's no big deal. I've never heard of this, and am pretty sure many others haven't, either. How can you be so indifferent about this and with other things you do? Not everyone lives – or even knows about – the kind of life you live."

She paused at his words. A touch of old defensiveness wove into her words, "All of this is old news, and normal, for me. I grew up with this."

He spread his hands out, palms facing her. "I know, but a lot of us didn't. It's not old news to me, and I'm sure, to others."

"Yeah. Well." She rubbed her temples. "I guess I still get a bit defensive." Old pain surfaced in her eyes. "I got frustrated trying to talk about his – you know, stuff that's normal for me – to other people over the years, only to have my words fall on deaf, or in some cases hostile, ears. I guess I use my attitude as a way to protect myself."

Morris rubbed the back of his neck. "I thought the world was more accepting of people with abilities. Doesn't WPO's world-wide presence help?"

A mirthless laugh set the tone for her words. "I think the only differences between the twenty-first and twenty-second centuries and now are the increase in the number of people with abilities. As our WPO Director, Mrs. Witherabbott said, "Bigotry, judgment, denial and fear still run rampant.' And, in my experience, it certainly is still very much out there."

The conversation halted with the arrival of the animal control officer. She instructed the dogs to follow the officer and to get in his truck. "Thank you, officer. I'm so glad that the euthanization laws changed. The animals know this, so they aren't as hesitant to go with you guys anymore."

"Yes ma'am. Thanks, Morris. See you later." He and the dogs climbed into his truck and took off.

"Shall we get back to work?" she inquired over her shoulder as she traipsed back into the office.

Chapter Twelve

Once settled in her office, Morris jumped in. "All right, partner. Start filling me in on your thoughts, hypotheses, and how we're going to help them. What's your role or objective and what'll mine be?"

"Bigfoot Bob said to push aside the UFO stuff and the animal mutilations, which was what Samuel pretty much stressed, so my guess is that the UFOs and mutilations are connected to one another and not necessarily connected to our portals. That points us towards paying attention to the portals and unknown animal sightings."

Clari explained what she'd discovered in her research and her energy scans about anomalies.

The breath he hadn't realized he was holding came out in a whoosh. "What a relief! I don't want to get sucked into the UFO realm. I'm the odd man out as it is. I don't need to be ridiculed for investigating UFOs."

Clari thought his joking tone had a serious edge.

He continued. "What unknown animals are being reported? Are they similar, or perhaps connected, to the case we looked at earlier?"

Even though he may be relieved about not working the UFO angle, she was pretty sure he wasn't going to be pleased with what she was preparing to share. "I can't say that they are definitively connected. However, after having said that, I don't believe there are such things as coincidences."

She watched as he leaned back and crossed his arms.

Nope, not going to like this at all, she thought right before she plowed on. "You heard about the large wolf sightings? Well, there have also been reports of blue dogs, little humanoid creatures, animals that resemble a cross between a bear and big dog, and of course, Bigfoot, plural and various other not-quite-sure-how-to-describe-them creatures."

"Wouldn't Bigfoot plural be Bigfeet?" Morris interjected with a smirk.

Eyes twinkling, she swatted at Morris. "Oh, great. Dad jokes. Be serious. There are also my favorite creature sightings...the dinosaurs. Velociraptor in Arizona. Thunderbirds, which have also been called giant eagles – as well as pterodactyls and pterosaurs – have been sighted in Texas, Georgia, Missouri, and Illinois. These sightings are from days of old to as recent as the beginning of this year."

"Dinosaurs?" he voiced his disbelief.

"Sure, think about it. Nessie and other water monsters are thought to be dinosaurs."

"I'm sorry. I'm having a hard time swallowing that."

"Why? What about Bigfoot sightings? Or dinosaurs? Some believe Yeti, the Abominable Snowman and Bigfoot may have belonged to Gigantopithecus, who supposedly lived millions of years ago."

"Exactly. Not nowadays, there's no proof that any of these beings and dinosaurs really exist in our time."

"As incredulous as it sounds, how else would you explain the drawings and stories — let's use Bigfoot and Thunderbird as examples — that began way back, before there was intercontinental communications, and continued all the way up to pre-internet? How did they share these experiences across the globe? Yet we have cave drawings and native lore about these beings at different locations around the globe, and we still have modern day sightings. There has to be some truth to it.

"As for proof, I think the scientists with Samuel's group might have that, but I don't think they're sure what to do with it. Quantum physics was slow in catching up with the metaphysical and paranormal beliefs."

He still wasn't convinced. "Let's just say that these creatures are real and that people have seen them. Do you know why we can't find hard proof, like bodies or their babies?"

"Yes, I do." Her eyes burned with conviction.

Morris shifted in his seat, his face showing that he was not comfortable with this conversation. "Well?"

"Much like ghosts do, they are traveling here via portals or wormholes and disappearing into the same to escape, or actually return, to their place of origin. I believe this is what Samuel and his team discovered and are asking if we can close them."

"Wormholes? Come on. You can't be serious?"

"What's wrong, Morris? A little too far out there for you?"

"So are the portals ghosts supposedly travel through the same ones as what Sam's team is investigating?"

"No. There are different dimensions, and within each dimension, there are different planes. For Earth, the Earthbounds, or the ghosts of those who didn't cross over, are seen with their feet standing on their ground, which is about three feet above our ground. Same dimension, different plane.

From the sound of it, the ones Sam's talking about are from a different dimension and that are visiting our dimension. However, both examples use portals, or wormholes, to move into our space. So when a house or location is thought to contain a portal, where ghosts travel as they please, it needs to be closed. Once closed and dismantled, the activity stops. If I'm correct, these beings are doing the same thing."

Morris scrubbed his chin. "You're saying that you're convinced they have portals where we're going on Friday?"

"Yes, that's what Samuel thinks and it makes sense to me."

"And you're going to close these portals? You can do that?" The cynicism in his voice wasn't lost on her.

"I think this one may be very old, and I'm pretty sure I've never worked one this old. Though it may be ancient and well established or rooted...but I don't see why not."

"Hm. And what am I supposed to do? I don't work energy like you."

"It's my hope that you'll protect me if any of those beasties decide to try to stop me. They're not going to be happy with me closing their entryways to their favorite hunting grounds and may physically come after me or others on site."

Morris cracked his knuckles. "Now you're talking about my kind of game."

Samuel, Morris, and Clari arrived at the hangar. "We need to bring out luggage over to our pilot so he can store it," Samuel pointed to the rear of the plane.

After the luggage was stored, Morris asked the young looking pilot, "What kind of plane is this?"

The pilot cheerfully provided the information, "It's a very light jet, or VLJ. This one's older, but is a good jet. It's a Cessna M2 with a cabin length of 11 feet, a width of four foot ten inches, and a height of just under 5 foot, so please be careful and mind your head when you enter the cabin."

Samuel guided Morris and Clari to the few steps leading up into the cabin. As Clari entered, she stood in front of a side-facing seat. To the left were the pilots' seats and the control panels. To the right was the passenger cabin with four slightly off-white luxury seats arranged in a standard club configuration with dual executive pull-out writing tables.

Clari picked a chair on the left side and sank into its generous comfort. Morris, with head tilted to avoid hitting the low ceiling, moved into place across from Clari, while Samuel moved to a seat on the right side. The pilots' soft muffled voices were heard through the closed cockpit door.

Samuel broke the eerie silence that accumulated within the main cabin, "Clari and Morris, our plan is to introduce you to the rest of the investigators and take a drive around the property to give you an idea of the layout before it gets dark. When we return, you both can talk to the investigators and get a feel of the environment and perhaps how we work as well.

"The ranch is an older home. The interior is rustic, but it does suit our needs. Oh, and the rule out here is no one goes anywhere outside of the house alone. Everyone travels in a group of at least two…always. When it gets dark, we gear up and start working."

After light chit-chatting, each person finally settled in and became immersed in their own thoughts as the private plane whisked them off to get them closer to the mysterious ranch.

A dark green jeep, which had seen better days, awaited them when they touched down. Clari pulled Morris aside. "Can you sit up front with

Samuel, please? I need to focus on scanning the energy of the land and area."

Morris dipped his head, "I got your back, partner," and smiled, and went off to help Samuel store their luggage into the jeep.

Samuel slid into the driver's seat, Morris in the front passenger and Clari climbed into the back seat.

She adjusted her Senses to open a bit wider to monitor, and learn, the local area's energy. She Looked over at Samuel and noted that his energy had a tinge of relief and excitement. It appeared that he had his hopes pinned on her and Morris.

She shifted her Sight to Morris and as usual, she couldn't See or Sense much from him. She tuned out their light chit-chat and stared out the window.

The landscape in some areas reminded her of home with its barren patches of red rocks, while other areas had trees, grass, and plants.

As the drive continued, she began feeling uneasy. She closed her eyes and focused on her body and what it was trying to tell her. The Feeling she had was that of something unpleasant and ancient uncoiling and her body was responding to this new-to-her possible threat. Her internal warning bells were stirring from their slumber as they prepared to sound the alarm if needed, though no specific reason made itself known to her. She opened her eyes.

Samuel regarded her in the rear view mirror. "Oh good, you're awake. You were so quiet that we'd thought you fell asleep. We're just on what we affectionately call 'the driveway', so we'll be at the ranch in about five minutes."

Her warning bells began to softly chime. A generic "be careful" warning.

The plan was for them to first visit the ranch home, the base of operations for Samuel and the rest of the team. Samuel informed Clari and

Morris pre-flight that they would be in a hotel located forty-five minutes away. However, Samuel informed them there were cots and sleeping bags available if they preferred to spend most of their time at the ranch.

Clari watched out of the window, keeping her energy feelers out for any energy weirdness or major disruptions, but the only thing she Felt, energy-wise, was an emptiness that carried twinges of desperation, isolation and hunger.

She shivered, remembering the last time she'd Felt a similar kind of intensity... from the cursed dagger.

She'd noticed a long time ago that incidents or topics came in waves, and within those waves were clusters. If someone contacted her and was, for example, grieving and having a hard time since their loved one passed, human or animal, she would inevitably have a cluster of people contacting her about their grief...usually all under a two-week period.

A short time of calm was usually afforded before another wave would roll in bringing another cluster of similar-typed energies, though she never knew in what form they would arrive.

Her thoughts brought her back to the energy, and incidents, surrounding the dagger event, reminding her that there were no such things as coincidences.

The cursed dagger that Clari had encountered had been programmed to suck out her energy and feed, as a sacrifice from a dark practitioner, Hecate. That incident shared some commonalities with the reported ranch incidents. Both involved someone harming another; included Other-World beings; and both took from others to feed. Her stomach soured and she sent a quiet prayer to her Team and Creator for strength and protection.

As they continued up the driveway, she saw a barn but no sign of the house yet. She noticed that the pens and turn-outs were empty.

A few minutes later, Samuel steered the jeep around a bend and she could see the ranch in the distance.

Clari felt the anticipation rise within the jeep as Samuel parked by the ranch house. Tall pine trees stood fifty feet out around the cabin, making the cabin feel like it was smack dab in the middle of a pine forest and protected from the outside world with an open patch of land in front of the cabin.

The house was a single floor ranch. The exterior was like that of an old cabin, but bigger with modern amenities which included the various types of scientific equipment settled on the front porch.

The front door opened. Three men filed out onto the porch and waited for the newly arrived to approach them. As Clari, Morris and Samuel walked toward the porch, she noticed that Samuel's gait was more confident — he was in his environment now.

"Clari Jones and Henry Morris, these are the other scientists that work here. I'll let them introduce themselves."

A tall and rather lanky man stepped forward. His shoulders were hunched as if his many years were spent ducking under door frames and his posture eventually stuck in that position. The hair that remained on his head was solid white and in little puffs as though someone took cotton balls, stretched them out thin and haphazardly glued them to his head. His white short sleeve shirt and grey pants were clean but threadbare. He spoke with a no-nonsense approach, short and to the point, yet not abrasive. "I am Dr. Jeffer, Dr. Randolph Jeffer."

He stepped back and a bald-headed, wide-berthed man with small deep set eyes, somewhat unkempt and had what she hoped was powdered sugar on his face, stepped forward. "Dr. Alberts," he stated brusquely. He reminded her of her history professor who had an overall rumpled appearance. As Dr. Alberts retreated, she sensed that he wasn't too pleased about her and Morris being there. His demeanor announced he didn't like any disruptions of any kind, including discussions beyond what his passion was. Anything else was a waste of his time and not to be tolerated.

After Dr. Alberts stepped back, the third person, the youngest, stepped forward. "Hi. Welcome. I'm Steven Gram. Don't mind the stuffed shirts here. They've lived, breathed and eaten science for so long, they've forgotten there's a world out that includes other people. Sometimes I think they've forgotten how to interact with people who aren't scientists. Heck, I'm a scientist too, but I do remember to have a life outside of my job." He shrugged, then continued, "Come on and we'll give you the grand tour of the house and then either Sam or I'll give you a tour of the grounds."

She decided right then that she liked Steven. His dark brown eyes were intelligent and playful. His black, almost shoulder-length hair was mussed. He wasn't quite as tall as Jeffer, and his physique spoke of nimbleness, indicating either regular exercise, sports, or perhaps both.

Steven turned back to the door and held it open. Morris and Clari forgotten, Alberts and Jeffer, already swallowed up by their science projects, faded back into the house.

Steven waved the rest forward. "Come on," he coaxed good-naturedly, "we're wasting sunlight."

As Clari entered through the front doorway, she immediately stood in the living room, slash dining room, slash kitchen area. An open floor plan made it appear to be comfortably large…well, except that every flat surface sprouted yet more scientific gadgetry.

Samuel led them to a hallway. There were a total of two guest bedrooms and one main with an ensuite bathroom. There was also a guest bath in the hallway.

The furnishings in the house were dated and a bit tired looking. Not her idea of rustic at all.

For the next half hour, each investigator played show and tell for them. She didn't understand even a third of what the gadgets were and what they did…except for the shotguns and cattle prods that were lined up against the wall by the door. She knew what those were for.

Just when she thought her brain couldn't handle any more information that it didn't understand, Steven announced it was time to tour the grounds. "I'll be your guide. Sam feels the need to get back to his research as quickly as possible since he's been away all week. Are you two ready?"

All three piled into a late 1970's F-100 model Ford pickup truck. The sorely faded turquoise paint hinted at the cheerful color it once had, but was now marred with scars and a fungal looking spread of rust. Clari, the smallest, sat between Morris and Steven.

Morris voice held a bit of reverence when he spoke, "Wow. I didn't know there were some of these still around."

Steven patted the worn dashboard and put the truck in drive. "I've only seen this one, but it's considered a farm truck, so haven't taken it out on the open road. My guess is that, if there are any others out there, they probably won't look any better than this one. But it does run just fine."

She openly watched Steven as he drove across the grounds. "You're different than the other three. What's your role here?"

"Well, we're considered the brightest in our individual fields, and we are each PhDs. I don't like the whole snobbish or stiff air these guys present — so I guess in that area, I'm the 'youthful rebellion'," he revealed while using air quotes.

He continued. "Basically, a simplified explanation is that we're all scientists that use our equipment to monitor, study, capture, document, and record the phenomena out here, with hopes that our PhD brains can figure out and explain the phenomena."

"Huh. That sounds just like any other paranormal, or ghost, investigation group."

Steven's good-natured guffaw filled the truck. "Yes, I guess it does sound like that. But seriously, we're all trying to find a scientific and quantifiable explanation as to what the heck is going on out here."

Morris spoke up. "Care to explain all the firepower? I noticed the shotguns lined up, and saw everyone but Samuel carrying a sidearm."

The energy within the truck shifted, becoming a bit heavier. "We've come across some rather...uh...aggressive entities as well as some stuff that we're not sure about. Nerves, after dark, are pretty jumpy. You'll probably find out tonight."

"What kind of stuff have you seen?" Morris asked him.

"We decided that rather than trying to explain, and convince you, we'd explain things as you witnessed them. Well, explain as much as we know. I'm sure that sounds a bit cold, but we've become quite used to others thinking that we're daft when we tell them what we've seen and experienced. Seeing is believing, right?"

They fell quiet as Steven continued driving. The silence broke when Steven announced that they had arrived at the Mesa. He stopped the truck and everyone got out. Steven stopped a few feet from the edge and stared down into the valley, transfixed by the sight before them. Clari stood between Steven and Morris. The deciduous trees below them were starting to turn colors. "Welcome to La Mesa de Almas Perdidas."

Clari followed his gaze. "Wow," she softly gasped, afraid to break the spell. "What does the name mean, Steven?" she asked in a quiet voice.

Steven answered, "Lost Souls Plateau."

The view was breathtaking. From the mesa, they could see the whole valley that contained the ranch and barn, both of which looked like tiny specks. And much further out..."Uh, Steven, are those ruins out there?" She pointed to the farthest point to the left of the land below them.

"Yes, that's the home and barn from the previous owners from the 1920's. They had some problems with unknown beings terrorizing them, so the story goes. They abandoned those buildings in the 1930's and built the cabin we're now using." Steven scratched his head, "I'm surprised some of the older buildings are still standing, but they were initially built with cinder blocks. Most of the blocks are still there, but don't wander out there. Weird things go on out there, and the buildings are in no way safe."

Intrigued, Clari asked, "What kind of weird things?"

Steven used his canvas tennis shoe toe to scuff up some of the dirt. "Well, things like lights going on within the building shells, hot spots on thermal imaging, and weirdly shaped beings are sometimes spotted in the trees nearby. And the place just feels spooky. We stay away from there as much as possible, though we occasionally have to go out when we see things out there, like when we see lights come on inside to make sure no one snuck onto the property. There's no electricity, so it may be someone's flashlight we're seeing. We don't want a lawsuit if someone sneaks onto the property and gets hurt."

"Got it, thanks."

Behind the ranch was a mountain. She and Morris shared a knowing look. The ranch, barn, and land were isolated, as though they had been cordoned off from the rest of the world. The buildings sat within a bowl, and that made everything within the valley trapped and vulnerable.

Morris moved next to Steven, "I believe I'll be in need of some of that firepower you guys have."

"Of course. I'll make sure you get some as soon as we return."

"I think we've got an idea of the lay of the land now. Should we head back now?" Morris suggested.

Steven nodded, "Let's do it. We'll grab a bite to eat before we head out tonight. But, fair warning, it's Dr. Alberts turn to make dinner and it's usually canned beef stew with biscuits."

Clari's stomach rumbled. Embarrassed, she rubbed her stomach. "Sounds good to me, eh, Morris?"

Morris displayed a wide grin, "Sounds perfect."

Steven shook his head, "Brave souls you two are," and chuckled.

Clari switched to her Other-Sight Saw that Steven's overlay showed Elf. She smiled. Having Elven attributes most likely meant he was unable to lie. She also Felt his energy was bright, which made his overlay that of a High Elf, not a Dark Elf. It occurred to her that she'd not Seen, or Sensed, an overlay for Jeffer or Alberts.

They entered the house to find the others in a flurry of action. Half eaten bowls of beef stew were beside the three scientists who were busy putting various pieces of their scientific equipment in backpacks and gear bags.

Alberts looked up long enough to say, "Bowls are on the counter next to the biscuits. It's serve yourself. I suggest you eat while it's still warm. We carry snacks, but I think you'll need this heavier food first."

Steven began to gather his gear. "Sunset isn't too far away, go ahead and eat, Morris and Clari. I'll join you in a minute."

After they scarfed their stew, Morris asked, "So the action begins when it gets dark? I'm itching to load up with fire power."

Steven shrugged. "It could be as soon as the last of the light disappears, or anytime between sunset and sunrise, or not at all." He addressed Samuel, "Sam, could you get Morris set up with weapons while I finish gearing up?"

Samuel motioned for Morris to follow him. Out of curiosity, Clari followed. Clari and Samuel stopped to watch as Morris surveyed the arsenal the scientists had. Like a kid in a candy store, Morris surveyed the arsenal in the gun cabinet, and then moved toward each firearm to see what flavor he wanted. He looked over some rifles and picked one, then moved on to handguns. He said to Samuel, "I'll take one of the 12 gauge Remington shotguns you have at the front door." He explained to Clari, "Those are good for close range. When you pull the trigger, it sprays double 00 pellets into your target." He held up a handgun, "This is a Glock 17 and uses a 9mm round. It's good up to about twenty feet." He held up the rifle, "This one, which I've not used in ages, is an AR15 semi-automatic rifle and is good for longer range, like up to 300 yards."

Clari wasn't sure if she was supposed to be impressed or not. "I'm not sure what to say, Morris. I really don't know much about firearms. I'm just glad you're armed. I'll feel safer and can concentrate on what I do and not have to worry about my surroundings, so, thank you."

Morris seemed to puff up a bit.

Samuel, Morris and Clari returned their focus to the scientists getting ready to move their backpacks and gear bags to the outside porch.

Steven turned his attention to Clari. "What will you be doing, Clari?"

"Observing visually to see what you all do if, or when, any phenomenon occurs. If it does, I'll also be Reading the event to see what I come up with. If there are no hostilities or when things quiet down, I'll work with my Team to see if I can come up with a plan of action."

While Steven and Clari had talked, Samuel, Jeffer and Alberts lugged their gear outside. Morris joined Steven and Clari. She thought Morris stood a taller now that he carried his own little armory.

"We usually start off on the front porch. We take baseline measurements for comparison. We split up, in pairs. One team goes mobile on the property. We have two way radios if we need to contact the other team. Sometimes they work, sometimes they don't. The other either stays on the porch or moves up to the Mesa and stays there unless the mobile team requests backup," Steven explained. "What we need to know is if you, Morris, are going to stay with Clari, or are you two going to split up?"

"I go where Clari goes. Period."

"Fair enough. Sam and I have the stationary position tonight while Jeffer and Alberts are mobile. You two will be with Sam and me. We'll be at this until about three or so in the morning. Then everyone'll come back here and crash until the early afternoon. We eat, review whatever recorded information we received, and share. We also have reports to write. Then we start all over again, except the teams swap positions. I suggest you grab some warm clothing and maybe a blanket. The nights are cold and when the wind blows, it can have a bit of a bite to it. Any questions?"

Clari and Morris answered in unison, "No." All three stepped onto the porch to begin their night.

After Jeffer and Alberts took off in the pickup, Steven showed Clari and Morris how to use the night vision goggles, thermal imaging and night cameras — both static and video. There was other equipment, but Steven and Samuel would be the only ones to handle those.

Each person grabbed a chair and some coffee and some buffalo jerky that Steven and Sam had supplied, and then settled in for the night.

She reinforced her shields, opened her other-senses and began monitoring as the sun finished sinking below the horizon in a beautiful display of golds and reds, then they were plunged into darkness. It took everyone a couple of minutes for their eyes to adjust to the partially moonlit night. When Clari's eyes adjusted, she watched as the stars made an appearance in the clear night sky. Like New Mexico's sky, some stars seemed close enough to reach out and touch.

Morris and Samuel spoke softly while Clari relaxed her body and stared at the star-filled sky. Clari heard the background sounds of the humming and occasional beeping that the monitoring equipment that Steven and Samuel set up. As she zoned out, she slowly became aware of an energy shift in the air. She sat up straighter, alert and listening.

Morris noticed. "Clari?"

"There is a sense of wrongness in the air. Something is changing...something is coming."

"Can you tell what it is?"

"I'm not sure. It's as if the barometric pressure is abruptly changing and there is movement in energy. Is something gathering energy to manifest? I don't know yet." Her unease continued to grow.

As the energy continued to build, her Senses began getting more information. "It's old, maybe ancient and possibly from before the time of Homo sapiens. It's pulling energy from every direction as it builds."

Samuel and Steven jumped up as several machines suddenly came to life, beeping and whirring, demanding the scientists' immediate attention.

She gasped as the energy she Felt sent out a large pulse, similar to a shockwave from a large explosion.

Morris stood and moved closer to her. She was nervous. "Morris, if that was the opening of a wormhole, I have to wonder if I was a bit too naïve. It's huge."

It was suddenly as though someone flipped a switch which caused the energy to halt; paused in mid-movement. It wasn't gone…just suspended.

Everybody else stopped what they were doing and stood still. They had felt the change too.

She stretched her Awareness outward, searching for any new energy signatures which might announce the arrival of another being. She skirted the edges of Alberts' and Jeffer's energies. Their signatures placed them as far away from the ranch as possible while still staying on the property.

She Felt the disturbance originated closer to Alberts and Jeffer than to the ranch, but no other new or unknown life-energies registered.

Even though he whispered, Morris' voice broke through Clari's concentration. "Got anything?"

"No. It feels like whatever was happening just stopped, but I can't get a Read on anyone or anything connected to the energy building, and can't even pinpoint exactly where it originated. It's baffling."

As she finished speaking, the air changed back to normal. No pressure, no movement, and the machines quieted.

Steven was excited. "Wow. The Electro-Magnetic Frequency detector went off the charts! I wonder if Alberts and Jeffer experienced anything."

Disappointed, Clari turned toward Morris. "This is not what I expected, how about you? Wasn't it kind of…"

Morris finished her sentence, "Anti-climactic?"

Clari's eyebrows came together, creating a crease between them. "Yeah."

"I didn't know what to expect, so…" Morris shrugged.

The rest of the night and early morning hours were uneventful. Alberts and Jeffer returned close to three in the morning.

While the investigators hauled their equipment back into the house, they ignored Clari and Morris as they excitedly compared their take on the evening's events.

Clari and Morris stayed outside to talk. She asked Morris if he wanted to drive out to the hotel, or spend the night out at the ranch.

"I think we need to stay the night. I'll ask someone to take us to town after we sleep. I can rent a car there so we can come and go as we please."

Steven, who had come out to check on Clari and Morris, overheard Morris' response. "No need for that, Morris. We have a company car out back that can be yours while the two of you are out here. Does that work for you?"

"That would be great, Steven, thank you."

"Good, now that transportation is settled, you two might want to pick out some bags and crash. Remember, we do this again tomorrow after we review what our equipment caught from this evening. Come on, I'll show you where the bags are."

Steven informed them that, since they were guests, they would have the main bedroom and bath, that way the rest of them wouldn't disturb Clari and Morris.

The main bedroom had no bed. Sleeping bags in hand, Clari and Morris each chose to nest on opposite sides of the room. *I wonder what else might be nesting here, like rodents and bugs.* She shook her head to shake out those thoughts. They each took turns in the bathroom to get ready for bed.

Clari wormed her way into the zipped up sleeping bag. It smelled clean, but a little musty.

Morris turned the lights out and crawled into his bag. Clari began to relax as she listened to Morris' deep breaths. She started when Morris spoke, "So this is the kind of stuff you do when you're not working with me?"

Clari smiled into the dark, "No. I've never done this before. I'm not even sure what I've gotten myself...uh, us, into."

Though only a moment passed, time seemed to drift in the dark. Morris startled her as replied, "Oh."

Clari sighed, "Yeah. Morris? It's nice knowing you've got my back."

She heard the smile in Morris' voice, "I'm really glad to be with you, Clari." Amusement tinged his voice, "Though I'm not quite sure what you've gotten us into either."

Morris' voice floated out of the darkness, "Hey, I wanted to ask you something."

"Shoot."

"I noticed that you talk to different people in different ways. I mean, you talk to each person differently. Did you know you do that?"

Clari squirmed in her sleeping bag. "Um, yeah. But I didn't think that anyone else realized it."

"I'm a detective," he teased. "Why do you do that?"

Clari played zipper on her sleeping bag. Two inches zipped down, and then zipped it back up. "It's a reaction to each individual's energy. For example, the Lieutenant has prickly energy towards me, and I respond most of the time by being prickly towards him. Well, that and I really don't like being told what to do."

Zip, unzip. "And J.R. – formerly Maestro – is so formal when he speaks, so I try to mirror it back to him." Zip, unzip. "Plus there's the whole sharing thing. My mother used everything I said against me – as narcissists are known to do. As a kid, I didn't understand that she had a disorder – I just learned that if I shared anything about me or my life, she'd find a way to use it, like a weapon, against me. I learned to not share much about myself to anyone. So I'm more relaxed and open with people trust.""Like Josie and me?" Morris asked.

Zip. "Yep." Unzip.

"Okay, I get it. Well, I'm going to get some shut eye. Night, Clari."

Zip. She heard him roll over in his bag, "Night, Morris."

Clari snuggled deeper into her sleeping bag. *It feels weird sleeping in a room with someone else. Especially Morris.* She eventually fell asleep, comforted by the rhythm of Morris' breathing.

Chapter Thirteen

Clari woke up and after hitting the shower, quietly left a still-sleeping Morris in search of some coffee.

She found the others busily attending to their equipment, each person absorbed in their task. She located the coffee and helped herself. A small portion of the dining table was available so she claimed it and started working to caffeinate her body.

Alberts broke away from his equipment to refill his coffee cup. He pulled a chair up next to Clari and, with a grunt, lowered his cumbersome body into it.

"Morning, Clari."

"Morning, Dr. Alberts."

"George, please. And I apologize for my grumpiness yesterday."

"Morning, George, and you're forgiven."

George sat quietly for a moment and contemplated the contents of his coffee cup. He voice was gentle, almost friendly. "How was your first night on the porch? I heard you guys didn't get any visuals but that the EMF detectors were pretty active."

"All true. How about you and Jeffer? Anything happen out where you two were?"

"No, nothing visual. We're preparing to go through all our devices to see what they picked up, but otherwise it was a pretty quiet evening. Maybe they didn't start up because you two came in. Maybe it'll kick off tonight. Just be thankful that the orbs didn't show up. Those are pretty terrifying."

Energetic spikes radiated out from Alberts, showing her that his memories, tinged with fear, haunted him. "How can orbs be terrifying?"

George shrugged. "They just are. Your whole body responds in terror and there is no logical explanation for it. You've no choice but to feel terror. You've no control. The orbs haven't done anything to any of us that we remember. It's just that they produce extreme fear. I nearly urinated on myself. Very nasty piece of business."

Morris found Clari on the front porch.

"Morning, Morris. Did you get your coffee yet?"

"Yep, I'm good."

Clari inhaled deeply. "Don't you love the smell out here? It smells earthy and clean."

Voice a little husky, Morris answered, "All I can smell is you. You smell nice, kind of like a warm hug."

Clari felt her ears warm up. "Oh. Um. Thank you, Morris. A warm hug, eh?"

He looked deep into her eyes, "Yep. A warm hug." Morris turned his head and look out across the land. "So, what are you up to now?"

The panic, or was it excitement, quickly evaporated when Morris broke eye contact. Clari didn't realize she'd been holding her breath until she opened her mouth to answer Morris. "I wanted to stroll around, but no one was free to go with me. Steven gave me a crash course on using a GPS locator, handed me one and a notebook and told me to take notes and get coordinates of the positions of anything of interest for their records. Are you up to it?"

"Sure, let's go."

They stepped off the porch and strolled away from the ranch, and as they did, she shared with Morris, "I had a little chat with George this morning."

"George? Who's George?"

"This morning Dr. Alberts apologized for yesterday's rudeness, and told me to call him George."

Morris snorted in amusement.

"What?" she demanded.

"I was wondering if George was another Bigfoot, or some other creature in need of a name. I was a bit surprised when you said it was Alberts."

Clari gave Morris a playful shove before she continued. "George told me that they've had orbs around here which, according to him, produced a dramatic reaction of fear in them."

"Orbs? Aren't those the balls of light that sometimes show up in photos and videos, and there's usually heated debates as to whether or not they are spirits or dust?"

Clari nodded. "Those are the ones. I've never heard of orbs producing fear. Well, besides the normal excitement of 'Ooh! What are they?' when someone sees them on photos or videos for the first time. George was talking about feeling terror and told me it was, to him, an illogical fear."

"So you've never experienced this? Was it a spirit orb? What could make this one different from the others witnessed or caught on tape? What are your experiences with orbs?"

She tittered. "Whoa there, dude! Slow down long enough for me to answer some of your questions." When Clari was sure he wouldn't start up with his rapid-fire questions again, she shared her thoughts on orbs. "While growing up, I never really paid attention to the orbs and light streaks in the photos of me, and I didn't have much to do with them in a paranormal sense until I began working with some paranormal investigation groups."

Morris interrupted. "You were a ghost hunter?"

"No. I helped instruct some groups, worked with them to help expand their intuitive or medium abilities to add more depth to their investigations and to teach them how to aid those beings who are ready, but weren't sure what to do, to cross over." Clari made a sour face. "I do not like the term 'ghost hunters'. I prefer 'ghost investigators' or 'paranormal investigators'. I'm not 'hunting' ghosts."

"Got it. Sorry, go on."

Clari's face smoothed out. "Ghosts – who are deceased but haven't crossed over – and spirits, who have crossed over or those who have never been human, can show themselves as orbs. This is how they transport themselves. It takes less energy to show themselves as orbs than it does to show as a whole body apparition."

She continued. "The only direct physical experience that I've had was with a blue orb. I'd been sitting on the back patio one night when my peripheral vision picked up a fast moving *something*, but never had a chance to process or identify it because it ended up hovering right in front of me by the time my brain registered movement. It was the size and shape of a football, and was cobalt blue. It wasn't a solid blue color. The blue within the orb undulated and swirled.

"It hovered about two feet off the ground in front of me. I had the feeling it possessed intelligence and that it was observing me. You know, checking me out.

"Then in a blink of an eye, it zoomed off. It didn't take long before it disappeared from sight.

"Oh, and there were, and still are, huge orbs in the sky out by my house. They usually show up several times a week. Some bear a resemblance to a huge ball of fire, except it hovers up in the sky.

"And there are others that move slowly, and aren't as bright, or as orange, as the big ones. These others are red, blue, green, or a soft white. They move slowly, as though they don't want to call attention to themselves."

"Did any of them ever create fear in you?"

"Nope. The only one that got near me was the blue football one. The others remained higher up and never approached me."

Morris slipped into detective mode. "So the one that hovered in front of you, you didn't Feel anything from it?"

"Only that it was observing — like it was trying to get a sense of me, just like I was doing to it. Curiosity, nothing else. That's why I don't understand why an orb created such fear in George and the others."

Morris was quiet as he mulled things over. He began thinking out loud. "Maybe if you're relaxed to begin with you don't have anything for the orb to react to. What if these guys were so tense, upset and scared already from some of their other experiences that the orb perceived them as aggressive and hostile?"

He became more animated as he worked his way through his thoughts. "Maybe it was trying to scare them off the property. Or," he continued, talking faster, "the orb amplified what emotions they already had. You were relaxed when your orb showed up and you were curious about it, so there weren't any emotions from you that would have been uncomfortable or detrimental if the orb had amped up...you know, intensified and mirrored what it saw in you."

Surprised once again, she snorted. "Well, Morris, there certainly is a lot more to you than meets the eye. You should think about becoming a detective. I think you'd be good at it." Clari mischievously challenged.

Morris rolled his eyes.

Her phone rang. She motioned to Morris to wait and answered. "Hi, J.R."

"Tahini. I have information for you."

"On what? And my name is Clari."

"Remember I told you that a woman was trying to find you?"

"Yes, J.R., I remember."

"I was able to find out more, and I am very concerned for you, Tahini."

"Why? What did you find out?"

J.R. revealed, "I did some digging by starting with the woman's contact number. It turns out that the phone number she provided has been linked to a known Grigori satellite office.

"The woman seeking you is most likely from the radical group called the Grigori. They were raised to seek and destroy anyone who shows any signs of abilities that could possibly mean the individual, or individuals, have some awakened trace of Nephilim blood in them. Are you familiar, Tahini, with Nephilims and Watchers?" J.R. queried.

Clari played with her earring. "Not really, J.R. I heard bits and pieces of information while growing up."

J.R. explained, "Fallen angels were cast out of heaven and fell to Earth, where they eventually mated with human females and produced offspring. These offspring were the Nephilim. The Nephilim were said to have abilities inherited from their fallen angel fathers. Some say the Nephilim were also the giants written about in the Bible, and are the same line of giants whose remains were discovered from the late 1700's or early 1800's on."

Clari interrupted. "Oh, so they have the skeletons? Could they do DNA testing and see who the descendants of the giants are?"

"No, Tahini. Many were turned over to – what had been called – the Smithsonian Institute and purposefully lost or destroyed. Their existence would have created all sorts of problems, from the standpoint of the Bible all the way to how the history of mankind is being taught."

"Are you serious?" Clari rolled her eyes. "Unbelievable."

"Yes. May I continue?" J.R. sounded miffed at the interruption.

"Yeah. Sorry."

J.R. discoursed, "The Watchers were said to be angels sent to kill off the Nephilim because they were never meant to exist. Another name for the Watchers was Grigori.

"The human Grigori group is a self-important, self-appointed and delusional group. The original Grigori, or Watchers, were not humans but rather angels created by God to be near or on Earth to do God's bidding — to administer punishment, to guide and to teach humans. Some stories say they were sent to eradicate the Nephilim. The written records state that when the Nephilim were destroyed, God called his Watchers back home.

"But some delusional human, in ancient days, took it upon himself to be judge, jury, and executioner. He decided to be a human-Grigori. To hunt and kill what he deemed as Nephilim, or the many-generations-removed peripheral offspring of the fallen angels and humans. He also trained others who held this same belief, and this cult-like organization continues that work today. Their life goal is to eradicate any chances of Nephilim blood or abilities from surfacing in the human world.

"In the real world, the angels who were sent to kill the offspring were completely different angels than the Watchers.

"Tahini, I believe the woman who contacted me is hunting you. I've not contacted her, but she's received information from someone about you, though I don't know who."

"I think I do, J.R. I'll bet Maria set this whole thing in motion. Even after she's gone, she's still trying to get me killed. Thank you for letting me know."

"Please be careful, Tahini. And tell your human..."

"J.R.!"

J.R. rumbled and continued, "...about our conversation so he can be on the watch and protect you."

"I will. Thanks again." She rang off. *Peachy*, she thought.

She and Morris hadn't wandered far from the ranch porch, they'd been too busy talking, but were still out of normal hearing range from those at the ranch. "Let's stay here Morris. I want to tell you about J.R.'s call, but don't need the others to hear this."

"Okay, spill."

She did. When she finished, Morris complained, "I don't like this one bit. And I'm not that comfortable with J.R. either. What's his story, anyway?"

Clari rubbed her forehead. "His story, Morris, is not mine to tell."

Morris crossed his arms across his chest. "Huh. I'm not sure I like him." He paused for a moment, and then thought out loud "Hm. We'll see." He turned his attention back to Clari. "Did he tell you if he got her name or any information on this woman...what did you call her?"

"Grigori," Clari offered.

"Right, Grigori. Did he get anything else?"

Clari shook her head. "No. He just inquires into the nature of the requested services. If he doesn't want to take their case, or isn't sure, he doesn't get their full names or any other information other than a contact phone number. That's how he works."

"Well, I'm glad he gave us a heads-up about it. I think you might want to ask Josie to join us on this little adventure."

Clari's eyebrows rose. "Oh? Why do you want to pull Josie in?"

"I'd like another person who'd have your best interests in mind — as opposed to those who only want you to be part of their investigation. Also, with this mystery lady hunting you, I think Josie would be a huge asset. Josie could protect you using energy methods and I'll have you covered physically."

"Good argument, Morris, but I would rather not drag Josie into this." Clari raised her hand to belay Morris' argument. "Having said that, I do remember your speech about letting others decide for themselves, not me deciding for them. I have to get Samuel's okay on this, and then inform J.R. as well. If all of that goes well, I'll ask Josie."

"Good. We have a plan. Let's go back and talk to Samuel."

"I have no problem authorizing another WPO member on the project. I'll email the confidentiality form to you and you can forward it to Josie if she agreed to come," Samuel informed Clari and Morris.

Clari called J.R. and explained their plan. He was supportive and told Clari that, at this point in time, Josie wouldn't need to sign his confidentiality agreement. "However," he warned, "if it changes, I'll fax the form to your hotel or to Samuel's, wherever you are at the time."

Her next call was to Josie. She took her phone outside for this one so she could talk freely with her. After filling Josie in, she had to pull the phone away from her ear as Josie screeched with delight, "Holy moly, yes!"

Samuel sent the jet for Josie, and he would make sure one of the scientists would bring her out to the hotel where Clari and Morris were staying.

She and Morris packed their belongings into the loaner car, and agreed to come back in two days with their newest team member in tow.

Clari and Morris spent the previous day catching Josie up and relaxing in the cool but fresh air pool side, and were now on their way to the ranch. The plan for the day was for Samuel and Steven to introduce Josie around and give her some lessons on the gear. Morris and Clari would tour the property, giving Clari some much needed personal getting-acquainted time with the land and its energy.

With Josie settled in with the science team, Morris and Clari walked the property. As they walked, Clari pointed out, "Have you noticed the lack of wildlife here? There are no birds or bird noises, no rustling in the undergrowth or treetops, no deer sightings and I haven't even seen any animal droppings."

"Yeah, I noticed, and it gives me the heebie-jeebies. What does the wildlife out here know that we don't? And is it just now, or is it always like this?"

She stopped, closed her eyes and focused. She expanded her awareness further out. Yes, she was being pulled north. "Is it okay with you if we go in a northerly direction? I have a little tug pulling me that way."

"Sure. Got anything specific?"

She pointed in the direction they were heading. "No, I just have a generic 'go this way' feeling."

There wasn't much to see. The trees began their release of their colored leaves which decorated the ground and the other plants were starting to look like the desert scrub brushes back home in New Mexico. The land was beginning to show signs of winter nipping at the heels of fall.

Soon they were far enough away that the cabin looked like a speck in the distance. Clari adjusted their direction by moving in a bit westerly. Driven by her end goal, wherever and whatever that might be, she wasn't consciously aware of her surroundings.

She stopped abruptly, Knowing that she had arrived. At first glance, she didn't see anything special about the area, but then noticed a big bare patch on the ground.

Morris noticed it, too. "There's no vegetation here. No trees, no grass. It's a big bare spot, a dead zone. What do you think?"

"My first thought would be it is a regular UFO landing spot, but Samuel was adamant they haven't had the typical UFOs on the property, only occasionally spotted high up. I think I want to sit in this area and see if I can get a Read. Will you step outside of the dead zone so your energies won't mix with the ones already here?" She handed Morris the GPS locator. "And would you mind? Steven will want the location."

"Sure. I'll be just outside the circle." He moved to the edge of the bare patch, ready to stand watch. Though it may have appeared to others that Morris was relaxed and watching Clari, she Knew that he was well aware of their surroundings, and that he'd keep her safe.

She sat crossed-legged in the center of the bare patch, closed her eyes, checked to make sure her shield was still up and strong, and did some deep slow breaths to calm her body and mind. She soon Felt the familiar stillness settle within her — her signal to start working. She opened her Other-Senses.

Curious. She smelled burnt ozone. *Is this what a wormhole site smells like?*

She focused on Seeking, and following, any energy signatures connected to the barren ground. Overcome by vertigo, she balanced herself by placing the palms of her hands on the ground, one hand on each side of her. The sense of spinning continued, followed by the feeling of coming against something that offered resistance. She couldn't follow the energy through this blockade.

She pulled away from that and refocused on her body. When she felt balanced again, she changed tactics and stretched back to the past, searching for the last incident memory of what had occurred there, and that's when she found the residue of hunger.

The hunger signature had spontaneously appeared where she sat. This meant the hunger had begun here, and then moved out. She followed the signature as it progressed in the direction of the Mesa and moved beyond it as it continued to move out towards the next town.

She shifted her focus to the hunger signature itself. Her body responded, giving her the sensation of stretching, getting larger and wider. Her spine didn't support standing up straight, like the upright position wasn't natural for this form. Next, her arms felt as though they were lengthening, and they were disproportionate to her "new" body.

In her mind, her fingers developed rather large claws that could be retracted at will, and sharp pointed teeth threatened to pierce her lips. Her senses sharpened to that of a predator on the hunt...a hungry predator.

She Pushed her energy to probe deeper.

She picked up the Feeling that this creature knew its way around the property, and Felt that it was the source of the missing animals, at least in this area. She also had the Sense that someone, or something, else had let the beast out. Someone had opened a wormhole to let out their pet predator for it to run and feed, and they'd been doing this for eons.

She at least had one piece of the puzzle, but this wasn't the source or entrance location of the orbs George mentioned, though Clari wasn't even convinced those orbs were connected to the beasts.

She extracted herself from the other energy, grounded herself, and stood to move towards Morris. When she reached his side, he raised his eyebrows in an unspoken question.

"I Saw a creature similar to the one described in the police report back home," she shared. "The creature enters the land here, via a wormhole, and hunts for its food, which can be cattle, horses, or any other accessible prey. It brings its prey back here. It stocks up enough 'food' to hold it for a while so that there's no set pattern or hunting schedule. This makes it harder for any human to stumble across it hunting here." She rubbed her upper arms. "It's scary and I'm pretty sure that this creature is where the werewolf image from horror movies came from."

Morris straightened. "Okay, you inform Steven and we'll work on a plan in case it comes back tonight. Did you have a sense of when it'll show up again? You think that's what we felt here the other night?"

"I honestly don't know. The hunger I Felt when we landed at the airport is more than likely this creature. But, there is one thing I'm sure of. I'm glad you're here and that you're armed. That thing is a predator and I don't think it would give a second thought to taking us down. I think those guns will come in handy."

Morris gave a little grunt of acknowledgment. "Do we need to continue exploring the property, or did you get what you needed?"

"I'm done for now, thanks." Clari shivered, trying to shake off all that she had Felt. "Let's go back."

After she told Samuel and Steven about her experience, she set off for the kitchen. She wanted to be alone, and other than hiding in the bathroom, this was as alone as she could get at the ranch.

She got a glass of water and leaned against the sink to drink while she let her mind wander. She pulled out of her reverie when she realized that she could hear the tick tock of the wall clock. The ticks and tocks sounded like they were getting louder each time.

Her water was momentarily forgotten as her attention centered on the clock. The time between the ticks and tocks was being stretched out longer and longer. A thought popped in. *The space between the tick and the tock is where time stands still. It is a place outside of time.*

Then time stood still.

A loud noise startled her, causing her to focus back on her surroundings. She glanced into the living room and saw Alberts picking something up off the floor. He gave Clari an apologetic look. "Sorry, I dropped this," he held up a hard-shelled camera case.

She turned back to the sink, washed and dried her glass and put it back into the cabinet. All of this was done without much thought. Her mind dwelled on what the clock had, in essence, just taught her. And why she would need this new information.

Conversation at dinner had centered on the hopeful speculation that something big might happen that night.

After dinner, when everyone became absorbed in readying themselves and their gear, Clari could feel the energy change. A serious sense of excitement and anticipation of their upcoming scientific hunt, and nervousness about what — if anything — would appear tonight. Gear ready, they made their way outside.

They all decided that Josie would be with the Alberts and Jeffer team on the porch for her first night. Morris and Clari would be on the mobile team, so they would be going out with Samuel and Steven. The two scientists decided to park near the dead zone. They would park far enough away to not be noticed but close enough to see and record when something happened.

Steven and Samuel put their gear up. A video recorder, mounted on a tripod, would stay focused on the dead zone.

Each person had either night vision goggles or night vision binoculars. Clari had the binoculars. She'd had a tutoring session her first day at the ranch with Samuel. He'd worked with her on wearing the night vision goggles, followed by lessons on how to walk while wearing the goggles. After she kept stumbling and falling, the scientists informed her that she, and everyone else, would be safer if she were wearing the night vision binoculars around her neck...while sitting. Though the guys' teasing was good natured, she still felt a bit embarrassed by the whole incident.

Everyone settled into a spot in, on, or beside the truck and waited.

Several hours passed and Clari began getting drowsy. She leaned back and closed her eyes. *Just for a moment,* she told herself.

She jerked awake, her internal alarms warning her that something had changed. Her eyes darted to each of the guys. Each was in the same spot they'd been in before she had dozed off, and no one was reacting to anything.

She closed her eyes and went inward to See what her body could tell her.

She Felt pressure building ever so slightly. Using her Other-Sight, she focused on the dead zone area. *There,* she Saw it. There was a small, slight shimmer in the air. It looked similar to the heat waves that come off the roads in New Mexico during the summer, except this was about four feet off the ground.

"Something's happening at the dead zone," she alerted the team. "There is a small shimmer about four feet off the ground, near the center."

The team was now alert. Samuel responded to her information. "What do you Feel?"

"It's similar to the pressure building around a person when they are preparing to trance channel," Clari informed Samuel.

Samuel was the first to admit confusion. "I don't know that that means."

Clari briefed Samuel, "Right before trance channeling occurs, a wormhole, or portal — which utilizes an energy bridge — opens which allows the entity to not only enter our dimension, but also to enter the channeler or host. This can create a feeling of pressure building in the air. It's almost tangible. You can physically feel it if you are sensitive to it.

"This is what I Feel now, only it has grown larger as we sat here and talked." While she'd been explaining to Samuel, Morris had moved closer to her. She Sensed him move into bodyguard mode, which was comforting to her.

"Remember Clari, we'd like this thing closed." Samuel reminded her.

"I remember. I'll do my best."

In the meantime, the pressure had built so much that she was yawning to pop her ears. Even with her ears popped open, she could hear a consistent whooshing sound. The sound was a longer and louder version of the blood rushing in her ears.

She closed her eyes and turned to her Other-Sight. She Saw that the portal had become big enough for someone, or something to step out.

Since she had never worked on a wormhole as it was opening, she had decided earlier that day that she'd wait for it to be fully open before she tackled it. That way the investigation team might be able to record everything.

She heard a gasp and opened her eyes. Everyone was staring at the sight before them. Clari saw a fire-orange orb like she had witnessed many times by her home, only this one was much closer. It was about ten feet in diameter, lit from within, and it looked like it was on the ground. The fire orb opened more and she could see the back lit silhouette of a long-armed, slightly hunched tall being as it trudged towards the opening...and headed straight for them. *If this is anything like what George Alberts experienced, no wonder he thought he would pee on himself.*

Clari shook her head and snapped into action. She focused on the wormhole. To her, the wormhole looked like an hourglass lying on its side. One end opened to where she was, the other opened to the Other dimension. The narrowing of the hourglass shape is considered to be the energy bridge – or the point where the two dimensions connect.

She called energy to her and Pushed with the intent to push the hunched being, or beast, back to its dimension.

As she Pushed, she Felt resistance, like someone on the Other Side was Pushing back on her. The hunched beast bellowed. The sound raised the hair on the back of Clari's neck. *That's the sound of a true predator...an angry predator.* Clari could Feel a mix of rage and frustration coming from the beast. She didn't believe it was the Beast that was Pushing back, but it certainly wasn't happy not being able to re-enter Clari's dimension.

Clari continued to Push, and located the center point where the part of the energy bridge in her dimension connected with their dimension. When she Pushed the being back behind the center point, she sealed off their portion of the dimensional energy bridge access to her location. Working fast, she snapped the tunnel into two separate pieces, like snapping the hourglass in half at the smallest point, disconnecting the two dimensions. She followed that by energetically disassembling the energy bridge in her dimension. She thought she saw, physically saw, a large but quick flash of bright white light where the wormhole had been and what sounded like a small sonic boom was heard, and felt. The pressure disappeared.

She immediately Felt someone on the other side attempting to rebuild the energy bridge connecting the dimensions. *Oh, no you don't!*

As she worked, she Received the knowledge that this side of the portal was ancient. The energy used to construct the wormhole tunnel had been programmed to hold its place, anchoring it at this location in this dimension. *Had this been created to be a permanent wormhole between the two worlds, and if so, by whom?*

Clari took a slow deep breath while concentrating on absorbing more energy so she could finish off the wormhole. She focused her attention on the deconstruction of the portal energy, and worked quickly to dismantle this dimension's part of the anchored wormhole. Her head began to hurt, but she kept at it until she Felt the energy give and then release. She gathered the energy from the wormhole's creation and sent the energy back to the Source to be recycled however the Creator deemed.

Clari next Scanned the area for any energy signatures of the beings, and beasts from the Other dimension. She could no longer Sense them. By now her head was screaming in pain.

She opened her eyes to see a concerned Morris closely watching her. "You back?"

She attempted to nod, and failed. "Morris? I need help," she whimpered, then passed out.

Chapter Fourteen

Cleaned and dressed, she opened the bathroom door, took two steps out, where she was greeted by Morris handing her a cup of coffee.

She took the cup. "Woah! I about ran you over." Clari took a sip. "Ah. Thanks, Morris, and good morning."

"Afternoon, Clari."

She took a couple of sips and enjoyed knowing it would soon jolt her completely awake. She noticed Morris hadn't moved. "Are you okay?"

"Yes, I'm fine." He scrutinized her.

She cocked an eyebrow. "You're giving me the creeps, Morris. Got something on your mind?"

"I want to talk to you before you leave the bedroom, but want you to have enough coffee in you so I can be assured you are coherent enough to understand me."

"Okay, shoot."

"Are you sure you have had enough coffee?"

"Morris, I'm starting to get annoyed, or scared. I'm not sure which just yet. Spit it out."

"You've been asleep for almost two days. I want to make sure you're okay."

The news startled her. "Did anyone try waking me up?"

Morris watched her face carefully while he spoke to her. "Yep, and you weren't having it. Does this happen often, Clari, or do you just pass out when you do some heavy duty energy work?"

"I don't know, Morris, I've never done something like this before. It's all new to me. Did I talk in my sleep or do anything weird or scary?'

"No, you just slept." His eyes gleamed as his signature smile tugged at his lips. "You laid there like a log."

"Okay...why do I feel there's a 'but' in there or that there's more than what you've told me?"

Morris motioned for her to sit down. With only sleeping bags and suitcases, Clari plopped down on top of her sleeping bag.

Morris sat on the floor next to her and asked, "What do you remember?"

"I remember you, me, Steven, and Samuel going out to the dead zone. I remember the wormhole and the being in it, and then Pushing the being back and disassembling the mother of all wormholes." She paused. "Nothing else until waking up this morning. Why?"

"You passed out after your work on the wormhole, but it's good your memory appears unaffected. The other thing is the guys out there are really keyed up about what happened." Morris stopped talking. He broke eye contact with a sudden interest in the floor.

A flutter of unease moved through her. "Morris? I'm getting nervous."

He looked up. "Is there something you want to tell me?" Morris studied her face.

"What are you talking about?"

"Is there anything you neglected to tell me about you and your abilities?"

Her posture stiffened. She began to panic. "No. What is going on, Morris?"

For the first time since she'd known him, Morris' voice and energy carried uncertainty. "Clari, do you know what you are?"

She dropped her head. Her hands were wrapped around the coffee mug settled in her lap. She stared into the coffee's liquid depth. Tears, which now pushed on the back of her eyes, threatened to spill.

She looked back up at Morris. "What happened, Morris? Why are you asking me this?"

Morris scooted closer to her and rested his hand on her upper arm. "We saw what you did, while just sitting in a chair. Samuel, Steven and I all saw the portal or wormhole open; we saw a creature inside of it, and we saw the portal abruptly disappear as if someone flipped a switch into its 'off' position. Next came a bright light and a – I don't know – sonic wave that blasted outward. We were almost thrown out of our chairs from the force of it. Then you passed out.

"I carried you to the truck, then went back to help the guys gather everything, pack up and load up their gear back into the truck.

"As we were driving back, we had weird...what looked like lightning strikes inside of some rather dark, ominous looking clouds which seemed to come out of nowhere.

"Sam and Steven said none of this stuff has ever happened before. You were out for two days.

"I'm still not exactly sure what you did, but I'm pretty sure it wasn't a common occurrence...for you, or anyone else." He removed his hand from her arm. "I know you said you do some things that are off the radar, but I'm beginning to suspect there's a heck of a lot more to you than I, and maybe you, realized. That's why I wanted to know if you know what you are."

Clari's stomach clenched and she felt her inner self curl up on itself, trying to become invisible to the outside world. She hadn't felt like this since she was a child. The fear of exposure and the fear of being rejected because people didn't understand her.

The tears that had threatened made good on the threat. They escaped and slid down her face. Morris encircled her in his arms and held her as she softly cried.

Morris handed her a warm, damp washcloth. Clari took it and covered her face with it, pleased with the soothing warmth as it seeped into her face. When it finally cooled, she removed it from her face. She opened her eyes and saw Morris once again sitting on the floor and facing her.

"Better?"

She wasn't sure if he meant since she'd cried or because of the calming effect of the warm washcloth, but it didn't really matter, the answer to both was "Yes".

"Thank you, Morris."

He stood up, took a few steps to the door, opened it, and called Josie in. Josie raced in, plopped down next to Clari and hugged her. Morris joined them on the floor. He and Josie waited for Clari to open up and share with them.

She explained how both Sebastian and J.R. had questioned her on what she was, continued on with Sebastian's warnings, and reminded them of the information J.R. had about the woman who was searching for her.

She told them she'd broached the topic with her Team, but they'd recommended she stay away from trying to label herself. "Other than occasionally feeling like an oddball every once in a while — like when I do something new and someone sees me do it, and they freak out — I'm just me. Even when I do something new, it doesn't seem unnatural to me. It feels totally organic, and right."

She played with her shoe laces as she continued. "When I was growing up, my Team always encouraged me to problem solve. If my answer didn't resolve the problem, I never saw it as failure. I just figured I hadn't observed or understood the situation fully or correctly, so I re-examined, re-evaluated, and tried a new possible resolution. I would eventually find a solution."

As Clari's old uncertainties resurfaced and the more agitated she became, the more her hands, which had abandoned the shoe laces, were in the air accentuating her words. Her hands were flying now. "It was the same thing the night we were out at the dead spot. I did what I thought needed to be done to close the wormhole. This is what Samuel hired me to do. I'd never attempted this before, with one that size and under those circumstances, but that didn't mean I couldn't do it. It just meant I'd try, and if the attempt didn't work, I needed to re-examine and try again."

Her hands fell back into her lap with a thud. She took a deep breath and released it in a puff of air. As she exhaled, she deflated as though defeated. "I don't know how else to be. I don't know how not to be me. And I didn't mean to scare anyone, or freak anyone out." The tears leaked out more slowly this time...even they were weary now.

"I don't know what I am. Growing up, I kept hearing 'the Watcher', but it never made any sense to me." Clari fidgeted.

Morris queried, "What's a 'Watcher'?"

Josie gave him a half shrug.

Clari brushed non-existent crumbs off of her jeans as she spoke. "Different sources say different things. The Keys of Enoch talk about how the Watchers are ascended masters who have returned in physical bodies. They are able to tell the light workers from dark workers. They've returned to the physical to help humans.

"Then in the Old Testament, you find the mention of the Grigorians. Grigori means 'Watcher' or 'those who are awake'. It can also mean 'those who carry out God's judgment'. They have also been called the Old Ones.

"The wiccan version of the Watcher is one who guards portals. It can also mean the guardian of one of the four directions. In that scenario, you need four Watchers.

"There are so many different views, stories, translations, interpretations. I'm at a loss on finding any solid answers." Clari stopped to catch her breath.

Josie took this break to put a question to Clari, "That's a lot, and you are right about differing information. So, which one are you?"

"As near as I can tell, I'm only a guardian of the dragon portal."

An incredulous snigger escaped Josie. "Seriously, Clari? Are you really going to sit there and tell me you are *just* the dragon portal guardian? People have been trying to use you and even kill you ...all over being a dragon portal guardian? Please. Would you quit being so naive? Morris, back me up on this."

"Stop and think, Clari. Have you ever been put in a position to put into effect God's judgment?" He ran a hand over his face. "I can't believe I just asked that. Boy, you certainly have changed my world, lady."

Clari let out a small nervous titter.

"Think about it though," he continued. "Have you?"

Clari pleaded her case. "I work hard to not judge others. I work to keep balance."

Josie jumped back in. "Wait! Didn't you tell me your Team trained you early on to remove entities who attempt to obsess or possess humans?"

Clari reluctantly nodded.

Josie was on a roll. "It only stands to reason then that you're a Watcher. You're enforcing God's Law of Free Will in those who the negative entities forced themselves onto or into." Josie jumped to her feet and raised her arms in the touchdown-triumphant stance.

Clari wasn't convinced. Her shoulders sagged and she hugged herself.

Morris, who had been watching the banter, noticed Clari was attempting to withdraw into herself and chose to re-enter the conversation. He spoke softly and evenly to bring her stress level down. "Clari, remember the lady at the restaurant back home? The one who gave you a hard time about your dietary restrictions?"

"Yes, I remember."

"The one you told she needed to be careful about judging you?"

Clari's curiosity peaked. "Yes, so?"

"Why did you tell her that?"

Fully enrapt with the new direction the conversation took, Josie sat back down.

Clari shrugged. "Because when people judge me, something usually happens."

"Like what?" inquired Josie.

"Well...when someone gives me a hard time, or attacks me out of meanness, it usually turns out they end up experiencing what it was they were giving me grief for...except in a more severe form."

Morris leaned forward. "Did you wish it on them?"

"Absolutely not! The first two times it happened, especially the one involving a so-called friend, I felt crushed. I cried over it when I was alone.

But never once did I wish it on them...any of them...ever. I never wish pain, suffering, or trials on anyone.

"After the second time it happened, I started warning people when they acted like I needed to be judged by them."

Josie was concentrating, putting pieces together. "What happened to them?"

Clari's hands had once again animatedly joined in the conversation. "Always a form of what I experienced, except more so. Once, a store clerk bumped into me hard enough to knock me off my feet. I ended up spraining my ankle. The store owner started yelling at me, telling me I was faking it to get money from him. I called a coworker to come help me and he took me to the doctor's and then drove me home.

"After my ankle healed enough, I went shopping at the same store. I noticed the owner near the back of the store. He was on crutches with his leg in a cast.

"When I was checking out, I asked the clerk what happened. She recalled that he had a freak accident. He was alone at home when it happened. He was in too much pain to move and couldn't reach his phone to call for help. It wasn't until the next day, when he failed to show up for work, that someone stopped by. They brought him to the hospital. His leg was broken and he suffered a bit of dehydration."

"One who carries out God's judgment," Josie replied softly and with reverence.

Clari abruptly stood and backed away. "No. You're wrong. I'm not that." Her pointer finger jabbed her own chest. "I'm just me, Clari." Her eyes pleaded with them, begging them to tell her she was right, but she saw no trace of either of them supporting her denials.

She pleaded. "What am I supposed to do? Hide even more? And now this whole thing was recorded, I'll be even more exposed."

Josie spoke tenderly, "We aren't trying to frighten or upset you. We're trying to help. We don't know what you are. Holy moly, Clari, you don't even know what all you're able to do. You moved some major energy, and then you were unresponsive for two days. How are Morris and I supposed to help if none of us knows what's going on with you? Unless you want to involve the WPO, I highly recommend you talk to your Team and seek guidance from them."

Clari recognized another fear pop up — the weight of the world on her unsure, confused, and frightened shoulders...or so it felt.

She vacillated from Morris to Josie, sighed, and sat back down. "I'm sorry. You're right. When we are back at the hotel, I'll seek some answers. Thank you both."

Morris decided a subject change was in order. "Let's revisit the investigation prior to your passing out. You don't need to worry about the recording. It disappeared, so you are safe there."

"What do you mean 'disappeared'?" Clari leaned forward, and in a hushed voice continued, "Did you erase the recording, Morris?"

In a conspiratorial tone, he disclosed, "They used an SD card in their camera to record it. When you passed out, I had Samuel and Steven help you. With their attention on you, I was able to remove the card and replace it with one I 'borrowed' from Samuel before we left the ranch. They have nothing. The card was blank. All they have now are their memories."

Josie's playful nature came out. "I didn't know you had it in you, copper."

He frowned as he crossed his arms over his chest. "Copper? Did you really just call me 'copper'?"

Clari leaned closer still, grabbed him, and gave him a quick hug. "Thank you, Morris. What did you do with the recorded one?"

With a mischievous glint in his eyes, he confided, "After I saw what you'd done, I decided I needed to destroy the proof. The recorded SD card had an unfortunate accident with the blowtorch I found in the shed out back. The guys are going over and over their equipment, trying to figure out what happened. I feel bad, sort of, but stand by what I did."

She shook her head. "Unbelievable. Thank you again, Morris."

"You're welcome, but this was only a Band-Aid fix. I think either you and I, or the three of us, need to figure out what to do to protect you. Can you ask your Team for some help with this?"

"I can, but I need to feel safe enough to relax and work with them. Right now, I don't feel safe or relaxed. What's our next move here, Morris?"

"Margaritas!" suggested Josie.

Morris chuckled, stood up and stretched. "Maybe we can have margaritas later. How about we let the science guys know you are okay and then find you something to eat?"

Relieved, she stood up. "That works for me." Her stomach growled in agreement.

Samuel sniffled, cleared his throat and was quick to wipe his eyes when Clari came out to the living room. Clari pretended to not notice his emotions. "We've missed you. I hope you're feeling better, Clari." He rushed to give Clari an awkward hug. "We've been worried about you. We weren't sure what to expect when you closed the wormhole, but I think it's safe to say that you passing out for two days never entered our minds.

"Josie kept tabs on you and told us your energy showed you were depleted but okay. I'm so glad you're okay." Samuel pushed his glasses up. "You are okay, right?"

Clari patted his arm. "I think I'm okay, Samuel. Thank you." She'd never heard Samuel talk so much at one time. She looked away from Samuel and noticed the rest of the scientists were focused on her. Question marks danced in their energy fields.

Samuel continued, "Good. After you eat, we'll all get together and review the night we all saw the portal. I know we're all curious to hear your perception of the experience."

Steven politely cleared his throat, "Uh, though we're dying to know what you experienced, we're also hopeful you can answer some questions." Steven shook his head and his eyes lit up. "I can't quite explain what all we saw that night," he chuckled, "but I do have a friend – a doctor in quantum physics – who I think would absolutely freak out about all of it." He went back to his science gadgets while chuckling to himself.

Samuel chimed in again. "It was my turn to cook. I hope you like tacos, Clari."

Clari rubbed her belly, "I do, Samuel. Thank you."

After Clari ate, everyone found a seat for Samuel's meeting.

Samuel started with, "We're all glad you are feeling better, Clari. Unfortunately, the unusual evening that you closed the portal wasn't recorded."

Steven stepped in and requested, "Clari, because Jeffer and Alberts were not with us, can you share what you Saw and experienced?"

Clari shifted in her seat. "Okay. In a nutshell, I saw a fire-orange orb, about ten feet in diameter, which appeared to be lit from within. Inside the orb I saw a beast worthy of a horror movie. I Pushed it back and went on to dismantle and seal off the portal. Someone on the other end of the portal was trying to reestablish the connection between our world and theirs."

Samuel nudged his glasses back up. "Thank you, Clari. Jeffer, Alberts and Josie, did any of you experience anything?"

Alberts head popped up from using a damp cloth on a stain on his shirt, "Jeffer, Josie and I were up on the Mesa. I don't know about Jeffer, but I personally experienced a change in pressure in the air, like a storm was moving in. However, it only registered a slight pressure change on our barometer. The timing coincided with witnessing a glow down below us, about where you all were."

Jeffer bobbed his head in agreement. "That is what I experienced as well. Nothing near what you I heard you guys experienced."

Josie shrugged, "I saw a glow, nothing else."

Samuel turned his attention to Morris, "Morris, is there anything you would like to share about that evening?"

Morris shook his head, "It was an amazing, and unsettling, sight for me. I pretty much saw what Clari shared."

Samuel remarked, "It's been quiet since, so we're sending you three back," he pointed to Morris, Clari and Josie, "to the hotel tonight. We want to see if anything will happen." He looked around. "Is everyone okay with that?"

Everyone appeared to agree. Clari, Morris, and Josie gathered their belongings and headed back to their hotel.

That evening while Josie was on the phone in her and Clari's room, Morris and Clari headed out to sit poolside. Clari was relieved the pool area was empty so she and Morris were able to sit at a table and relax. They were both quiet, staring at the stars and enjoying the peace.

Morris waited a few minutes before speaking. "I have a question, Clari. When you look at the stars, what do you see?"

Eyes twinkling with mischievousness, Clari said, "My guess is I see the same thing you do."

Morris rubbed day old beard growth. "No. Well, yeah, probably. But I want you to describe what you see when you look at the stars and what emotions or thoughts are brought up."

Clari looked up at the night sky. "I see a reminder that we are – our planet and all of its inhabitants – just a small piece of a very vast system. We are nothing but a speck.

"I see millions and millions of years of history beyond Earth's narrative of being inhabited.

"I see there is so much more to life than our daily grinds.

"I see where we can go if we ever lose the whole 3rd dimension duality crap so many – out of fear – hold on to for dear life.

"I See, with Other Sight, so many dimensions, planes or levels the human eyes cannot yet perceive.

"I Feel the expansion available to us all when we aren't busy limiting ourselves to just a physical existence.

"I Feel the beauty of it All.

"I Feel connected.

"I Feel hope." As if shaking off a dream, Clari shook her head and looked at Morris. "There. What do you see?"

Morris smiled. "I see sparkly lights against a dark background."

Clari snickered. "Be serious."

"Okay." Morris shared, "I see you."

Clari frowned. "I don't get it. I'm not out there."

With a pensive look, Morris leaned forward, "I see you. Vast, with hidden gems yet to be discovered. I see the beauty and wonder of the Universe in you. I see you shine and sparkle. I see you, Clari."

Panic raced up her spine. Rarely speechless, her mouth dropped open. Clari was afraid to blink much less say anything.

Morris continued, "I know getting close – emotionally – to people is hard and scary for you. I've seen you shrink when someone tries. I won't push you, Clari, but I want you to know how I feel about you."

Don't blow this, Clari! Say something! Her mind shouted. Clari opened her mouth to speak...

The moment was shattered by Josie when she sang out, "There you two are!" as she opened the pool gate. Josie plopped down at the table. Josie looked at Clari, then at Morris. "Um, did I interrupt something?"

Clari brushed imaginary crumbs off the table.

"No, Josie," Morris answered, "we were just enjoying the stars."

"Oh, okay. Clari, my mom said everything's fine back home, so we shouldn't worry. Oh, and she said she hopes we're having fun. If only she knew." Josie rolled her eyes.

Clari stood. "Thanks, Josie. I think I'm going to head up and go to bed now. Night, Morris. I'll see you, Josie, when you come back up to the room." Clari didn't miss the look Morris and Josie shared before Clari fled.

Chapter Fifteen

Clari was exhausted when they arrived back at the hotel, but she needed answers – sooner rather than later.

The connecting door to the adjoining hotel rooms remained wide open during the day and cracked open at night to allow everyone access to both rooms. When they got back to their rooms, Josie and Morris moved into his room to give Clari a bit more privacy for meditating.

Clari lay down and as her body relaxed, she shielded herself and the room. She was ready. She reached her mind out to her Team, seeking guidance and information. She asked her Team, "Am I a Watcher?"

* Yes — no *

She sighed. She needed definitive answers, not more ambiguity.

Her Team replied to that thought. * Seek your Council *

Now that makes sense, she thought. She took a few more slow deep breaths and sought an audience with her Council.

Clari stood before her Council of Twelve. The large room was dark, except for the crescent moon shaped dais that she stood before.

Eleven beings sat facing her. The twelfth chair stood vacant.

In thought form, it took mere seconds to convey all that had transpired as well as her uncertainty, fears, confusion, and desire to know more.

She also sent them her questions, suspicions, and requested clarity in the answers.

The Feeling from the Council was equivalent to concurrence. They agreed it was time and began downloading the Cliff notes version.

Her mind translated it into: "Clari was an experiment; one of a thousand of 'new' type humans. Her 'creation', her role, for this life's body took eons of training and experiences, as well as living and working with many cultures and beings to prepare her for her life as Clari.

"She is a being from the eleventh dimension. That's four dimensions over to the right, turn ninety degrees, a slight left angle, jump, and you arrive at the eleventh dimension.

"Clarima was trained by, and worked with, Archangels as well as with the Arcturians, Pleiadians, Sirians, and other planetary beings. She was a member — and still is — of the Star Council and a member of the Dragon Council.

"She trained with the Watchers, who were overseen, in part, by the Archangels Michael, Raphael, and Gabriel, and sat in on the Supreme Judgment Council of the Heavenly Court.

"She spent time with each group to become well versed in their duties and their ways.

"She entered a human body and promptly erased those memories from her newly physical conscious mind. Her subconscious mind, her higher self, and her Team had remembered for her and urged and guided her through this life.

"And all of this was to prepare her for where she is today in her life as Clarima Syd Jones."

Almost as a side note, Clari received an answer to her "unspoken" question about her council. Others have a Council of Twelve. Clari also had a Council of Twelve, but the twelfth chair was vacant.

The Council explained that because of her unique situation, she is the twelfth member of her own Council. The chair was hers.

When Clari came out of her meditation, she got out of bed and found Morris and Josie playing cards in Morris' room.

Clari dropped into a chair and shared her experience, and the answers she received. "I know what they told me, but I still feel like just plain old Clari."

Morris rubbed his chin in thought before speaking. "I think Sebastian was right. If the wrong person finds out what you can do, they may try to use you for their own selfish goals."

Clari's phone chimed announcing a text message. Her breath caught when she read the message from J.R. "Forms for Henry and Josie are at the front desk. Explain the Dragon Pact before they sign them. I'll arrive tomorrow."

Clari typed back, "What's going on J.R.? Why are you coming here?"

"Received word that war has been declared. Will explain more when I get there."

Explain the Dragon Pact? War? Crap.

As she bolted to the door, she yelled over her shoulder, "Be right back!"

Once she retrieved the contracts and was back in the room, she told Josie and Morris what she had.

"Why do we have to sign another one from J.R.?" Morris grumped.

"This one is different," she began, "and I need to explain some things before you two sign anything. What I'm about to say just might be the strangest thing I've ever told either of you."

With reluctance, she continued, "What's being asked of you shouldn't be taken lightly. These new forms are a Dragon Pact."

"Holy moly!" Josie exclaimed in an exaggerated whisper.

Morris turned to Josie. "What's a Dragon Pact?"

Josie stared at Clari. "I thought that Dragon Pacts were a myth. You're telling me that they are real?"

Morris tried again, this time asking Clari, "What is a Dragon Pact?"

"Yes, Josie, they are real. Morris, a Dragon Pact is a type of supernatural contract that binds the parties involved. This means that you sign it and you face the penalty of death if you break it. The good news is that breaking it is difficult. The bad news is it is difficult because you have to survive the pain of trying to break it."

Morris paled. His eyes darted back and forth between the two women, attempting to figure out if they were pulling a prank or not. Clari's face was serious and Josie's was pasty.

He felt stunned as the truth sank in. "You aren't kidding, are you?"

"No, Morris, I'm not kidding. The other beings, such as dragons, take their promises, or contracts, seriously. A verbal agreement between two dragons may appear only verbal, but carries the same penalties as a signed Dragon Pact if one tries to break the agreement.

"Because humans in general are known to try to find loopholes in human contracts, the dragons use the Dragon Pact forms with humans or other beings who have a history of trying to worm out of agreements. It is a contract that is magically enforced. Once you sign it, you're bound to the agreement under a penalty of death for breach of contract.

"In this case, you're signing to agree that you'll not divulge to anyone, other than J.R., me, and the two of you if you decide to sign, anything about the beings or abilities you may encounter while working alongside of, or with, J.R. and his peers.

"But, before you sign anything, I need you to read it thoroughly. If something is on the contract you don't understand, underline it and say, 'Clarify.' An explanation will reveal itself to you. You can ask me questions when you have finished."

Morris' mouth hung open.

Concerned, Clari asked, "Are you okay? Did I push you over the edge?"

Morris closed his mouth and shook his head. He took his contract and began reading.

Clari asked Josie, "How about you? Are you okay?"

Josie beamed. "Holy moly! Are you kidding me? This is fantastic!" Using the adjoining door, Josie took her contract and moved back into her and Clari's room, and sat down on her bed. Clari followed her.

Morris stepped back into Clari's room. "Can I ask questions now, or do I have to sign it first?"

"I can answer questions about the contract, but can't provide any details unless you sign it."

"Okay, I have one pre-signing question for you. Do you trust J.R.?"

Her answer was immediate. "Yes. I trust him with my life."

"Good enough for me." Morris signed the contract.

With both signed contracts in hand, she motioned Morris to sit. "I'll tell you what I know. You aren't obligated to participate. You're only obligated to not talk about any of this to others. Okay?"

Morris and Josie nodded their assent, so Clari opened with, "J.R. is a dragon." She waited for a response.

"Holy moly!" yelled Josie.

Morris cocked one eyebrow. "Seriously?"

"Seriously." Though forbidden to use a dragon's true name (even if she could remember it), Clari wasn't going to muddy the waters or create confusion by introducing his dragon pseudo-name of M. She would just stick with J.R.

She related the experience she'd had with Michael and the dragons, and explained what she understood about her dragon aspect and being a dragon portal gatekeeper.

Morris asked, "So does that mean no dragon can come here without you opening an entrance for them?"

"Well, there are some dragons that have stayed. They've been asleep here for probably millennia. Many are located deep within the mountains on Earth. What being a gatekeeper means is that I, or any other dragon portal gatekeeper, have the ability to allow dragons to pass through. Right now there is no free coming and going between the two worlds, or dimensions."

Morris voiced his concern. "Are they so dangerous we have to be protected from them?"

"What? No. It's the dragons that need to be protected from humans. You know how just about every civilization has dragon stories that are independent of one another? Each civilization has passed down dragon stories over time. Have you ever wondered how so many 'isolated' civilizations could all have dragon stories of old? It was because we all once shared this land. The humans and dragons lived in harmony and peace together. This was before we humans became totally bound to Earth."

Morris watched Josie, who sat on the bed like a little kid listening to her favorite bedtime story

He looked back at Clari. "What do you mean 'totally bound to Earth'?"

"This is a very watered-down version, and pre-dates the biblical flood, but here goes. The beings of Earth, who eventually became humans, used to be lighter energy beings, as in a whole lot less dense than we are now. We didn't maintain human bodies. We remembered our connection to the Creator. We remembered our creation abilities.

"Over time, we wanted a more sensory involved experience, so we made ourselves more and more dense until we eventually forgot our true selves, and we became three dimensional humans. We became dense energy, living a full sensory existence.

"Dragons remained with us until we completely forgot who, and what, we were. They tried to stay on to continue to work with us, but as we lost touch with our energy selves, we began living 'blind'. We discovered fear. And, generalized as a species, we became fearful of the dragons.

"And that's when humans began slaughtering the dragons. The majority of dragons that were still alive shifted to another dimension. The humans who were still able, worked the energies to seal off the connection between the Dragon Realm and Earth. It was decided that it was the only way to save the dragons.

"It was hoped that one day the portals would be permanently unsealed so that dragons and humans would peacefully coexist once again."

"But you said J.R. is a dragon. How is it that he's on this side?" Morris inquired.

"Uh uh. Again, not my story to tell. If and when J.R. wants to share, he'll let you know."

"What has happened to precipitate exposing himself to Josie and me? Why now?" Morris demanded.

"Your 'detective-ness' is showing, Morris," she affectionately teased.

Not amused, he cocked an eyebrow once again, indicating he was waiting for an answer.

Clari noticed Josie's energy sparkled and vibrated. "Josie?"

Josie's face morphed into a full-faced grin. "That's what I'm talking about! Is your life always this exciting?"

Clari rolled her eyes. "I don't consider my life 'exciting'…but it's certainly never dull."

Morris cleared his throat.

She realized she couldn't procrastinate any longer. "J.R. texted me. He's on his way here. He wanted me to explain the Dragon Pact and have you sign his forms so he could fill us in when he arrived, then you both could decide to stay or leave."

As Clari pulled her thoughts inward, she twirled her silver earring. She did not want to expose her friends to war. Heck, *she* didn't want to be in a war. She struggled once again with the drive to protect her friends versus informing them and letting them make their own decisions.

Morris knew Clari well enough to recognize she was having an internal debate, though he wasn't sure what prompted it. Morris prodded her. "Clari?"

She let out a puff of air, releasing the internal struggle. "J.R. announced war has been declared." She raised her hand to halt the possible onslaught of questions. "That's all I know. We'll all learn more when J.R. gets here."

They sat by the poolside waiting for J.R. to arrive. As they lightly chatted, both Clari's and Morris' phones rang. Her call was from J.R.

"Hi, J.R." As Clari listened to J.R., she tuned out Morris while he spoke on his phone.

"Tahini, I will be at your hotel in about fifteen minutes. I've already alerted Samuel, so he'll be there shortly, as well. I have secured the hotel's conference room. I've also requested catering, so please be at the conference room in about ten minutes to make sure they are set up. Okay?"

"Got it, J.R. See you soon."

As Clari put away her phone, Morris finished up his call.

Josie looked back and forth, trying to read either of their faces. "So what's going on?"

Morris nodded to Clari, indicating that she should go first. After she caught them up, she asked, "What do you have, Morris?"

"That was Samuel letting me know that he's on his way, and that this morning the air felt malevolent at the ranch, though they have had no visual activity."

"Hm. Thanks, Morris. I guess I'll go upstairs, grab my notebook and head down to the conference room." Clari stood. "Is everyone ready?"

* * *

The hotel staff showed the trio to the conference room. As they opened the door, they were greeted by wonderful mouthwatering smells. The offerings ranged from breakfast to dinner foods. Several tables lined the wall, all covered with off-white linen table clothes and laden with food and drink. Though Clari was only expecting there to be the eight of them, including herself, but Clari thought the amount of food provided was enough to feed more like 24 people.

A long banquet table with ten chairs took up the rest of the room. Everyone was to be seated at the same table.

Josie's eyes widened as they entered the room. "Holy moly, would you take a gander at this spread. How many people are coming?"

"Maybe this is our proverbial 'last meal', so he went all out," Morris replied sarcastically.

Clari frowned. "Thanks for that cheerful thought, Morbid Morris."

Clari, Morris and Josie looked over the foods. The caterers had brought fried chicken, baked chickens and Cornish hens, steaks, link sausages, roast beef, and other meats. There was also a variety of vegetables, enchiladas, tortillas with Mexican fixings on the side, breakfast foods, biscuits and gravies.

While they perused the food tables, the door opened. J.R. led the way, followed by Samuel, George, Steven, and Dr. Jeffer.

Clari waited to see if anyone else was coming. No one else came in. Josie was right. It was a lot of food.

"Thank you all for meeting here. Please, we have a lot to discuss, but I'd rather we eat first, so let us dine." J.R. motioned towards the food spread.

Morris was still prickly. "That's a lot of food, J.R. Are you expecting more people or is this to be our last meal?"

Everyone froze. His question reminded everyone of the reason they'd gathered. That realization made the room feel heavy.

Everyone's heads turned to J.R., waiting to hear what he had to say. "Don't be morose, Morris. I wanted to make sure we all had a healthy meal. Everyone here has some type of food preference, so I tried to address them all, the best I could. So please, let us prepare our plates." J.R. once again motioned towards the food tables.

Clari watched as each person loaded up their plates. She chuckled when she saw that both J.R. and Morris piled their plates with different types of meat...a lot of meat, both red meats and fowl. Clari stared at a meat she didn't recognize.

J.R. saddled up next to Clari and whispered, "Oryx."

Intrigued, Clari asked, "You had Oryx brought in from New Mexico?"

J.R., following a one shouldered shrug, smiled unapologetically, "I wanted Oryx meat."

Clari knew that East African Oryx had been released from 1969 to 1977 on the White Sands Missile Range in New Mexico. She'd heard that the News Mexico Game and Fish back then wanted to establish some big game out on the range, but Federal laws prohibited wild animals being released into the wild there – however, they were allowed to release the offspring of the wild Oryx onto the missile range. The gorgeous, large – around 450 pounds – long-horned Oryx, some of the larger members of the gazelle family, thrived in the New Mexico desert.

J.R. continued, "Have some, Tahini?"

Clari shook her head. "Ugh, no thanks. A little too red for me." She held up her plate, "I'm good." J.R. smiled, turned and went to sit down with dripping red meat feast.

Clari sat with her plate and looked around. George had a stack of pancakes with maple syrup and another plate with several biscuits on it. He'd also taken a coffee cup and filled it with gravy.

Steven had a plate heavy with vegetables and a Cornish Hen. Samuel and Dr. Jeffer appeared to have similar tastes as Clari...their plates held a slice of roast beef, mashed potatoes with a touch of gravy, a biscuit and green beans. Though Samuel did add a couple of fried chicken legs to his plate.

Josie opted for more from-home foods. She had rolled enchiladas – one hot green chile and cheese, one red chile and cheese, and what looked like sirloin enchilada and a side of Mexican slaw.

Though trepidation hung in the air, the communication was light and intermittent as everyone sat and ate. After the meal, some hit the desserts table, some hit the coffee, and some hit both.

Everyone's attention then shifted to J.R. when he rose. His pose, strong and tall, conveyed his well-tuned confidence and ability to lead others. He made eye contact with each person before addressing everyone in the room. He saved Morris for last, and when J.R. locked eyes with Morris, he said, "Thank you for all for signing the agreement."

Morris returned maintained the eye contact, his face hard and a distrustful edge in his eyes.

"Trust me," J.R. told Morris, "it is just as distasteful for me as it is for you. I'm not completely fond of, nor comfortable with, being bound to any human."

Morris was startled by J.R.'s rather intimate disclosure, and acknowledged J.R.'s brief show of vulnerability with a short head nod.

J.R. continued speaking. "Now for the reason we're here today. War has been declared. More specifically, war has been declared on all of you," he pointed to the four scientists, "and you, Clarima."

Everyone's eyes turned to Clari. "Why? I mean, why declare war on us?"

"They," he pointed once again to the four scientists, "meddled with and messed up the hunter being's portal." Samuel cringed.

J.R. then turned and pointed to Clari. "You cut them off. Those beings, the hunters, have been using that entry point for as long as they can remember. You come by and destroy, or erase, something that has been in existence for...well, probably for many centuries. I guess they felt they owned it or had rights to utilize it for their 'pets' hunting grounds. Whatever their reason, they've declared war. It's been my experience that when someone declares war, it's for one base reason...fear."

Clari's spine stiffened as she interrupted J.R. "Fear?" The disdain was noticeable in her voice. "They had ancient doorways to *our* continent on *our* planet in *our* dimension. They have large, scary killing beasts. Aren't *we* the ones who should be scared? What the heck do they have to fear?"

Unperturbed by her outburst, J.R. continued. "Fear of losing control. Fear of having to change. Fear of the unknown that they suddenly face. Also, we don't know if they actually had anything to do with the creation of the wormhole. Perhaps they happened upon it and discovered their beasts could dine here. Maybe, now that it's closed, they have nowhere to bring their beasts and whose hunger will grow. And maybe they are now in jeopardy of being harmed by their own beasts."

Clari shifted uncomfortably in her seat as murmurs rose around her.

J.R. resumed. "You closed it, Tahini. Do they fear the one who's able to so completely dismantle the doorway? Do they fear you?"

Clari was at a loss for words. She felt her food wanting to sour in her stomach.

Morris spoke up. "How are they able to declare war on the ranch inhabitants if Clari closed the wormhole? How are they going to be able to get to the ranch?"

Samuel slightly raised his hand. "I think I can answer that. Clari closed the enlarged wormhole. It's the one that we had been experimenting on — the one we accidentally made larger. However, there are numerous other similar smaller wormholes on the property. I imagine they could enlarge them enough to let the beings or their beasts through. And, if all were activated at one time, a lot of beings would be able to pass through. They could do a lot of damage."

During the momentary lull following Samuel's explanation, Josie turned to J.R. "How did you hear about a possible declaration of war?"

"There are more dimensions than the two you have consciously been involved in. And there are many other beings that visit Earth and visit with me. I guess you could say I heard it through the dimensional grapevine. And, before you ask, I unequivocally trust the being that passed this information on to me. There is no guesswork here. War has been declared."

"So what does that mean for us? I mean, why are we here now?" George grumbled as he mopped up the maple syrup and bread crumbs on his shirt.

J.R. shared, "I wanted to let you know what I had learned. I also need each of you to decide if you are staying to fight or if you are leaving."

Randolph Jeffer sneered, "I didn't sign up for this crap! I'm a scientist, for heaven's sake! This is not my fight."

Unperturbed by Jeffer's outburst, Steven commented, "But how many other scientists get to experience all of this? Not only do we have front row seats to this, we may be the only ones to stop these things from over-running our planet. Think about that."

Jeffer rolled his eyes, "Yeah, right. No pressure."

When it was obvious that the two scientists were finished with their side conversation, J.R. cleared his throat to bring attention back to him, and took a moment to make eye contact with each person in the room. "I can't force anyone to join in this battle. I can't guarantee anyone's safety. I can't tell you what to expect. We'll be going in blind and," his eyes locked onto Clari as he finished his sentence, "stepping forward in faith."

J.R. pointed towards the food tables. "You will find takeout boxes. I recommend you each prepare a box to take with you. Samuel, there are more rooms available at the hotel for you and the others. You're welcome to stay here or return to the ranch. However, any of you who do not wish to be involved in this war, please be gone from the ranch by ten tomorrow morning. If you aren't going to fight, you will need to be somewhere safe...away from the ranch.

"Please think this over tonight. If any of you are going to stay to help, please join me here, in this conference room, tomorrow morning at eight. Breakfast will be provided. If there are no further questions, gather your takeout, think everything over."

Back in the room, Clari spoke with Morris and Josie. "I'm not going to ask you to stay. If you leave, there'll be no hard feelings. I'm staying to see this thing through."

Morris' eyes hardened as he crossed his arms across his chest. "Hey, I'm your partner. You stay, I stay. I've got your back."

"Holy moly. We certainly can't break up the three musketeers, now can we? I'm in!" Josie proclaimed.

Chapter Sixteen

Reader Level X – Deadly, dangerous or uncontrollable. They usually are not seen again. ~ As understood and described by Clarima Syd Jones

Awakened by the incessant ringing of her phone, Clari struggled to make the noise stop. Through the sleep haze, she realized J.R.'s name was on the screen. In the next bed over Josie whined, "Shut it off."

Clari's hand, searching for the source of the noise, slapped its way across the nightstand. Finding the source, she whined into her phone, "What?"

"Tahini, those at the ranch are in grave danger. If you and the others are staying to fight, you need to hurry and get out there." His serious tone brooked no argument, but that didn't faze her.

"What? Crap, J.R., it's in the middle of the night!"

"I understand, but they've decided to attack tonight instead of tomorrow night. I believe we've about two hours before they arrive. Wake the others. Decide, and get out there if you are staying. Oh, and Tahini? You must call on, or request help from the others. They can't help unless you ask them to do so."

She had trouble making sense of what he was telling her. "Who, J.R.? Who am I supposed to ask?"

He'd already hung up.

"Josie, wake up." Clari gently shook Josie. "Come on, Josie, I need you to wake up."

Moaning her displeasure, Josie unwound herself from the bed covers and stumbled towards the bathroom, muttering, "This had better be important! I swear you're like my mother's tenacious terrier!" She slammed the bathroom door behind her.

Clari moved into Morris' room, approached his bed, leaned over and gently shook his shoulder as she whispered his name. Next thing she knew, Morris was sitting upright with one hand clamped around her neck and the other held a gun in her face.

She pleaded through her constricted windpipe, "Morris", it's me!"

"Oh, gods, Clari!" His hand abruptly left her neck with the gun disappearing at the same time. "Are you okay? Crap! I'm so sorry!"

Morris reached over and turned the bedside lamp on. He paled when he saw the red marks on her throat...marks he put there. His face turned green.

In the meantime, Clari was sucking in air and gently rubbing her neck. "I'm okay," she croaked. "Just give me a minute."

Morris threw off the covers and jumped out of bed. He stood beside Clari. "Um. Dang it! I need to..." Morris dashed into the bathroom where he filled a glass with water.

Clari blushed as she watched him, shirtless and in his boxers. As he turned to leave the bathroom, Clari dropped her eyes as though she was afraid of getting caught looking. *And appreciating*. Her blush deepened.

As Morris raced back to Clari, Josie lugged her tired body into his room.

Alarmed at the scene before her, Josie, no longer sleepy, demanded, "What the heck....what happened?" She glared at Morris. "What. Did. You. Do?"

Clari sipped the offered water which helped soothe her throat some, though her voice strained and sounded a gravelly, "It's okay. I woke Morris up by touching him, apparently triggering his combat training responses."

Josie jammed her clenched fists on her hips and envisioned shooting laser beams from her eyes into Morris', "That's no excuse! You could've killed her!"

Morris hung his head and sputtered, "I didn't...I should've...oh, god, Clari. I am so sorry!"

Clari waved his apology away, cleared her throat and with a raspy voice, spoke to them, "Enough. We'll discuss how I should wake you, for future reference, later. But for now, we need to get ourselves together. I'm sorry to do this, but the ranch is going to be under attack tonight. I'm afraid that if you are staying for the battle, we have to go...now. You're going to need to bring your coffee."

The air in the car was tense for the next forty-five minutes — each person buried in thought. Clari appreciated the full moon illuminating the night. *Maybe things won't be as scary seeing them in bright moonlight*, Clari tried to convince herself.

Clari inched the car forward as they made the turn-off for the property. Everyone's attention was focused on the sudden appearance of a wall of fog in front of them. Clari let the brake off and eased into fog. She held her breath as the outside world disappeared when their vehicle was consumed by the thick fallen cloud.

"I don't like how it makes me feel," complained Josie. "Holy moly, it makes me feel isolated, ya' know? It absorbs sound, cuts us off from everyone, like we've been cocooned and the rest of the world just ceased to be," she shared.

"Creepy," Morris interjected.

Josie continued, "This can't be good. We're going to war and we can't even see three feet in front of us. Even the moonlight disappeared."

Morris grunted his agreement while Clari kept her attention on driving.

The fog left a large expanse open in the area in front of the cabin, leaving an area of hard packed dirt available. *A clearing large enough to have a small battle*, Clari thought.

When they pulled up at the cabin, they found J.R. and Samuel armed and standing watch on the porch. Samuel looked like a deer caught in the headlights while J.R.'s troubled frown and rigid stance made Clari nervous.

"Do you feel it?" J.R. questioned as the car emptied. "Morris, why don't you go in and get geared up. Both Jeffer and Alberts are inside. They've decided to stay and help us." J.R. turned to Clari and Josie. "I want you two to be armed as well, but only carry items that are second nature to you. Now is not the time to better learn a weapon."

"I'm okay with both handguns and knives. Oh, and really good with staff work," Josie informed him.

"I don't know if they have any staffs, but there should be knives and handguns. Talk to one of the guys inside," J.R. motioned towards the door.

Clari shrugged when J.R. turned to her, and explained. "I don't do weapons, J.R. I never felt comfortable with them. Besides, I'm not so sure they'll be effective. Remember the giant wolf incident? Where the ranchers tried to kill the wolf. The guy shot at it repeatedly. The story made it sound as though the bullets were ineffectual. They didn't seem to affect the wolf."

Listening to J.R. and Clari's conversation, Samuel frowned. "She's right."

J.R.'s intense gaze penetrated Clari's brave façade, like he was speaking directly to her soul, "Perhaps that needs to be changed."

Before Clari could question him about what he meant, a surge of adrenaline pulsed through her...a primal survival response to something she couldn't see.

Clari turned, looking outward. The moonlight was still blocked enough to leave a pretense of diffused lighting above them. The porch lights couldn't penetrate the wall of fog beyond the clearing.

"What the heck?" Samuel pointed. Muted orange glows littered the fog surrounding them. An eerie groan radiated out as the fog appeared to give birth to less than graceful dark shapes.

It was time. An explosion of activity erupted around her. Making room to fight, the other humans spread out a bit from Clari, and without saying a word, had moved in such a way as to make a protective circle around Clari with Morris standing at her back.

Fear cemented Clari's feet in place and she felt detached not only from her body, but from everything going on around her. It was as though she were watching a movie. She turned her head to catch glimpses of the humans preparing to fight with Beasts of nightmares. As the Beasts neared, an unclean musk smell with sour undertones of something foreign to her, mingled with the gunpowder smell growing in the air.

These creatures, these Beasts, truly looked like what one could envision werewolves to look like. They alternated between an unsteady two-legged gait and a smoother lope on four legs with their front legs being dispro portionately longer.

The Beasts' hair, which bristled as they moved, shone full and stiff in the muted light while their black eyes occasionally refracted any available light, making them appear to glow red. Their exaggerated lupine faces resembled those from old werewolf movies. Easily pushing seven feet tall when standing upright, they even sported the hump on their back at the base of the neck like Hollywood had portrayed their werewolves.

Their freakishly long arms ended in terrifying extended razor claws. These were killing machines...total predators.

Clari's ears, now deafened by a mix of gunfire from handguns, explosion of the shotguns, screams, growls surrounding her, and the sound of her blood pounding in her ears meant she needed to rely on her eyes to make sense of the chaos around her.

Clari watched in front of her as Samuel raced to help Jeffer at the same time a Beast closed in on Jeffer. The Beast raised its arm and swung aiming his curved scythe-like claws at Jeffer.

Jeffer, in an attempt to stave off one of the Beasts, raised his left arm. Clari forgot to breathe as she watched the Beast's claw effortlessly slice across Jeffer's forearm. Clari's fists clenched and bile rose in her throat. While the Beast was still in contact with Jeffer, Samuel shoved a hot cattle prod at the Beast's head. The smell of rancid meat burning added into the mix of all the other smells as the Beast roared in rage and pain. Samuel prod the Beast again, and the Beast dropped to the ground.

Blood flowed as Jeffer dropped his now useless left arm, filling the air with the tang of copper. After tearing a strip off of his own shirt, Samuel made a light tourniquet for Jeffer's arm. Next, Samuel took his belt off and made a sling to prop Jeffer's arm in. The two men stood back to back, walking a tight circle to have each other's backs and to watch the area all around them. Samuel continued to use the cattle prod to keep any Beasts from approaching.

Clari felt she just received an important piece of information from that exchange, but with adrenaline racing through her making her heart pound, she couldn't quite grasp why what she just saw was important.

Clari looked toward Alberts. His breath was labored and his heavy sweating made the kicked up dust stick more heavily to him and his pale face. Alberts seemed quite agile despite his wide girth as he ducked and wove out of reach of a Beast.

She found Steven when she tracked a crazed battle cry. Apparently out of ammunition, Steven whipped out a hunting knife to fight off the Beasts. His face reddened when he bellowed another challenge to the Beasts.

Clari couldn't see Morris, but Knew he was behind her, protecting her, but she couldn't spot J.R. in the melee. She could Feel her group's energy levels lagging as they tired.

Each of the humans had one Beast attempting to engage them, but it looked more like the human side was playing a dangerous game of keep-a-way. No one was sure what would work to hurt the Beasts, or when something might work.

No other Beasts joined the battle unless one of their Beasts went down. *Why aren't they all attacking at once?* Clari also noticed the Beasts kept moving in, forcing the humans to shrink their circle.

Time seemed to stand still as she watched the fighting going on all around her. Her mind screamed, *there has to be something I can do! But what?*

She noted the bullets slowed the Beasts down a bit, but didn't damage or wound them as they moved in closer, though it seemed like the beasts weren't in a hurry to attack. *What are they waiting for? OMG, are they doing this as a type of sport, or are they playing with their potential prey?* she thought.

As Clari looked around, she noticed that the fog had thickened the air so much around the perimeter of the battlefield, that the dust being kicked up was suspended in the air as if it was displaced from time and space. It was acting as if it were a barrier, hiding the fight from the outside world.

Clari's mind turned as she sought an answer to give them all a chance against these Beasts. *How could these Beasts be here and not be here at the same time? Are they phasing? Jumping back and forth between their dimension and ours? Is that why our bullets aren't fatal to them? Do the bullets slow them a bit because the energy forces of the bullets are slamming against the Beast's energy field causing them to be momentarily stunned?*

Clari's feet were finally responsive, so she turned around and found Josie, and not far from her friend was J.R.

A Beast had visually locked onto Josie. It moved slowly, but steadily on all fours. Clari could see the muscles as they rippled under its hair. It exposed large canines when it snarled, and began closing in on Josie as Josie emptied her handgun.

Clari's attention shifted from the Beast and back to Josie and saw a look of terror on her friend's face as her friend realized the bullets weren't going to stop the Beast. Something primitive rose from within Clari. That Beast not only scared Josie, but had the audacity to go after her?

Clari's only thought was to protect Josie. Without a second thought she moved toward Josie and that's when the Beast launched itself into the air. Clari thought, *Displaced from time and space? That's it! I need to keep them in this dimension!* She concentrated and Pulled that Beast completely into her dimension.

As the Beast sailed towards its target, Josie dropped to her knees forcing the Beast to sail over her. She thrust her knife upward and sliced the Beast chin to groin. It dropped dead behind Josie.

Josie, coated in the Beast's blood, yelled, "How did that happen?"

Clari had made it susceptible to death.

J.R. moved closer to Clari. He stopped to take in the sight of the dead Beast at Josie's feet. Clari's quick glance his way showed the light in his silver eyes dancing with excitement as he called out, "Keep going, Tahini!"

Clari Pulled the Beasts closest to the humans, but she knew she wouldn't be able to get them all. It was as if those other beings had an unending supply of Beasts – they just kept coming and she was tiring.

Clari's shoulders sagged and she scraped the hair that stuck to the sweat on her face. Taking a deep breath, she closed her eyes, blocked out the surrounding din and raised her arms towards the heavens. With an energy pulse, Clari Pushed a request out to the universe for assistance. She Called the dragons, the mythological, the wee folk, the higher beings and more, beseeching for aid.

Clari felt her whole body as it became suffused with a beautiful energy. Her supplication had been heard...and answered. With renewed energy, she opened her eyes and once again worked on Pulling Beasts into her dimension.

Amidst the sounds of battle, Clari heard J.R. shout, "Yee-haw! You did it, Tahini!"

Amused, Clari thought, *what in the world would make J.R. drop his demeanor?* That's when she heard a new sound. No, sounds — plural. Roars.

Clari guessed that forty dragons of all sizes and colors arrived. Each dragon was a different size and color. The colors ranged from black to midnight blue, opalescent pearl, even dark forest green and more. Each of their teeth looked to Clari to each be easily the size of her hand.

Even the smallest dragon towered several feet above the Beasts. The dragons, eager to engage, spread out and encircled the outer edge of the, hopefully temporary, battlegrounds. The dragon's scales quivered with anticipation as the dragons moved in to fight. The scales created a hypnotic shimmering effect across their bodies.

As with any apex predator's deep guttural roar, the dragon's roars turned Clari's blood to ice, yet something primitive stirred within her in response to them; dragon calling to dragon. She stood taller, and if anyone happen to look at her at that moment, they would've seen her eyes, just for a moment, glow from an internal flame.

The Beasts, realizing they were in danger from the dragons, swarmed in to fight. It was no longer one-to-one fighting. Each dragon faced multiple Beasts. The Beasts found that their deadly claws made climbing the dragons easy, but they were unable to penetrate the dragon scales. The dragons shook the Beasts off as easily as a horse shaking off a pesky fly.

Clari's mind struggled to find a match in her memory to a new sound that accompanied the fighting. The loud crunching noise. It sounded like a really large dog biting and chewing on a bone. She turned and saw the dragons were eating, stomping on, or using fire to kill the Beasts.

Clari clutched her stomach and felt the blood drain from her face.

The magnificent dragons crushed their opponents as they worked their way toward where the humans fought. With their powerful bodies and their scaled armor, the dragons made quick work of the werewolf-like creatures.

Clari, so intent on watching the Beasts and dragons battle, forgot about the dangers closer to her.

She heard a low, deep growl. As she swung around to locate the source of the growl, something slammed into her hard, knocking her off her feet. She sailed five feet before she collided with the unforgiving earth. Having had the air knocked out of her, she felt as though she'd never be able to breathe again. White stars danced in her vision.

After a few shaky tries, oxygen flooded her body as she was finally able to suck in precious air. That's when she realized that the Beast's black eyes locked on to her. Clari Felt the Beast wanted her completely coherent before it killed her.

Another low menacing growl reverberated, directed at her, came from deep within the Beast. It was on all fours with its head lowered like a cat creeping up on its prey. Sitting up, she saw the Beast taking a slow step towards her. *It's playing with me*, she thought, *like a cat toys with a mouse before killing it.* Unfortunately, getting up, much less running, was not an option for her quite yet.

When the Beast took another sinister step towards her, Clari drew her knees to her chest, trying to put a bit more distance between it and her. She could smell its putrid breath as the stench reached her, getting stronger as the Beast continued its slow approach.

The Beast tensed. Clari Knew it had finished playing with her was preparing to spring. Clari held her breath as she waited for the inevitable. She heard someone yell "No!" as the Beast leapt. Clari's vision became tunnel-vision, showing her nothing but vast darkness of the Beast's eyes.

But before the Beast reached Clari, something, or someone, hurtled between the Beast and her. Her vision relaxed and returned to normal, but Clari, still somewhat disassociated, was confused by what she was looking at. *Surely the Beast hadn't just put his oversized clawed hand right through someone's chest? Whose chest was that?*

The scene before her changed again when a huge wolf charged the Beast. The Beast, as though removing a formal dress glove, slid Clari's protector's body off its arm, and the body collapsed onto the ground. Then the Beast turned to face the new threat...the wolf.

The wolf vaulted through the air aiming for the intruder's neck. Slightly smaller than the werewolf-like creature, the wolf's jaws were easily able to clamp down on the Beast's throat and shook it vigorously, as though it attempted to rip the Beast's throat out. When the wolf was convinced that the Beast was indeed dead, it released its hold. The Beast crumpled.

The wolf turned his attention to Clari. His bloodied muzzle severely contrasted his lolling tongue and wagging tail. Clari blinked, and her eyes widened in disbelief when she realized that the wolf was grinning at her. She stood as the wolf moved to her. The top of his head came to her chin. *He's huge,* she thought.

The wolf gently pushed against her body. Clari released a sound which was between a soft laugh and awe at the sight of this massive wolf. With another wide dog grin, it plopped down on its butt like a little puppy. She opened up Communication.

Thank you for saving me.

* Happy *

Who are you?

* Companion *

My companion?

* My pack *

I'm part of your pack?

* Yes - rest of pack protect *

Who else is in our pack?

* Not as happy, but will allow *

Allow who?

* Big kitty *

You can See him?

* Big kitty cranky *

Show me.

The wolf Showed her Clari's large black panther spirit animal that stayed by her right side. Clari Felt a reluctant acceptance of the wolf from her black panther spirit animal. No one else had ever mentioned Seeing her spirit animal totem. Clari turned her attention back to the wolf.

Are you the wolf that the previous ranch owners had shot?

* Confirmed – confused *

Confused about what? Saw the men eat cows – cows are food – took food to eat – men got angry – I left *

We have different rules here which probably don't make sense to you. You can't just grab an animal like that and eat it.

The wolf's response was equivalent to a human's "harrumph," followed by the intent to try to follow the dimension's rules when he was here.

Thank you again for your help.

* Pleasure *

Wolf stood and shook himself. He hesitated, turned to give a nod good-bye to Clari then faded into nothingness as he loped off.

Clari's mind retreated to a safer place. Her feet took it upon themselves to move her toward the figure on the ground. The one that saved her lay face down, body twisted – a carelessly tossed aside rag doll. Some part of her knew who had saved her, but another part refused to believe it. As if her hands had a life of their own, they moved to roll the body over. When she had it on its side, she saw the face. She fell to her knees and yelled, "Josie! Josie! J.R.'s hurt! Josie!"

Chapter Seventeen

Josie appeared, knelt beside J.R. and blanched when she saw the gaping hole in his chest. "Clari, he's gone."

Clari reached over and grabbed Josie's shoulder, her eyes pleaded. "Help him, Josie! You have to help him!"

Josie shook her head. "He's dead, Clari. There's nothing I can do. He's beyond help."

Clari's breathing became irregular and her face turned ashy. She could hear a primal gut-wrenching scream, but it sounded far away. It hadn't registered that the screaming came from her.

"No!" She screamed her pain again and again, until she was mentally and physically exhausted, though she couldn't stop the tears, even if she wanted to. Her heart hardened in her chest. J.R. was dead. She failed him. He died because of her.

Numb, she tuned back into her surroundings and realized she wasn't hearing much noise. She looked to the battle, only to find there was no battle. The fog was gone, and even the dragons had disappeared.

Everyone else stood where they had battled while they surveyed the battlefield. Clari saw the four scientists sagged in exhaustion, barely on their feet. Morris was still hyped up on adrenaline and standing guard, while J.R....her tears began again.

Josie scooted up against Clari, wrapped her arms around Clari and gently rocked her to soothe her. Josie released Clari when some of Clari's color came back and Clari begun to engage again.

The rest of the humans there merged where Clari and Josie sat.

Clari's voice was raw, distant and flat. "He's dead. He died trying to save me from a Beast," she explained. It hurt to breathe. "He died because of me."

Clari's began trembling again. Josie wrapped her in her arms again and joined her tears with Clari's. When the sobbing slowed, Clari whispered her thanks to Josie and pulled away.

Steven disappeared into the house and came back carrying a sheet which he draped over J.R.'s body. He then broke the silence and asked, "I know we're all shocked and saddened by J.R.'s death and we're all exhausted, but we have a lot of dead Beasts to deal with. Since this is not something we can call the police for, does anyone have any ideas?"

Clari looked out over the land. Ground soaked in blood and bodies lay where they fell. A lot of bodies. Rage seeped into Clari, enabling her to reconnect with her reality. She took a weighted breath and raised her hand. "I do. I want to try to Push them back to their dimension." Bitterness rose and she sniped, "Or would I be provoking another war?"

Josie stood up, lent a hand to Clari, and then Josie followed Morris onto the porch.

"Clari," an exhausted Morris said, "if you can do it, then do it. Let them deal with their dead." Then he slipped into officer mode. "Everyone else, please go inside and get checked out by Josie. Josie, let me know if anyone needs to get to a hospital."

No one questioned Morris, and left Clari and Morris to deal with the dead. Everyone else went inside.

His voice softening, Morris asked, "Are you ready, Clari?"

Taking a deep, jagged breath, Clari nodded to Morris. She forced the pain and grief to the side so she could remove the horrors that lay strewn over the impromptu battlefield. She concentrated to Push all of the remains back to their own dimension. There were too many to do all at once, so she had to Push smaller groups of three or four at a time.

As she worked she became aware of a live energy by the tree line. She turned to face whoever stood out there. A man stepped from the trees.

* Peace * he broadcasted * Want to understand *

She Recognized that the stranger's energy was connected to the big portal she'd closed the night she passed out. *The Beast Master*, her mind hissed as her fists clenched. She felt something within herself slithering below the surface. Something caustic, alive and seeking. She now understood the saying "seeing red". Her distress became all-consuming. Her head buzzed and her blood sought vengeance. Her anguish sought a way out.

The agony flared from the depths of her soul as her mind screamed, *Peace? Want to understand?* Her rage found a target. She wanted to destroy this being, to make him suffer for J.R.'s death. She raised her hands with the intent to energetically rip this man's body apart.

Morris spoke from the porch. "Clari?"

He tried again, "Hey, Clari!" he barked.

The buzzing in her head pushed everything away. Some part of her knew that Morris was talking, but not only didn't she understand the words, she didn't care. Tunnel vision helped her this time as she locked onto her target...on the being she thought of as the Beast Master. Small pieces of debris and dust began to swirl around her. The more the fury consumed her, the faster the swirling became.

Morris shouted, "Clari!" He grabbed a pair of binoculars, threw them at Clari and hit her leg.

Morris' voice finally penetrated her anger. Clari blinked, looked down at the binoculars at her feet and shook her head. "What?" she spat out without looking at Morris. The swirling vortex of debris came crashing to the ground.

"Clari," his voice wasn't as demanding now, "Are you okay?"

"What?" His words weren't making any sense to her.

"Clari, you're eyes are glowing red and are looking pretty scary right now. How about you take a few deep breaths and calm down a bit?"

Seething, she whirled on him. "Calm down? Calm down!" she screeched. Once again responding to her emotions, wind, debris and dirt began swirling. Clari raged, "Why should I calm down? That...that *man* orchestrated the death of J.R. and the injuries of everyone else. He deserves to die!" Her beet red face matched her glowing eyes. Her veins stood out. She spat, "He. Deserves. It. I will decimate him."

Morris quickly stepped off the porch, walked through the building debris whirlwind, breaking its momentum. He gently grasped Clari's shoulders. "Clari, if you do this, there's no going back. This is not self-defense, this is revenge. Revenge will stain your soul. Clari, you're better than this. Please don't do this. It'll make you the same as them. Please. I'm begging you."

It worked.

She forced a deep breath and fought to maintain control as tears once again ran down her face. The fire in her eyes flickered and went out. Morris' words finally penetrated her conscious mind and she realized he was right…destroying the Beast Master wouldn't change what had happened, and it wouldn't bring J.R. back. Her breathing became more steady. She spoke so only he could hear her. "Thank you, Morris."

Satisfied, Morris dipped his head and returned to the porch where he resumed watching over her.

Clari telepathically confronted the Other-Dimension man – the Beast Master. Seeing him triggered Clari. With control of her rage, she demanded, *Why did you send those Beasts here?*

He Sent back, * I, and my comrades, have every right to send our Beasts here to eat. We understood that the beings here were nothing but primitives, and that they had no connections, no feelings. *

The Beast Master, and his people, saw humans as merely food for their Beasts, much like how humans perceived cattle.

A question popped into Clari's head that she wanted to ask him. She showed him a picture of sightings of Beasts and portals being heavily reported in a scattering across the States. *Why are you all popping up all over the place?*

* The dimensional walls have thinned – easier to access now – and our Beasts grow in numbers and need more food *

Clari Shared emotions and connections of those the Beasts hurt and killed. Knowing and not really caring that her energy message carried the near toxic feelings she had for him and his, she Told him, *Your race may have appeared to excel in understanding energy manipulations, but you have lost compassion. As far as I am concerned, that makes your race the backward, challenged, and primitive race.*

She ended her tirade with: *We will continue to fight you on this.*

She Felt his startled reaction to her message. She then energetically slammed the door in his face.

Having ended Communication, she dismissed him and went back to her task of returning the bodies to their dimension of origin.

The Beast Master disappeared.

When she finished sending the bodies of the Beasts back to their dimension, she turned back to the house and saw Morris on the porch, once again armed with a rifle.

"Thank you for stopping me, Morris. I was so angry and hurt that I wanted to make him pay for what happened to J.R. I think I would've killed him."

Understanding backed his words. "I know."

"What do I do now?"

"We grieve. We begin again. It's a new day. Are you okay?"

Clari saw that it was indeed early morning. The sun had begun to peek over the horizon. "I'm sad. I'm angry. I'm hungry." She looked down at her blood stained hands. "And sorely in need of a shower."

A somber Samuel joined them. "I'm sorry about J.R., Clari. He was a good man."

So she wouldn't start sobbing again, Clari just nodded.

Pushing his glasses up, he told Clari, "There were a lot of 'impossibles' that happened today. I, and the rest of my team, really need to discuss this with you all."

Morris agreed, "Good idea. Let's go back to the hotel. I'd also like to be able to talk to everyone about what happened after we've all had a chance to clean up." Morris spoke more softly. "I'm sorry about J.R. I'll call the local police and report his death."

Samuel put his hand on Morris' arm. "That won't be necessary, Morris."

Morris bristled as he shrugged Samuel's hand off his arm. "Why not? He died and the authorities need to know."

"One, how do we even begin to explain this without all of us being taken in for psychiatric observations and evaluations? And two, because we don't have a body, Morris." Unfazed by Morris' attitude, Samuel motioned to the area where J.R.'s body had lain.

"Where did it go?" Morris demanded.

"We had some guests while Clari was...umm...cleaning up. None of us wanted to disturb you two, so the guests talked with me instead." Samuel looked star struck as he continued. "Two dragons stayed behind when the other dragons left." While pushing his glasses up, Samuel rocked back and forth on his heels. "I know we've experienced the loss of a good man today, but we also saw, at least for me, a new representation of the law of conservation of energy."

Morris bristled, "What are you going on about?"

Samuel focused on Morris, "The law of conservation of energy states that energy cannot be created or destroyed, but it can be transformed from one form to another..."

Morris growled in frustration and interrupted Samuel, "I know what the law of conservation of energy is, Samuel. What does that have to do with J.R.'s body?"

Samuel's face reddened, "Oh. Well, the two dragons that stayed behind shifted into people! Right there in front of me!"

As Morris growled again as he took a step toward Samuel.

Samuel took a step back and stammered, "J.R.'s body was removed from our dimension and taken back to the Dragon Council. Oh, and Clari? They said that they would contact you soon."

"Why? For what?" Clari was secretly hopeful that the Dragon Council could perform miracles and revive her dead friend.

Samuel shoved his glasses up higher on his nose. "I don't know." Clari grumbled and stomped her foot. Samuel continued, "I believe that you'll find out when they contact you."

As Samuel spoke with Morris and Clari, the rest of the investigation team coalesced on the patio. Everyone agreed to go clean up and meet back at the conference room at the hotel for breakfast that J.R. had prearranged and to discuss what had transpired.

Josie must have had heard Clari softly sobbing in the shower earlier, because as they were about to enter the conference room, Josie whispered, "Are you okay?"

Clari's shoulders sagged. She answered Josie as she opened the conference room door, "Yeah. A little numb. My tears come in waves. I'm okay one moment, and crying the next. How are you, Josie? Are you okay with all that happened last night?"

Josie's eyes hardened as they made their way to the buffet. "No. No, I'm not okay with it. We were attacked and J.R. killed. And we had to kill those things coming through." Josie took a shaky breath and her shoulders dropped. "It's just all so senseless. I'll probably feel better in a few days, but right now I'm just so angry." She took a slow deep breath and expelled it with force then shook her head, as though to shake out the memories.

After they fixed their plates, Josie and Clari joined the others at the table. Everyone looked battle-weary and sported cuts, scrapes and bruises.

Clari saw Jeffer moving slowly while he ate. "Shouldn't you be in the hospital, Jeffer?"

He looked up from his plate. "Technically, yes. They had to do a lot of stitching and wanted me to stay overnight – but I refused. I'd rather be uncomfortable in more comfortable surroundings."

"I'm sorry about what happened to you," Clari looked around the table, "to all of you."

Jeffer responded, "Thank you, but why are you apologizing? You didn't do this to me – to any of us."

Clari sighed, "But it's my fault all of this happened."

Samuel spoke up, "Poppycock, Clari! You did what I asked of you. I'm the one that started this whole mess by screwing around with their portal orb. What happened, happened."

Clari bristled, "J.R. died because of me. All of you are hurt because of me. Don't tell me 'Poppycock!' "

Steven's eyes softened as he spoke to Clari, "Clari, I don't think anyone here holds you responsible. No one here feels J.R.'s death is on you. We each made a decision, and I for one stand by it. I am sorry about J.R. But, please remember, it was his choice. Not yours."

Everyone around the table nodded or murmured their agreement of Steven's words.

After a few moments of uncomfortable silence, everyone went back to eating.

When Samuel finished his meal, he looked over the group and said, "I'd like to open the floor to sharing, or discussing, today's events. We've all seen things today that, at least for me, have never been seen before. I know we lost a good man today, but, I mean, *dragons!*"

Clari chuckled to herself about Samuel's enthusiasm.

Samuel continued, "And to see not only dragons, but then some of them shifted into a human form!" His face fell, "But we did sign the non-disclosure contract with J.R., so we can only discuss it amongst those of us at this table."

George looked up from his slowly reducing mound of food, "Unless J.R.'s death nulled the contracts?"

Clari shook her head. "No, it doesn't null the contracts. Those contracts were designed to protect the dragon's existence – to keep humans from finding out."

Steven added, "But they were amazing to see! This whole thing, the orbs, multi-dimensional beings, the Beasts, the dragons...those are all supposedly hypothetical – or even mythical – and yet we're all actual witnesses to all of it. They're real!"

Jeffer complained, "Yes, and a lot of good it does us – we can't tell anyone else about any of it."

Alberts voiced, "I'm relatively sure if we could scientifically prove any of this – outside of sharing this experience and what's covered in the contracts – we should be safe."

Around the table, several heads nodded. Steven offered, "Yeah, but all of us here experienced it, and that can't be taken away from us. And, it was terrifying as well as pretty mind-blowing."

Morris grumbled, "I'm an officer of the law. I still don't like not calling the authorities about J.R.'s death."

"I know, Morris," Samuel sympathized, "but what would you tell them? We can't disclose what really happened, under penalty of death, and the dragons removed the body. Oh, I almost forgot! After you, Clari and Josie left, two dragons, in human form, came back. They told us they were going to purge the property of any traces of the Beasts, including blood, DNA, and so forth. They also took anything that had any chance of having had contact with the Beasts or J.R.

"They then changed into their dragon form and cleansed the battle area with their fire. Again, something that should be physically impossible. Anyway, there are no traces of what happened out there. Only blackened earth."

"Holy moly," Josie uttered.

Clari was quiet as the others talked amongst themselves.

Samuel cleared his throat and the room quieted. "I'd like to revisit our battle. Clari, your hypothesis of bullets being ineffective against those from the portal orbs, at least for our purposes and our event, was correct."

Josie asked, "But why did the Beasts suddenly become mortal in our realm? What happened to make them vulnerable?"

Alberts piped up, "I think I can answer that. I propose that Clari displaced the space-time continuum, collapsing the distance between the dimensions. The space-time continuum theory states that the universe can be seen as having three space dimensions comprised of up/down, left/right, and forward/backward. Oh, and one time dimension. These four dimensions together are called a space-time continuum. This is a theory, of course.

"A link was created between time and space with Einstein's theory of special relativity. Having said that, in 1848, Edgar Allan Poe wrote an essay, EUREKA in which he stated 'Space and 'duration' are one.' So, if you think about it, Poe was ahead of Einstein.

"However, quantum physics contends that energy and matter exists in multiple states at the same time."

Josie's eyebrows rose. She looked around the room, searching other's faces. She turned her attention back to Alberts, "Um...what? Can you explain in less scientific jargon?"

Alberts sat a little straighter, "The thing that makes time-space bend is gravity. Clari made the Beasts have more gravity, thereby making them mortal like us."

Eyebrows now furrowed, Josie asked, "Holy moly. You mean they were gods?"

"No," Alberts answered, "they just weren't from our space-time. That meant we couldn't touch or harm them because we were separated. Clari took that barrier away and forced them to be in our space-time, which meant they were forced into our world, subject to our world's rules. We were able to hurt them in our dimension."

Josie's mind was spinning with the new-to-her information, "But how come they could hurt us? And how did Clari get them here? Did she break the space-time thingy?"

Albert chuckled, "No. She probably used wormholes, like they did. Wormholes are shortcuts – the compress space and time to make the distance between the two locations, or dimensions – shorter."

Everyone turned their attention to Clari. "Uh. Okay, I guess you want me to explain? I'll try, but I'm not even sure about what I did.

"I noticed that the Beasts would strike out at us and make contact, but when you all tried to fight back, you couldn't touch them. However, when you shot your firearms, the bullets were able to stun them temporarily even though the bullets never touched them. So I figured the bullets created a bit of a shock wave, disrupting the energy between our reality and theirs...or as Alberts put it, the barrier between their dimension and ours. I thought the Beasts might have been phasing in and out of our reality. I thought if I could make them stay in our dimension, then we had a fighting chance.

"The best way I can describe it is that I Pulled them into our dimension, making them susceptible to our dimension's rules. We could defend our-selves against them. So I Pulled the Beast I saw going after Josie, and she was able to kill it. And I was happy when the dragons, who can also function in multiple dimensions, joined in the fight." Clari looked down at her lap, remembering J.R.'s intervention to save her.

Some of the group started talking amongst themselves.

"Oh, speaking of today's experiences, I meant to ask you, Clari. Did you make a new friend?" The room became silent following Josie's question.

Clari's head popped up. "You could see him?"

Morris spoke up, "Yeah, until he disappeared as he moved away from you. Wasn't it a wolf?"

"Yeah," Clari snickered. "Apparently he adopted me and I'm now part of his pack. He jumped in after one of the Beasts killed J.R. I guess I'll be seeing more of him."

George spoke up as he attempted to clean white gravy with biscuit off of his pants, "It reminded me of the description of the wolf the old rancher ran into."

"He's the one." Clari shared with the group the conversation that transpired between her and the wolf.

Much to everyone's surprise, the stodgy Dr. Jeffer, voice tinged with amusement, muttered, "You mean that old coot, the rancher, had been telling the truth?"

Chapter Eighteen

Back at their hotel room, Josie asked Clari, "I have to get back to work, so Steven and Samuel are bringing me back home. Are you two good?"

"Yeah, Josie, thanks. Morris is on the phone with his boss. We should be out of here later today. How about a hug?"

As they embraced, Clari told Josie, "Thank you for coming, Josie. And thank you for everything. I really do appreciate you."

Josie pulled back from the hug. "You're welcome, Clari. But, whew! Had I known beforehand what we were getting into…"

Clari pulled a thread on the hem of her shirt. "I know. I'm not sure I would've come had I known, much less involved you and Morris. But, I'm glad you both were here with me."

Josie grinned. "Oh, I won't mind working with you and Morris again, except maybe not so intense – or dangerous – next time?"

Clari smiled, "No promises, but I'll try."

Josie smirked, "Tell your man 'Bye' for me when he gets off the phone!" and headed out of the room.

Morris phoned Lieutenant Avery and shared that he thought the animal disappearances were due to the supernatural.

"How did he take the news?" Clari asked him after his call to the lieutenant.

"I explained to him that you may be able to help stop the disappearances, or at least slow them down, and that I was going to stay on vacation and go with you to visit the nearby locations.

"Lieutenant Avery sounded a bit relieved and said, 'I'll be happy if the disappearances 'mysteriously' stopped'."

Clari told Morris, "Before we hit the road, I'd like to take some time to pop over to the Dragon Realm and thank them for their help. We wouldn't have survived without them."

"Roger that. I'll be in my room until you let me know you're done." He went into his room and closed the door.

Clari Pulled herself to the Dragon Realm. She thought she was going to be bowled over when Michael ran full steam towards her. She laughed as he stopped right in front of her.

"Clari! Hi! How are you? What was it like at the fight? Are you okay? Are you here to fly?"

Clari chuckled. "I'm here to thank the Dragons for their help in the battle." Sorrow attempted to seep back in as she continued, "And to see how everyone's doing with M's death."

A large maroon colored female dragon stepped forward, "It was our honor to aid you and your friends. It felt good to be able to cross dimensions and work with humans again. You may call me Aria."

"Thank you, Aria. We are very grateful to you all for coming and helping us. I don't think we would've made it out alive without you all. How is it that you all could dispatch them so easily?"

The female puffed out her chest, "We are multi-dimensional beings. It was nothing to work your dimension and theirs at the same time. We could match their frequency. This allowed us to remove their presence quite easily. We were honored to assist."

Aria gave Clari a slight head dip, and in that one gesture, Aria ended the conversation and dismissed Clari. With a grace which contrasted the dragon's size, Aria turned and regally strode away.

"She's pretty cool, huh?" Michael's eyes shined with a bit of hero worship as he watched Aria leave.

Clari mentally rolled her eyes *Teens*. "Yeah, Michael. She's pretty cool."

"I'm sorry to have to leave you, but I've got my defensive flying class and I don't want to be late. I'll see you later, Clari."

Clari, proud of Michael's enthusiasm and growth as a dragon, shooed him away. "Go, be an amazing dragon."

Michael hurried off to his class.

Clari closed her eyes and Pulled herself back to her hotel room.

Clari and Morris traveled from one location to another that reported animal disappearances as well as the ones that had sightings of unusual animals.

After leaving one ranch, Morris stated, "You seem to close these portals a lot faster."

Clari bobbed her head. "These portals aren't as old, rooted or as big as the one at Samuel's, so I could close them more easily. And it helps that I can dismantle most of them while they're dormant."

Ranch, home and field after field, Morris would speak with the land or home owner, while Clari concentrated on closing the portals.

Working kept her mind busy, which sometimes helped to keep the memories of J.R.'s death at a distance. Though she felt she was beginning to accept J.R. being gone, it didn't make the pain of his loss any easier.

As he drove, Morris asked, "Have you seen your Bigfoot friend since the battle?"

"No. Bob had no reason to contact me again once the portals there were closed."

Morris kept his eyes on the road. "What do you mean? What did Bob have to do with the portals out at Samuel's ranch?"

"Oh, because Bob's a Bigfoot. The Bigfoot, or Sasquatch, are protectors of the land. He had actually summoned me to close the portals because they — and the Beasts that caused so much damage — had upset the balance of the land."

"So his appearances were to ask you for help?"

"Not necessarily 'ask'. The first time he ran across my energy signature at my house was the universe 'introducing' Bob and me. Bob actually sought me out at the retreat with the intent to get me on the portal case. My energy, to him, read that I could aid him in his job to restore balance in the land."

He glanced at her. "Okay, but what about all of these other portals? Why are they popping up?"

Clari stared out the passenger window, watching the landscape pass by. "The Beast Master out at the ranch that night said the natural barriers between dimensions had thinned, making it easier for others to open portals. Because access was easier, the Beast population rose and so did the need to feed them. Bob showed me numerous unusual animal sightings reported, which I think is probably Beast sightings, across the United States as well. Bob also shared that some portals are made on purpose — like the ones at the mystery ranch – and some are made accidentally."

"How can a portal be made accidentally?"

She half-shrugged. "Some people are able to open portals, though they usually aren't aware of it. It takes people like me to go around and close them."

"Strange."

Clari shrugged again. "I don't know what to say."

After Clari showered at home, she put on fresh clothes and dumped her travel clothes into the washer.

After pouring a tall glass of pomegranate juice, she took a sip, sank into her big comfy couch, closed her eyes and leaned her head back. She concentrated on the welcoming home energies and the sweet-tart flavor in her mouth. It was good to be home.

Sasha jumped up on the couch, chirped a greeting, and lay down next to Clari. Sasha purred, lulling Clari even more.

Clari startled awake. She hadn't realized that she had fallen asleep, and then remembered she had been dreaming of Sebastian, but couldn't remember any details.

She got up, put the clothes in the dryer, and moved to her home office. It was time to play catch up once again. *Nothing like the last two weeks' experiences to make one appreciate the mundane.*

The dryer buzzer reminded her to finish her clothes. She was in route to the laundry room when she heard a knock on her door. Changing direction, she went to the door and opened it. She froze, unable to believe her eyes.

"J.R.?" she stammered.

J.R., in his human form, beamed.

"But...but...I saw that Beast kill you. Wait, you're dead." Clari slapped her forehead. "Duh! You're a ghost! Ah, I'm relieved. That makes perfect sense." She frowned. "It would make perfect sense except ghosts don't usually knock on the front door and stand there waiting for someone to open it."

"No Tahini, I am not a ghost." He held out his arm to her. "Touch me."

Clari reached out and felt his solid arm. "I don't get it."

"May I come in, Tahini? I would rather have a discussion inside and not with me standing out on your front porch."

"Oh. Um..." Clari swept her arm towards the kitchen, "...okay."

They sat at the kitchen table. Her brain was too shocked to remember her manners; she didn't think to offer tea or anything else. She was too busy being confused by a dead, who didn't seem dead, J.R. sitting in her kitchen.

"Tahini, my physical human illusion form known as J.R. did die out at the ranch that night." He preempted her question. "Do you remember what I told you about my curse and how my essence had been split up?"

"Yeah?"

J.R. continued. "Well, my body went back to the Dragon Council, where it and my dragon self were summoned. And I have you to thank."

"Huh? Thank me for what?"

"Because I tried to save you..."

Clari interrupted. "You *did* save me, and you died because of it."

"Yes, I died from that action. After that, the Dragon Council revoked my punishment."

She gave him a blank look.

He opened his arms wide. "I'm whole again. I'm a dimensional-walker again. I can be either dragon or human. I'm no longer cursed."

Still stunned by his miraculous reappearance, it took a moment or two for her to react. Her mouth was one step ahead, so it spoke slowly, as if allowing her brain time to catch up. "So you are saying that, because you sacrificed your physical life to save me, they have dropped your curse?"

J.R. nodded.

She spoke a little faster now. "It was your segmented, cursed human illusion aspect that died?"

Again, J.R. nodded.

Her eyes lit up as the reality finally sunk in. "Oh J.R., that's wonderful! You can go back and forth now between dimensions. This is great news!" She stood up, leaned over and slugged him in the arm. "You scared the crap out of me! I saw you die. And you waited this long to tell me? Wait, so is this why the Dragon Council wanted to talk to me?"

J.R. stood. He spoke softly and with regret. "I'm sorry for the pain I caused you, Tahini. And yes, that is why the Dragon Council wanted to talk to you, but I asked them to allow me the joy of informing you." He rubbed his upper arm where she had punched him. "Though I hadn't anticipated this reaction. Perhaps I should've let the Dragon Council tell you."

Tears welled as she grabbed and hugged him, savoring hearing his heart beating as her head rested on his chest.

J.R. rumbled. Clari smiled, remembering that his rumbling was his dragon aspect chuckling.

Aware she hugged a little too long, she pulled away, wiped her tears and stepped back. "I'm allowed to let the others know? Morris and Josie? And are you still going to work in our dimension as J.R.? Oh, and what about Maestro? How often do you need to be back in the Dragon Realm?"

His laughter filled her heart. She'd never heard him do this before, and it pleasantly surprised her. "There's the Tahini I know and love."

Undeterred by J.R.'s good looks, she continued as she excitedly paced back and forth. "Oh, maybe we'll have a dinner. We can all get together here and celebrate your un-death and now curse-free life. Maybe a potluck. Yeah, that will work." She turned her attention back to J.R. "Will a potluck dinner celebration work? Of course, I'll need to tell Josie and Morris that you're alive again, or none of it will make any sense. And I don't want to just spring it on them when they come for dinner."

J.R. shook his head, sat back down at the table and waited for her to wind down.

She stopped, walked back to her chair, and dropped down into it. "Well?"

"Oh, is it my turn now?"

She nodded.

"Yes, you can tell Morris and Josie, privately though, Tahini. All of this still falls under the Dragon Pact everyone signed. And for your other questions...yes; probably let him fade away; whenever I want, unless there is a problem there; and yes."

"What?"

He chuckled. "Yes, I will still work here as J.R. As for Maestro, I'll probably let him fade away. I can go back to the Dragon Realm whenever I want, unless I get called back because of a problem there...and yes, I think a potluck celebratory dinner would be fine."

They decided that she would set a potluck dinner date after talking with Morris and Josie, and then let J.R. know where and when.

As a side note, J.R. said, "I heard you met my second in command, Aria. How did that go?"

Clari shrugged, "Good, I guess. She was nice. She seems...formidable."

J.R. smiled, "She makes a good second in command. I'm lucky to have her in my clan." J.R. hugged Clari. "I'm going to go to the office now, and see what needs my attention."

"J.R.? Thank you for saving my life...and for not permanently dying."

"My pleasure, Tahini," he grinned as he exited.

Clari, feeling lighter than she had in a while, went to finish her laundry.

She could see Sebastian off in the distance, and recognized that they were still in the southwestern desert, though she didn't know exactly where.

"What? I can't understand you, Sebastian," she yelled as she continued to take large strides towards him. She could tell he was yelling as he ran towards her, and she could hear the urgency in his voice, she just couldn't make out the words.

Sebastian began to wildly wave his arms.

"I don't know what you're trying to tell me, Sebastian," she grumbled to herself.

Sebastian's waving became even more frantic.

A shadow of something big darkened the landscape.

When she stopped to find the source of the shadow, she heard a horrendous screech and then she was flying backwards. She landed with a sickening thud on the rock hard desert floor.

Clari sat up. *Ugh! I really don't like being slammed into the hard earth!* As she shook her head to clear it, a rather large foot appeared in her vision. Her eyes followed it up to the knee, up past the torso, and upwards toward a rather big head. A black-winged female, ten to twelve feet tall, stood before her. The face was humanesque, but its mouth appeared to have the beginnings of forming a beak. Its deep set eyes were an unnatural flat black. *I wonder if they swallow light like two eye-sized black holes.*

The entire face was covered in small black soft-looking feathers. The hands were proportional to the large body, but had also had a light covering of small black feathers on the backs of each hand.

Clari's attention was drawn back to the black feathers on the large wings. Each feather rippled with iridescent light as the being breathed and moved. While Clari was lost in the feather's beauty, the being opened its mouth and the screeching began again.

The pain from the screeching was too much — it cut right through her brain. Clari screamed, "Stop!" The startled being ceased its screeching. "I can't understand you. I don't know who you are, why you're attacking me, or even where we are or how I got here," she complained.

"Vile," the winged woman spat.

"Yeah, I got that you didn't like me."

"You mussst die," she hissed.

Clari was hurt, confused, and annoyed. "I don't know you, so why do you feel I need to die? And please, quit spitting on me when you talk."

"Abomination mussst die." A really large sword appeared in the winged being's hand.

"What are you?" Clari demanded as she stood and began dusting herself off, still keeping an eye on the creature.

"Grigori," she hissed proudly.

Clari froze. *Oh crap.*

Clari heard Sebastian's voice again, only this time she could make out his words. "Clari! Clari, wake up. Wake up now!"

Wake up? Clari thought. *There's too much pain for me to be sleeping.*

"Clari, please! Wake. Up. Now!"

Clari gasped as she bolted upright. She worked to calm her breathing and reached over to switch on her nightstand lamp. The clock showed it was three in the morning.

She scooted into a seated position noting how sore her body was. *That was one heck of a bad dream*, she thought. She flung the covers off and swung her legs over the side of her bed.

"What the heck?" she yelped. She saw scrapes, cuts, bruises and dirt on her. The sheets, where she had just been laying, had small pebbles, desert dirt and smears of blood from the various scrapes and cuts.

Oh boy, she thought, *I think I'm in trouble.* She shuffled to her bathroom and took a long hot shower.

After she dressed, she made for the kitchen in search of caffeine.

She sat at the table and stared into her coffee cup. She watched the light reflected in the swirling liquid while she tried to understand her "dream".

Once she had enough coffee, she cooked some scrambled eggs, fried bacon, and toasted an English muffin. She continued to mull over what had happened as she ate.

Most often the body goes into sleep paralysis to avoid harm when sleeping, but she knew that sometimes people can scratch or cut themselves when they act out during sleep. However, that didn't explain the injuries on her back where she couldn't reach, or the dirt and rocks in her bed. She had no history of sleepwalking. That left bilocation, which she did have a history of doing occasionally.

She remembered how her bi-locating ability had been brought to her attention by a stranger in a store. The stranger greeted Clari by name, and thanked her for showing up at the house just when they needed help. Not only did she not know who the person was, but she had been at home visiting with Josie at the time frame this stranger was talking about. Even more odd was that when the stranger shared details about Clari's visit, she actually began getting memories of that visit...including what that person's house, and its occupants, looked like.

That's how it went each time. She would be at home or with a friend during the times the strangers thanked her for coming over and helping them.

It was a little creepy that she was physically seen at two places at one time, and that it was only when they spoke to her that she would develop memories.

She wasn't sure how many other people bilocated and knew about it. It was just another of those topics that she kept to herself. She didn't think bi-locating fit here though.

While she worked to put the experience into terms that felt right to her, she was alerted to someone's energy on the property. At five-fifteen in the morning, Clari couldn't think of anyone who would come to her house so early. She scanned the being for any signs of it being a threat to her, but didn't find any negative intent. She also didn't recognize the being's energy.

The doorbell rang. Clari opened her door to someone who could've been Sebastian's clone, but with subtle differences. "Yes?"

"Are you Clarima Jones?" Clari noticed his voice carried a similar soft lilt like Sebastian's.

"Yes. And you are...?"

"Bartholomew. I'm Sebastian's cousin. I have come with a message from Sebastian."

She pounced. "Why are you bringing a message from him? Is he okay? Where is he?"

"Sebastian is fine and he is...away. He asked me to convey to you that it was not a dream. It was real. That was a human Grigori, and it has abilities. One of its abilities is being able to show itself to you in the manner that you experienced.

"Sebastian asked that you be extra diligent and to not ignore the reality of what happened. That's the end of his message." Bartholomew turned to leave.

"Wait, Bartholomew! Is Sebastian really okay? When is he coming back?"

"Sebastian's fine. I'm not at liberty to discuss his whereabouts or his return. I simply came to deliver his message. Good day, Ms. Jones."

Clari watched the Sebastian look-alike leave. She had received some answers, but now had a whole slew of new questions.

I'd better let everyone know what had happened. That thought startled her. When had she started feeling the need to include others? *Oh, right,* she giggled as she answered herself. *Since the whole almost dying, having a partner, bringing Josie into the fray, watching J.R. die — oh, and come back again — stuff.*

She waited until she was sure they would be awake, grabbed the phone and called Morris and Josie. All three settled on having a pizza night at her house that evening.

Chapter Nineteen

Morris stopped at their favorite Greek cuisine restaurant to pick up dinner.

Clari laughed when Morris started pulling food out of the bag. "Are you hungry, Morris?" she teased.

Having just pulled another food container out of one of three bags, Morris stopped and looked up at Clari, "Yeah. Why'd you ask?"

Josie chimed in, "Because you ordered so much food!"

The tips of Morris' ears turned pink. He resumed extracting food containers out of the bags. "I couldn't decide what everyone would want, so I got Dolmades with pita bread and Tzatziki dip with pita for our appetizers."

Clari and Josie sat at the table. Morris pulled another box out and handed it to Josie, "Greek sausage sandwich with a side of french fries for you."

"Mmm, thanks Morris," Josie said with appreciation.

"And for you, Clari, Moussaka and Greek salad." Morris handed her a box.

Clari popped a Greek olive from her salad in her mouth. "Yum! My mouth is watering. Thank you, Morris. What are you having?

Morris took the last container and sat down. He opened the lid of his box, "I'm having the roast beef brisket plate with Greek potatoes."

As they ate their dinners, Josie asked Clari, "Are you going to the International Conference?"

"Where is it this year?" Clari took another bite of Moussaka.

"El Paso, and I really want to go. Will you go too?" Josie sounded hopeful.

"What's the International Conference?" Morris inquired.

Josie asked Morris, "You've heard of the WPO meetings?"

"I vaguely remember reading something about it," he answered.

"Well, the meetings are free and are for the local registered Readers to get to know each other. It also is where we get to find out the latest news, policy changes, and updates. But, once a year, the WPO has an International Conference. It's open to all registered Readers. It gives us a chance to meet different Readers from all over the world, and this year it's close by, in El Paso." Josie popped a couple of fries in her mouth.

Clari picked up where Josie's explanation had stopped. "And it means I, or we, can afford to attend this year. It's a three day conference, and we can drive down each morning and come back home each night." Clari turned to Josie. "When is it?"

"It starts in four days."

"Yeah, I want to go." Clari couldn't stall anymore. "Thanks for coming over, guys. I want to catch you up on what's been happening."

Clari reminded them of J.R.'s information about the Grigori and moved on to what she thought had been a dream. She told them about the scratches, smeared blood, and dirt in her bed, then went on to describe the Sebastian clone and his message for her.

Morris was concerned about this new development. "What do we need to do?"

"I've no clue. I've never been in this position before. I only know that the woman Grigori called me an abomination and said that I 'mussst' die. I mean, really. I wasn't the so called abominated giant woman thing with black wings."

Josie, remembering J.R.'s death, frowned. "Too bad J.R. isn't alive. He could have told us more about what that woman might look like in human form or maybe how to find her."

"Uh...yeah, about that." Nervous and not sure what to do with her hands, she clasped and unclasped them she spoke. "I have some news. Um..." she stammered, "I'm not sure how to give this news gently, so I'm just going to say it."

No one spoke.

"Yeah, okay. Here goes...J.R. isn't dead."

"What?" Josie screeched.

"What do you mean? We all saw his body. You saw him get killed." Morris frowned and shifted in his seat.

"Well, he did die, he just isn't dead anymore."

"Holy moly. A zombie?" whispered Josie.

"What? No, not a zombie, Josie."

Confused, Josie's attention bounced from Clari to Morris and back again. "Am I missing something? He's not an undead zombie. I don't understand."

"No, you aren't missing anything. Let me explain, but we are all still bound by the Dragon's Pact, so you cannot repeat this to outsiders." Clari waited for them to confirm that they understood, and continued. "J.R. used to be a dimensional-walker, which meant that he could switch back and forth between the Dragon Realm, where he was a dragon known as 'M', and this world, where he was a human that went by the name J.R.

"About seven hundred and fifty years ago, the Dragon Council discovered that J.R.'s human self was evil, greedy, and didn't care who he used or hurt. This came as a surprise to the Dragon Council since J.R.'s dragon self was a fair and just leader.

"As punishment, his essence was forcibly split. One part remained a dragon. The other part had to remain human until he worked off his crimes against humans. He could no longer switch between the two realms. He was no longer capable of being a dimensional-walker.

"And, there was a catch. He was cloaked in his former evil, greedy energy. That's why people who Sense energy dislike J.R. so much in his Maestro persona. Yes, Josie, it was J.R. all along. But he wasn't evil anymore. He just had to wear that energy as punishment. It made it a lot harder to right his wrongs when no one trusted the energy cloak of evil he had to wear. He worked hard to help others, without profiting from it himself.

"J.R. saved me that night. He threw himself between me and the Beast, and the Beast killed him. The Dragon Council summoned his human aspect and his dragon aspect to meet with them. The Dragon Council proclaimed J.R.'s debt paid and his punishment revoked. His essence is once again whole. He is a dimensional-walker again.

"I asked him if he was going to continue to work here as J.R. and he said he would." Clari paused.

"Holy moly!" Josie exclaimed.

"That's...uh..." Morris' eyes searched for the right word, "...different."

"But this is good news. J.R. redeemed himself, he is whole again. Oh, and that brings me to the next thing. I would like to have a celebratory party. The three of us with J.R., are you two okay with that? I figured you could see for yourself and ask him your questions at the party."

She anxiously drummed her fingers on the sofa pillow as she waited for their answers.

Morris broke the silence first. "Just when I thought you couldn't possibly surprise me with any more...um...uniqueness about your life, you tell me a dragon man, who I saw dead, has come back to life. Oh, and you want to hold a celebratory dinner for him. Did I get it right?"

"Yes," she frowned, "but when you say it with all that sarcasm, it just sounds weird."

Josie's enthusiasm filled the room. "I'm so glad to be in your life, Clari! It just makes me wonder what I missed before you included me in your adventures."

Morris rolled his eyes.

Josie pounced. "I'm in! I can't wait to see Dragon boy! Do you think he'll let me see his dragon body?"

Amused at her friend's optimistic outlook, she good-naturedly shook her head and then turned her attention to Morris. "Morris, are you okay with this? Do you want to do the party?"

She Felt his energy fluctuate between annoyance, relief, protectiveness, and jealousy. With such a mix of emotions, she wasn't sure what he would decide. He started thinking out loud. "I didn't really like him, and I didn't trust him. Now I'm wondering if it was because of his dual nature and the curse. And he did save Clari, so he gets points for that…"

The fluctuations stopped.

Morris continued. "Okay. I'm glad he is not still dead, and yes, let's do the party."

After they worked out the party details, Josie turned to Clari. "I meant to ask you, why does J.R. call you 'Tahini'? What does it mean?"

"I have no frattlin' idea why he calls me that. 'Tahini', at least in our dimension, is a paste made from ground sesame seeds."

Both Morris and Josie cracked up.

"I'm glad you both find that amusing," Clari playfully grumbled.

And on that note, the get-together broke up.

The un-death, curse-free celebratory potluck dinner party went well. After everyone ate, they all cleared the table and the serious discussions began.

J.R. explained to Morris and Josie what had happened to him and answered their many questions.

After the discussions about J.R.'s return had exhausted itself, Morris told J.R. about Clari's incident with the human Grigori.

Clari Watched J.R.'s energy flare. J.R. had become as protective of his human clan as Morris was of Clari.

Morris, unaware of J.R.'s energy change, continued to talk. "I was wondering if you have any information to help us physically locate the Grigori who attacked Clari. She needs to be restrained before she does more harm."

J.R. rebuked Morris. "You are thinking as a human."

Morris bristled. "I *am* human!"

"Agreed, but you are a human who has delved into the non-human and para-human realms. Arresting or detaining the Grigori is only capturing the physical human aspect. The attack on Tahini, though the ramifications did carry over to the physical, happened in another dimension.

"Now, don't get me wrong. If the Grigori kills Clari in another dimension, Clari will die here. She is a dimensional-walker, and is still tied to her physical body. While Clari Walks, her physical body suffers the damage she receives elsewhere.

"As for what the Grigori's human aspect looks like…your guess is as good as mine. Our dealings were via phone and email. I never laid eyes on her." Clari noticed a dangerous glint surface in J.R.'s eyes as he continued to speak. "But I promise you, I will work to find her and now that I'm a non-human dimensional-walker again, it will be a lot easier."

Frustrated and conflicted, Morris lit into him. "I'm a sworn officer of the law. I'm all for protecting Clari, I really am. But as a law officer, I can't sit here and listen to you possibly threatening to kill someone and not do anything about it." Morris and J.R.'s eyes locked.

J.R. raised his hand to stave off Morris. "I did not once say I was going to kill the Grigori, though I won't hesitate if it comes to protecting Clarima, Josie, or you.

"I understand all too well having to live with two sets of rules. For me, it is this dimension's and my Dragon Realm's. Add in other dimensions, which have their own rules and laws as well, and things get more and more complicated. I really do understand. And I work my best to keep everyone's laws and rules in my head. But, just like you, I will do what I must to keep 'mine' safe."

Both looked away for a moment, breaking eye contact. An unspoken understanding between the two alpha males had been reached.

"I have further news," J.R. announced. "The night of the fight at the ranch, when Tahini called the Dragons..." he turned to face Clari, "...you opened the portal to allow them to cross over here."

"Yeah, we know that. So?"

"You not only opened the portal gate and allowed passage — you also demolished the portal gate."

Clari paled.

J.R. continued. "The portal gate is no more. The portal is now permanently open."

"Oh, no!" she gasped. "They are no longer protected! They will be slaughtered and it will be my fault."

"Dragons are not naïve and will be careful about exposing themselves in this dimension. You've done nothing wrong. Keep in mind, it happened the way it was meant to happen.

"Some who are old enough and have the ability will appear as human when they visit here."

Clari's eyes lit up. "Will Michael be able to visit as a human then?"

"No, he must be a dragon for at least three hundred years before he'll be able to come back here as a human."

Clari frowned. "I don't think I'll be Clari in three hundred years."

"Ew. I don't even know what to think about a three-hundred-year-old Clari...beyond wrinkly!" Josie's disgust was displayed on her scrunched up face.

Laughter broke the tension in the room.

That night, Clari Pulled herself back into the Dragon Realm. A warm glow filled Clari and she felt like she was back home.

She turned her head to the left and then to her right, admiring her wings as she flexed them. She thought that the universe surely had a perverse sense of humor...why else would she be a pink dragon?

She took flight and began to seek M and Michael. She soon saw the ledge where she had last been with them, but it was empty, so she continued on.

It wasn't long before she saw another large plateau holding a large group of dragons. She maneuvered her way to them.

She hoped she was graceful as she came in for her landing. She searched for the two dragons that she knew, and when she caught sight of Michael, she thought as he raced to her, *my, he has grown*.

Michael teasingly scolded her, "Of course I've grown. Did you think I'd remain a mere pup my whole life?"

Clari projected amusement towards him. She really enjoyed the freedom mind-speaking gave them. "I missed you too, Michael."

Clari's mind registered an abrupt silence. The dragon's telepathic communication created a background buzz in her head, and for some reason, it had ceased all at once.

While she tried to figure out what happened, she noticed Dragons moved either to the left or right, creating a path.

The leader of the Avonish Clan, a breath-taking, immense silver dragon, strode forward. "Tahini."

"M! It's so good to see you. How are you?"

M rumbled. "I am well, Tahini." He moved to situate himself between Clari and Michael. She was sure some statement of claim had just been made in that one single gesture.

She was just about to ask him about it when Michael mind-whispered, "Look, Clari."

Clari turned back to the dragons. Each dragon was bowing. "M?" she queried with a hint of panic in her voice.

Clari could hear his amusement. "My clan honors you." He purred into her mind.

"Why?"

"Tahini, please bow back so that they can relax."

Horrified, Clari bowed. The dragons relaxed and began milling around. The background buzz returned as the dragons resumed their inner communications with one another. Clari repeated her question. "Why, M?"

"You battled the Beasts and destroyed the dragon's portal gate. The portal is an open travel path now. The clan honors and respects you."

Michael teased her. "You are royalty now."

"Royalty my behind! I'm just me."

"How about we go catch some thermals, Clari?" Michael offered as he moved toward the ledge.

Clari, M, and Michael spread their wings and took to the air.

Sometime during the night, Clari returned to her body and drifted off to sleep.

The next morning, jarred awake by the alarm clock, Clari reached over to shut it off, and lay back down, relishing the memory of the dragon dream.

No matter how many times Clari entered the police station, she was acutely aware of the not-so-pleasant energy directed towards her by some of the officers. Their fear of the unknown hung in the air like the lingering stench of Limburger cheese. But the smell was temporary and she wouldn't allow it to stick to her.

Although their dislike always hit her hard, Clari energetically swept away their fears and presented the officers with an air of nonchalance when she passed through to get to Morris' office.

When she reached his door, she took a slow cleansing breath to finish releasing any tension that may have lingered, and knocked on his closed door.

"In!" he barked at the door.

Oh goodie, the bear is cranky today. She smiled at her own sarcastic thoughts and entered the cranky bear's den. Clari didn't try to clear the cranky energy in the room since she didn't yet know the reason for his bad mood.

"Morning, Morris!" she chirped.

Morris scowled at her. "Good, you're here."

"Well, yeah. We agreed to meet at your office today at 9 a.m.," like a magician revealing the completion of his trick, Clari flashed him a big smile while she raised her hands up, "ta-da! Here I am! And, on time, no less."

Morris grunted. Clari plopped down in the chair across from his desk.

Time to poke the bear. "Care to share why you're so grumpy today?"

"None of your business," he snapped.

"Okay, then. Shall we reschedule for another day...say when you won't bite my head off?" she asked sweetly.

Morris stilled and Clari felt some of the tension dissipate. "I'm sorry."

She leaned forward. "What's going on, Morris?"

He scrubbed his face before he spoke. "You're in danger and I just don't know what the heck to do to find the crazy Grigori thing and make you safe. I mean, it's attacked you on a non-physical level. How am I supposed to help with that?"

"Morris, I don't have those answers. This is all new to me as well. Usually the ones I battle from the Other-Side stay on the Other-Side. So all I can say...no, all I can ask is for you to continue to be my partner and maybe we'll figure this out together."

Though nothing had been resolved, a somewhat mollified Morris replied, "Okay."

"Thank you." She scooted back into the chair. "Are you ready to review some cases?"

"Yeah. We're set up in the conference room."

Once in the conference room, Morris sat down and began grabbing files for them to work on. Still standing, Clari set her stuff in a chair and turned to talk to Morris, and froze. Fear shot up her spine. Behind Morris stood the specter of Death, the Grim Reaper. "No, you can't have him," she whispered.

"What?" Morris asked absently, as he continued shuffling through the files. He glanced up when she didn't answer and saw that she looked scared. But her attention wasn't on him – she was focused on something behind his left shoulder.

He swung around to face the threat...and saw nothing. Confused, he turned back to her.

She had turned again and was now concentrating on something behind her. Clari cocked her head to the side as she Listened to someone from the Other Side. Then her body relaxed a bit.

"Clari? Clari, what's going on? I'm getting major heebie-jeebies right now."

She turned back towards him, but again looked behind him. She nodded, then turned her attention back to Morris and made eye contact. He noticed the moment she really saw him, and was no longer using her Other-Sight.

"Clari?"

Clari sighed heavily before she spoke. "I'm sorry. I was just startled."

"Well, what happened?"

"I Saw…" She stopped and shook her head. "It doesn't matter. But, I do have a question for you."

"Okay." He wasn't quite sure he wanted to hear the question.

"Have you asked, wished, or desired to understand more, more than you do now, about what I Do or how I See?"

"Yeah, it's been on my mind a lot lately. How did you know? You know what, scratch that question." He nervously scanned the room. "Does that have something to do with the creepiness that just happened?"

"Sometimes when we ask for guidance, direction or understanding, it may not come in a form that we had ever imagined when we asked. So when your requests are answered, Morris, please hold your faith and Know it will work out just fine."

"You're making me nervous. What are you not telling me?"

As he asked this, Clari Saw the being behind Morris move closer to him. The being's hand reached into Morris' chest and then withdrew.

Anguish filled her. "I'm so sorry, Morris," she whispered. Tears sprang to her eyes as she watched Morris grab his left shoulder, his face lose color, and his breathing became labored.

Clari flung open the conference room door and yelled, "Someone call an ambulance. Officer down!"

The station broke into a flurry of action.

Chapter Twenty

"We've got him stabilized now. You can go in, but don't get him agitated or excited," the tired and frumpy looking doctor sternly instructed her.

Clari went into Morris' hospital room. He appeared so small and vulnerable in the hospital bed. His face sagged a bit and looked waxy. The wires attached to him kept the nurses apprised of his heart's function. The beep-beep of the monitor was both reassuring and terrifying.

Clari pulled the guest chair closer to Morris. She grabbed his hand and sat quietly and waited while he slept.

After a while she dozed on the chair and slipped effortlessly into a dream.

"I haven't seen you in a long time, Solamba. What are you doing here?" Clari found Solamba inside one of her rooms of her mind-house. Clari's mind-house was a visualization of a house full of rooms where she was able to organize her life experiences and store memories. One room was where she kept the traumas from childhood; another room was where she placed her cherished moments from her childhood. She also had rooms for experiences she drew on to help others; and another for Other-Experiences. She also had some empty rooms which were waiting for new experiences, memories and information. Solamba had a broom in his hand he used to sweep out an empty room. Well, empty except for the light dust and debris on the floor from the room not being used.

Solamba was a guide who came and went in her life. He was always dressed in a long coarse-looking robe and wore sandals. His presence was always welcome and his energy was soothing and calming. He usually showed up when things were going to change in some way.

"I'm finishing cleaning out this room so that we can bring in the new. It won't be long now. The new should be arriving shortly." Solamba propped the broom against a wall and took her hand and brought it to the inside of his elbow, a gentleman escorting a lady.

As they strolled, Clari softly asked, "Solamba, what is going on?"

"Like I said, Clarima, we were cleaning out the old so that the new can come in."

"But that usually means something 'old' of mine leaves and something 'new' comes into my life. Nothing 'old' has left me."

"No? Are you so sure about that, Clarima? Yes, Morris is the one in the hospital bed. Yes, he has some changes coming, but so do you."

"You're scaring me, Solamba."

He had a warm chuckle. "You know by now that fear has no place in all of this. Faith. Oh, and for Morris? More faith." He released her hand, went back to the broom, and continued sweeping.

He paused, as if listening to something. "He's waking now, and he's going to have a lot of questions for you." Looking like the cat that ate the canary, he turned his back on her and went back to his sweeping.

"Clari? What happened?" Morris' voice was scratchy and dry.

Clari started. "Morris, hi. How are you?"

He frowned. "Where am I, and what happened?"

"Hang on, Morris, let me get the nurse." Clari ran to the door and called out to the nurse, "He's awake!"

The nurse came in and shooed Clari out.

Morris protested, "I want her here."

"Nope, not until the doctor sees you, Mr. Morris. She can wait outside the room. It won't take long. Then, if it's okay with the doctor, we'll let her back in."

She watched the doctor enter Morris' room. After a bit he left again. The nurse exited shortly after the doctor.

"Can I go back in now?" she asked the nurse.

"No, doctor's orders. No more visits today."

Clari whined, "It's only 4 p.m. I've been here since he arrived this morning! He's finally awake, and I'd really like to stay with him."

The nurse shook her head, "Nope. But the doctor did say you could come back in the morning, but eight in the morning at the earliest." The nurse smiled, and in her best don't-mess-with-the-nurse voice, ordered, "Now go home and get some rest."

When Clari got home she immediately took her shoes off in the front hallway and scooted to the kitchen. *It's not even 5 p.m., and I seriously need a pomegranate juice fix.* As she took her first sip, her phone rang. "Hello?"

"Clari, it's me. How's Morris? Are you okay?"

"Hi, Josie. I'm fine and they think Morris is going to be fine."

"So it was a heart attack?"

"Yes. They wouldn't let me back in, but told me I could come back in the morning."

"Do you want me to come stay with you?"

"No thanks, Josie. I'm fine. I'll give you a call tomorrow if anything changes, okay?"

"Okay. And call me if you need me for anything, Clari."

"You bet. Thanks again, Josie."

Clari, juice in hand, moved to the couch. She felt the couch sink a bit under her. She always thought of it as a welcome-home couch-hug. She took another sip and the doorbell rang. Clari started. *Dang, I must be losing my touch...I didn't Sense or Feel anyone approaching.*

Clari squinted through her front door's peephole. She frowned as she opened the door. "Lieutenant Avery?"

"Can I talk to you?" he asked in the brusque, no-nonsense manner for which he was known.

"Please come in, Lieutenant." Clari led him to the living room. "Make yourself comfortable. Would you like some pomegranate juice?"

Avery's eyes drilled into her. "A what? Did you say 'pomegranate juice'?"

"Yes, Pomegranate juice. Or perhaps some water?"

Frowning, Avery shook his head, "No. I want to ask you a question. What the heck did you do to Morris?"

Affronted, Clari countered. "What makes you think I did anything to him?"

"I understand that he was fine until you two went into the conference room."

Clari's voice slowed and deepened in warning. "Are you blaming me for his heart attack, Lieutenant Avery?"

"Yes, I'm asking you if you are the reason he had a heart attack."

Clari huffed. "When you put it that way, I guess I am the reason."

Apparently Clari's answer threw the lieutenant for a loop.

"Explain," he ordered.

She motioned for him to sit. She curled up on the couch.

"What I mean is that, metaphysically, Morris' heart attack may have come about because of his contact with me."

Avery growled. "And what the devil is that supposed to mean?"

"It means changes are occurring, Lieutenant."

"You could've prevented this...so why didn't you?" Accusation dripped from his words.

"I'm not God, Lieutenant." She looked into Avery's eyes. Her voice quivered, "He is my partner, Avery." Disheartened, she added, "I'm scared too."

Lieutenant Avery growled, though more gently. "My apologies, Clari, I don't like my people getting harmed. What do you mean about his heart attack?"

"If I understood it correctly, his heart attack happened so something could change for him. I don't understand it all, so I guess we all need to wait and see what happens."

Avery rubbed his chin, "Is Morris going to be okay?"

"I'm counting on it."

After the lieutenant left, she was even more tired and a bit worn down. She sipped her juice as her thoughts, not wanting to land anywhere, floated.

"I still don't know how you can drink that stuff."

Clari jumped, flinging juice as she swung around to face the newest intruder, who once again had not only approached, but entered into her home undetected.

"Sebastian! What the heck? You scared me half to death!" She yelled as she scrambled around the couch. She reached Sebastian, grabbed him and folded him into a hug and in the process transferred some of the spilled juice from her shirt to his.

"Belle," he whispered.

Clari pulled back. "Where have you been? Are you okay? Are you staying this time? I have missed you!"

Charmed by her exuberance, Sebastian reminded her. "Breathe, Belle. Let's get this cleaned up and we'll talk."

After the spill was cleaned up in the living room, Clari left Sebastian at the kitchen sink with a wet rag to dab at the juice in his shirt while she went to her room to change her clothes.

They both met up at the kitchen table. Sebastian smiled, but to her it seemed a bittersweet smile.

Clari crossed her arms. "You sent your cousin to warn me. Your *cousin*, Sebastian. What's going on?"

"Among other things, I've been tracking the Grigori, Belle."

Exasperated, Clari threw her arms up. "But how did you even know about her?"

"It's my job to know, Belle."

Clari rubbed her temple. "I don't get it, Sebastian. What is your job?"

"You. Your safety."

Agitated, she demanded, "What the heck does that mean? Why does everyone think they need to protect me? Let me correct that...why does every male think he needs to protect me?"

"Haven't you noticed that if one of us isn't able to be around, another one of us steps in?"

"What do you mean?"

"When Morris is with you, I'm usually leaving or am away. Something happened and Morris isn't with you right now. And now I'm back. Sometimes we overlap, but it's usually just one of us. It's not necessarily a conscious thing, but it is the pattern. Why do you think that is, Belle?"

Stunned, Clari thought, *Is he serious? Is he right?* It had been one or another of the three men with her. Sometimes there was an overlap, but it didn't last long. "I don't get it."

"We are your guardians. We cannot stop you from what you're to do, but we're allowed to support you, and we wish to protect you."

Clari's chest tightened. She felt betrayed and devastated. Her voice got louder and angrier as she spoke to Sebastian. "Are you saying that you three – you, Morris and J.R. – are just my bodyguards? That's all I am to you three, a cosmic job?"

Clari was now standing — she felt like her world was crashing down around her. "Our friendships are lies?" she spat.

Panicked, Sebastian begged, "Belle! Clari! Stop and listen, please. No, it's not a lie. No, you are not just a job. No, we are not just your bodyguards." He was desperate to be heard. "We. Are. Your. Friends. Actually, I see us as more than just your friends."

She focused on Sebastian. Her arms hung along each side of her body, hands in tight fists. In a low, angry voice, she demanded, "Start explaining."

"Belle, we are your friends, first and foremost. You are a special person. You don't know how special we each feel that you chose us to be your friends. Each and every one of us. Your relationship with each of us is real. And for whatever reason, the Powers-That-Be asked us to help watch over you. It is not necessarily a conscious calling, but a calling nonetheless. It doesn't mean our love isn't genuine.

"For Morris, it was a feeling, to protect you – or maybe it was a soul call.

"For J.R., it was protectiveness as fierce as he would have for his dragon mate — except that you two are not bonded that way.

"For me, it is a deep protective love.

"And we know that though you care for each of us, you probably don't have the same love we have for you. And that's okay. On some level of understanding, we totally get it. But we will each continue to love you and protect you to the best of our abilities nonetheless."

Clari was quiet as she worked to process Sebastian's words. Part of her, deep inside, knew exactly what he was talking about. Another part of her, the stubborn human part, felt misled and betrayed and wanted to cry.

She finished her glass of juice. She demanded, "Why?"

"Why what, Belle?"

"Why do you three weave in and out of my life? Why are you back now? And why did you tell me all of this? Just 'why'?"

"We care for you and your safety. But, don't you care for our safety as well? Isn't that what friends do?"

"Yes," she conceded.

"Perhaps the universe has us weave in and out so that we don't get all macho and drive each other, and you, crazy. Or maybe it's so you don't get tired of us."

Clari rolled her eyes. "Yeah, like that would ever happen."

"As for where I've been, I was visiting some distant relatives. After my sister...well, I needed some healing time for myself, and time to forgive myself for not seeing what was happening."

Clari opened her mouth to protest, but he raised his hand, and continued, "I also learned that I was holding myself responsible for someone else's

actions and had to learn to let that go. And that included me feeling guilty
for failing to see it in time to protect you. Again, I had been holding myself
responsible for another's action.

"So after I began healing, I started having dreams of a tall, winged, ugly,
and hateful being that was focused on harming you. I followed that being's
energy to Italy. Next thing I knew, I was on a plane heading back to you.
In route to your house I heard that Morris was in the hospital.

"And finally, I told you all of this so you would have a better understanding of the unusual dynamics of your adopted family...which I understand
now officially includes Josie."

Clari may not understand everything happening in her life, but Sebastian was right. Her heart warmed. She had a family.

Morris' face lit up when Clari strolled into his hospital room. "Morning,
Morris! How 'ya doing today?"

His smile fell, "Good considering the doctor wants to keep me here to
make sure I'm balanced out." Clari dragged the chair to the side of his bed
while he continued," They're also going to send in a nutritionist," Morris
used finger quotes, "'to teach me the right way to eat' now. I just want to
go home, change and get back to work."

Clari patted his arm. "I wish I could snap my fingers and everything
would be fine. Did the doctor tell you how long you have to be in here?"

Shaking his head, "No, but I'm hoping he'll tell me soon. I don't like
being here. And, I am so bored!"

Clari chuckled, "I have just the thing! I got you a present!" She plopped a bag on his bedside table.

Morris' hand moved toward the bag, "What's in here?"

Clari's eyes twinkled, "Open it and see!"

Morris put his hand in the bag and pulled out a book of puzzles. He looked up at Clari.

"Keep going, there's more."

Morris pulled out a deck of cards, two coloring books, and colored pencils. His eyebrows rose, "Coloring books and pencils?"

"Yep. Those are for instant gratification and to help while away the time here."

Morris smirked as he put his goodies back in the bag.

Clari shook her finger, "Don't knock it until you try it. You may be surprised."

He smiled, "I'm not convinced, but we'll see. Thank you, Clari. Hey, aren't you supposed to be at the WPO Conference today?"

"That's not until tomorrow. Are you going to be okay with me not being here for the next three days? I could cancel and stay here."

Morris held up his goodie bag and gave Clari a cheesy grin. "Sure, I'll be fine. My friend – you may know her, her name is Clari – brought me a bag full of fun stuff to do."

Morris and Clari talked, ate hospital food together and played cards until the nurse kicked Clari out at the end of the day.

The clamor of different languages and dialects, along with the diverse assembly of abilities inside the hotel ballroom that contained the International Conference, was overwhelming the first day. Tired, but pleased, Josie and Clari shared their experiences and thoughts with each other as they drove back home that evening.

Clari barely remembered dropping Josie off at her place and driving home. She climbed into bed and was quickly whisked away to the land of sleep.

Suddenly alert, Clari sat up. Her heart was racing, she was panting and her night shirt felt cold and was plastered to her skin. She Scanned the room to find the source of her panic. She Saw and Felt nothing — the house was quiet.

She leaned back, trying to remember what had awakened her. She realized it was like the other night and Sebastian's voice had once again awakened her. Bits and pieces began to filter back in.

She remembered...it was that Grigori woman again.

Clari reached over and turned on the bedside lamp. The clock read four thirty-five. She threw the covers back, and saw cuts, scrapes, and dirt in her bed.

Annoyed, she showered and changed her sheets. Again.

This had to stop.

Josie playfully slapped Clari's upper arm. "Isn't that right, Clari?" Josie waited for Clari to answer.

"I'm sorry. What?"

Concern etched Josie's face. She leaned in towards Clari and whispered, "Are you okay? You aren't really here today. Are you worried about Morris? The doctor said he is healing well."

"Sorry. No. Well, yes, I'm concerned for Morris, but that's not why I was distracted. I must've been daydreaming." She gave what she hoped was a reassuring smile, and tuned back into the conversation at the table.

Josie and Clari sat with two women from Greece, Elena and Kora. As they discussed the similarities and differences between the local meetings of those from Kora and Elena's area and the one Josie and Clari attended, Clari felt the familiar energy signature of that same Grigori woman.

That's impossible, Clari thought. *There is no way the Grigori could be here. Only registered Readers are allowed here.*

No sooner had Clari finished that thought when she felt the sharp sting from a lash of an unseen whip as it struck her left shoulder. Her eyes watered from the pain.

"Clari? Clari, what's wrong?" Josie's voice sounded far away.

Part of her brain registered hearing fear in Josie's voice, but the unseen attack consumed her. Unable to answer, Clari gasped as she was struck again. She leaned over to grab her right thigh where blood began to ooze where it had been sliced.

Confused by what was happening, Clari blindly reacted. She energetically reached out, grabbed the Grigori's signature, and Pulled both the Grigori woman's energy and her own out of the hotel ballroom.

The two found themselves standing on a plateau...in the Dragon Realm. Clari did a quick check to see the surrounding area. Dragons stood still in a semicircle around the two women. The huge wolf that saved Clari during the battle with the Beasts – the wolf that had adopted Clari – made an appearance as well, and paced around the perimeter, keeping a watchful eye on the Grigori. No one made a move towards either the Grigori or Clari.

The Grigori-woman was in what Clari guessed was full Grigori-mode with black wings, flourishing a big sword and a bloodied whip secured to its hip. It was ten feet tall, and hissing and spitting. The look in its eyes let Clari know the Grigori was done messing around. This time it intended to kill her. The Grigori screamed and charged.

The battle began.

Well, actually, the Grigori began the battle while Clari was busy trying to not get stomped by big feet or cut by the big Grigorian sword. Clari had no weapons or fighting skills. All she could do was dive, roll, swerve, run and occasionally throw a small rock.

The Grigori was getting frustrated. She wheezed, "I command you to sstand sstill and fight me weakling! Fight me and at leasst die with a little dignity!"

While Clari played dodge-the-angry-Grigori-woman-thing, her mind scrambled to try to think of something, anything, that might help to defeat the Grigori...but she kept drawing a blank. Well, except for the part about how if the Grigori killed her here, she would die for real.

Her lungs burning and her body tiring, Clari knew she was in trouble.

"You are a weak nothing," mocked the Grigori. "Abomination. Foul creature."

Great, now I'm being insulted by the thing, Clari complained to herself.

The Grigori stopped chasing her and began swinging her sword, showing off and hiss-talking. Clari pretended to listen to the Grigori while she was bent over trying to catch her breath and come up with a plan, preferably one where she stayed alive.

While panicking and working to not hyperventilate, her attention snapped back to the Grigori's ranting. Something changed.

The Grigori was pointing the sword at the nearby dragons. An unbefitting and warped smile grew on the Grigori's face as it revealed, "And when I'm finisshed killing you, I sshall bring my wrath upon thosse who dared to befriend and protect you. I'll ssstart with thosse here, work my way through your friendsss in the human realm. I'll finisssh off with killing your man. You can die knowing that your presssence killed thossse you care about."

Nothing existed but the Grigori when Clari heard the threats against her friends. Tunnel vision brought everything in her view into sharp focus. She watched spittle drip from the Grigori's twisted mouth. The drop of spittle landed on the ground poofing some of the dirt dust up. At the same moment the Grigori snarled, "Sstarting with the dragon filth."

Fed up with being bullied by scary Beasts wanting to kill not only her, but also kill those she loved, something shifted. A crack appeared within her. A new strength surged up. She stood tall. "Enough," she commanded in the voice that was felt within others' bodies. The world stood still and waited for her to declare her intent. "I. Don't. Think. So. You are so done, self-proclaimed Grigori."

She transformed into her hot pink dragon self...her ticked off hot pink dragon self.

Shocked by Clari's transformation, the Grigori's sword arm dropped, and then the sword tip came to rest on the ground. The Grigori's beady eyes transfixed on the growing hot pink dragon.

No longer a small dragon, Clari's body grew bigger and taller until she easily out-matched the Grigori in both height and width, but Clari knew she lacked skill and was no match for the Grigori in a physical battle.

Clari concentrated on the place outside of time — the place between the tick and tock. After a slow deep breath, time stood still. She reached down, grabbed the Grigori's head, released time, and gave a sharp twist. A sickening wet crunch filled the air. Some disconnected part of her brain whispered, *Her hair feels as soft as feather down*. Clari let go of the Grigori and the Grigori crumpled to the ground.

Clari shrunk back to her human self, grabbed the Grigori by her hair, and Pulled them both back into the ballroom in El Paso.

Clari looked down and wondered why the dead woman was still in Grigori form. She saw that Wolf had come back with her and was now seated beside her with his tongue dangling out one side of his mouth. He appeared to be pleased with his pack member.

Then she heard the screams in the ballroom and realized that the screams were directed at her.

Chaos ensued.

Oh crap!

~ End of *Cursed Dagger and Dragon* ~

~ Up next: A Prophecy Revealed ~

Chapter Twenty-One

Terms As They Are Used by Clari

Abilities – Every human has an ability. The ability/abilities can be any-where from the ability to be an awesome teacher or doctor, to any of the "Clairs".

Astral travel – the ability to travel using your astral energetic body. Can sometimes be seen by humans and energy Readers.

Bi-Locating – the ability to be at two physical places at the same time and to interact, especially with people at those locations.

Clairaudience – the ability to Hear beyond the physical hearing; such as voices, music and sounds.

Clairempathy – an ability to Sense, Feel or Know others emotions, or residual emotions. For those empaths who are untrained, the emotions can feel like their own which can be confusing. Public places and/or large crowds can be overwhelming.

Clairgustant – the ability to Taste something without putting it in their mouth.

Clairscent – the ability to Smell beyond the physical sense of smell. This can present as smelling a deceased loved ones perfume or the scent of flowers where there are none.

Clairsentient – ability to Feel or Sense beyond the physical; a Knowing within one's own body such as intuition or 'gut feelings'. Can also present as an overwhelming urge to physically move or to speak without knowing where the information is coming from.

Clairvoyance – ability to See beyond the physical sight. Could present as telepathy or precognition. Can receive information in the form of symbols, mind pictures or overlays (see "Overlay").

Council or Council of Twelve – each being who comes to Earth to be a human is assigned a council of twelve elders or advisors. They help through the human life planning phase and are available for offering guidance and advice during the human's physical lifetime.

Earthbounds – those who have died, but didn't cross over into the Light. Their reasons for staying connected to the third dimension can be as varied as the individuals. But because they are still connected to third dimension, they still carry emotions and possibly their addictions.

Energy Bridge – see Wormholes. Same.

Gatekeeper – An assigned physical person who has the ability to control – open and close – portals/wormholes, such as the portal connecting the Dragon Realm to Earth.

Ghosts – See Earthbounds. Same.

Guides – being who voluntarily agreed to be with their human during their human's lifetime. Life guides are hand-picked by the human prior to coming into their current human body. The Life guides are with their human from conception until physical death.

There are also Specialty guides who come into one's life for a specific purpose – such as during the loss of a loved one, to aid with the grieving process. Specialty guides leave when finished or task is completed.

Higher Beings – non-physical beings of a higher frequency; usually have attained knowledge and understanding on a broader spiritual sense. They are not perfect. Can include guides and ascended masters.

Law of Conservation of Energy – The 1st Law of Thermodynamics states that energy can neither be created nor destroyed; rather, it can only be transformed from one form to another.

Medium – one who has the ability to See, Sense and/or Hear and Speak with non-physical beings, typically those who have physically died; both earthbounds and spirits.

Mind-house – Each person has an energetic mind-house. It is where one stores memories, experiences, beliefs, etc. Some may visualize their mind-house as a card catalog, file cabinet, multi-roomed house, or a computer and is where their experiences can be organized or cataloged.

Non-Physical Beings – those who do not have a third dimensional physical body. Can include ghosts, spirits, angels, other dimensional beings, etc. Sometimes those who do astral travel or remote viewing can be perceived as being a non-physical being.

Other Beings – life essences from other dimensions; not of Earth.

Other Senses – using the non-physical senses. Seeing, Hearing, Feeling, and Knowing beyond the physical senses.

Overlay – is a glimpse of another time and/or place that can be seen simultaneously with the here and now.

Portals – See Wormholes. Same.

Psychometry – the ability to hold or touch an item, object or person and energetically receive information about the item, object or person.

Pull or Push – the ability to energetically pull in, or push out, someone or something from one dimension, time-space or frequency to another.

Reader/Energy Reader – one who can recognize and interpret energy and energy patterns. It is one who can, using Other-Senses, See, Feel, Hear, Know and/or manipulate energy in different forms/manners. See "Clairs".

Scan/Scanning – energetically searching and/or Feeling a place, person or being and receiving energetic information (see "Readers") such as imbalances, new energies, energy disruptions.

Scrying – the ability to relax one's eyes and See in reflective surfaces, such as a bowl of water, a mirror, or a shiny surface. Depending on the scryer, they may See the past, future or possible outcomes.

Shielding – the act of calling in and directing White Light (Source, frequency, or whatever you choose to call it) into one's own body and directing it to remove, and transform, any and all negative energy. Then one can call down White Light and create a bubble around themselves, and sealing the bubble with an affirmation, such as, "Only that which is highest and holiest may enter within". Shielding can also be used for one's own property, vehicle, etc.

Spirits – those who have crossed over into the Light, are free of third dimensional anchors, and come back to occasionally visit and/or aid a remaining loved one.

Team – a group that can consist of deceased loved ones, including pets, ancestors and guides (including animal spirit guides), who help support and guide their human during the human's Earth experiences.

Voice of God – the ability to have the Source back up your spoken word. Not many people know about this right that we each have, and even less believe in it or use it.

Wormholes – Portals. Energy vortices created and used to move between two points in time and/or space. Usually used to move between different dimensions and/or planes. An energetic shortcut between two places or spaces.

The World Paranormal Organization Pamphlet

The WPO was created in response to the increase of paranormal talents and abilities that gained strength and began to show up across the globe after the major energy shift of December 21, 2012 settled.

The WPO had developed standardized tests to help recognize and label the known Readers and Healers (those who have abilities); this also helps keep track of potential threats.

The WPO instituted a level standard to certify Readers and Healers, and is where WPO is mainly focused. This certification process legitimizes the process of hiring certified Readers and Healers. The WPO's certifications are recognized and are an accepted as the standard worldwide. New abilities and talents have the possibility to spring up at any time, and anywhere, so our list is not inclusive.

Reader Levels:

Reader Level I - Those who are able to Perceive positive and negative energy and can Sense lying/deception.

Reader Level II - Includes Level I plus: light psychometry; can Sense non-physical beings in their space (rarely with details).

Reader Level III - Includes Levels I & II plus: ability for at least Arch 1 level energy healing.

Reader Level IV - Includes Levels I, II & III plus: energy manipulation and will include one or more of the following:

1. Telepathy

2. Ability to See/Sense non-physical beings with some details and communicate with same

3. Channeling higher beings

4. Ability to Sense/Know others abilities potential

5. Seeing paranormal energy manipulation and the ability to trace the stronger energy signatures

6. Trace imbalances back to the initiating accident, event, or incident.

Reader Level V - Most of all the Levels plus: able to trace the weaker energy manipulation signatures. Usually Level V's work at WPO as investigators, researchers, or instructors or they police WPO certified members.

Energy Healer Levels:

Arch 1 – Beginner or low level Energy Healers. Hands-on healing; healing may be temporary; and can usually provide short-term pain relief and relaxation or stress relief.

Arch 2 – Intermediate Energy Healers. Can provide pain relief; re-establish energy flow and some circulation; stress relief; chakra balancing; distant healing. Arch 2 Healers can be either Hands-on or Hands-off.

Arch 3 – Advanced Energy Healers. Each individual is unique and may have one or more specialties. Each practitioner must be able to easily accomplish Arch 2 level abilities as well as: do a health scan and provide client and their medical doctor, if applicable, with a chart pinpointing imbalances; work with medical staff, if applicable, and their recommendations; accomplish subtle body clearing and balancing. Arch 3 will also include at least one Reader Level IV skill.

WPO Meetings – Regularly scheduled local meetings for registered WPO members. These are not only to meet and greet other WPO Readers and Healers in your area, but also where Readers and Healers can share organizational news and updates. Open and free to all registered WPO members.

<u>WPO International Conferences</u> – Open to all registered WPO members, the WPO International Conferences bring together registered members from all over the world. The location changes yearly, allowing different countries to host. Most countries have a different conference site each time they host, bringing even more variety to those attending the conferences

WPO believes in a family atmosphere in regards to their registered members and works to support their members and assist where they can. They have mentor programs, practice halls, and others services available to members worldwide.

Do you feel you have an ability or two? Testing is free. Certification and registration have feasible fees.

Other WPO Classifications

Other WPO classifications not shared with the public and explained by Clarima Syd Jones' understanding.

Reader Level C – Wild Readers. Untested, unregistered. Not certified.

Reader Level D – Classified Certified Readers.

Reader Level M – Certification or certification renewal is pending. Certification dependent on investigation results.

Reader Level X – Deadly, dangerous or uncontrollable. Usually are not seen again.

In Appreciation

I appreciate you, the reader. Thank you for reading *Cursed Dagger and Dragon*.

I appreciate the Earth Angels who never gave up on me to finish this book. Ana Maria Quezada for her wonderful support; Kendall Love for her enthusiasm; Christy Trevino for grammatical guidance; and a great big shout out to fellow author, Mary C. Smith. Her enthusiasm, questions, her ponderings as well as her requests for "More!" that kept me moving forward. And Anthony Quezada for the beautiful cover work.

And I appreciate my loving husband who has been my foundation, quiet strength, gentle urging me to keep going, patience and his support.

And I mustn't forget...a big thank you to my Team.

About the Author

Jan Toomer resides with her husband in the desert Southwest in the United States. Jan is a writer and author; a Metaphysical, Spiritual and Paranormal Consultant; Reiki Master; creator of New Dimension Energy Session; as well as Founder and Owner of Reality Undefined LLC.

Born a multi-talented sensitive, Jan has literally been doing energy work for most of her life. Some of her abilities are energy healing, medium and channeler, animal communicator, energy reader and interpreter.

She also studied Metaphysics, Ho'oponopono and the Akashic Records.

She aids others to see a different perspective to help expand their awareness and consciousness; to bring reality-creating consciously into their lives.

Jan writes and shares a few articles a week, since 2008, on Metaphysical, Spiritual and Paranormal topics for her blog Reality Undefined at https://www.metaphysical-studies.com/ and also does videos on Rumble (@janToomer), Tiktok (@jantoomer) and YouTube (@jantoomer3828) as well.

Also by Jan Toomer

Prophecy Revealed: Clarima Syd Jones

This is the second book in the World Paranormal Organization series.

The story continues with Morris recovering in the hospital while an investigation is ongoing to determine Clari's part in the death of a Grigori.

Since Clari neglected to tell the World Paranormal Organization about her other abilities, the WPO suspended Clari's certification until she retested with them. When the testing concluded, Clari began training to control her other abilities. One of the training sessions was for her to learn how to control her dragon aspect; but this led to Clari inciting a revolution in the Dragon Realm.

With Detective Morris released from the hospital, Clari digs deeper into why the Grigori want her dead. Clari is informed about the Avatar Prophecy, and her friends think the prophecy is talking about her.

Ghosts from the 1940's ask Clari for help in crossing over; they are trapped. She and Morris begin looking into each individual ghost's story to see what the commonality is and how to help them.

After yet another attempt on her life, Clari discovers that not only are the Grigori connections close to home, but also that the Grigori are more widespread than anyone thought.

Can she put all the pieces together and expose the Grigori before another attempt on her life; an attempt that may succeed this time?

Prophecy Revealed: Clarima Syd Jones is available on Amazon

Re-Writing My Future: A Stroke in Time

Jan's memoir shares her journey from growing up with active abilities while wanting her abilities removed so she could be deemed "normal". Then, as she developed a tenuous relationship with her abilities, she had a stroke in her 30's and lost touch with her abilities. She struggled to not only find her new "norm", but to get her abilities back while she explores the question, "Who am I now?"

Jan shares her experiences and offer some insights from her own journey in hopes that her story may they help you through yours. This book for stroke survivors, caretakers of survivors, those interested in the paranormal, spiritual and metaphysical, as well as anyone who has or is facing major changes in their life.

Re-Writing My Future: A Stroke in Time is available on Amazon